YOUNG CAPE COD PUBLIC DEFENDER and commercial fisherman Michael Decastro ventures to Saigon with his father, a Vietnam War vet, to come to the aid of his long-lost client and love-interest Tuki Aparecio.

The half-Vietnamese, half-African American diva is in a fight of her life with a mysterious dragon lady from Indochina's underworld. At stake is an antique ruby in Tuki's possession … and the mortal souls of everyone Decastro loves.

Ghosts that the Decastros and Tuki carry with them from Cape Cod and Southeast Asia will have their day.

ALSO BY RANDALL PEFFER

CAPE ISLANDS NOVELS:
Killing Neptune's Daughter
Provincetown Follies, Bangkok Blues
Old School Bones
Bangkok Dragons, Cape Cod Tears
Listen to the Dead

CIVIL WAR AT SEA:
Southern Seahawk
Seahawk Hunting

NON-FICTION:
Watermen
Logs of the Dead Pirate's Society

SCREAMS & WHISPERS

A CAPE ISLANDS NOVEL

BY RANDALL PEFFER

TYRUS
BOOKS

Published by
TYRUS BOOKS
1213 N. Sherman Ave. #306
Madison, WI 53704
www.tyrusbooks.com

This is a work of fiction.
Any similarities to people or places,
living or dead, is purely coincidental.

Library of Congress Cataloging-In-Publication Data has been applied for.

15 12 13 12 11 1 2 3 4 5 6 7 8 9 10

978-1-935562-36-8 (hardcover)
978-1-935562-53-5 (paperback)

For Hong, Khiem, Trung …
Cam on, ban toi

Prologue

THE TEARS ARE COMING so hard they're choking him. So thick he's gasping in loud sobs ... as if someone's hammering on his heart.

"Come on, Michael," the cop says to him. "Give me the gun. You're scaring these poor people."

Michael Decastro—failed public defender, commercial fisherman, lost lover—hardly knows where he is. He can't remember how he got out on this jetty in Woods Hole's Great Harbor, can't remember how much rum he drank at Captain Kidd's or when he sat down in the lotus position on this granite boulder. Especially can't remember why he's got the Remington twelve-gauge cradled in his lap. The shotgun his father usually keeps behind his berth on the family trawler Rosa Lee.

All he knows is that it's a dark, foggy night. Early November. Getting cold. The tide's so high that the eight Vietnamese immigrants who have been casting for scup off the end of the jetty are now huddled together—no longer fishing. They look at him anxiously, holding their white, plastic buckets of fish or hugging their own shoulders for warmth, clucking softly in their strange, tonal language. One's whispering into his cell phone. They are up to their calves in the water. Sitting here with his gun—halfway between shore and the light on the tip of the jetty—he has effectively trapped the Vietnamese at sea in the rising tide.

"Give me the gun, Rambo." State Police Detective Lou Votolatto gestures for the Remington with his fingers.

"Michael, come on. Snap out of it. Get a grip," the detective's partner says.

Her name's Yemanjá Colón. She has her Glock pointed at Michael's chest. She had quit the state troopers for an investigative job with local Cape police in Slocums Harbor. But now, it seems, she's back, partnered with Votolatto again.

"Leave me alone." He bites his lip to quell the sobs, looks up at Colón. Sees she's on the edge of crying, too.

Jesus. Not again.

Something starts to crumble in his chest. He turns to the Vietnamese at the end of the jetty, then back to Colón. Wants to say something to them all. "I'm sorry. I'm … really sorry."

For a second he just stares at the fishers. Then he looks at Colón, who has lowered her weapon just a bit and is wiping tears from her cheek. Those brown eyes, those high cheekbones, the long, dark wavy hair remind him of his mother Maria. His sweet mother, dead to cancer more than two years ago. And … they reminded him, too, of the woman lost to him somewhere on the other side of the planet.

"*Jesus Cristo.*"

He tries not to remember what happened the last time he saw Colón a year ago, what happened at the Chatham Bars Inn one October night.

"What's wrong with me?" He can't stop looking into those midnight eyes.

"I think you Portagees call it *saudade*," says Votolatto. He's a crusty old state dick in a tattered, brown overcoat.

Yeah, Michael thinks. Saudade. *That's what it must be that brought me here.* He pictures black nights when his father Caesar Decastro sits in the wheelhouse of the *Rosa Lee* chain smoking, swilling glass after glass of *vinho tinto*, clutching his dead wife's silk chemise. He stares out into the gloom of a Cape Cod harbor for hours. *Saudade*— unbearable longing. He wonders if Puerto Ricans and Cubans like Colón have a word for it, too.

And what about the Vietnamese …? What if right now Tuki's nights in Saigon are as black as his nights here? Does she, like him, have nightmares that a mysterious Asian woman named Wen-Ling is still stalking her, still chasing after that stolen ruby Tuki has? Does she still think of Wen-Ling as the Dragon Lady, fear her as if she were some kind of superhero villain from a 1930s comic strip? Does Tuki wrestle with a heart full of guilt, too?

Or has the one-time princess of Bangkok's Patpong, the diva of Provincetown Follies, re-invented herself yet again? Cleaned her emotional slate so thoroughly that she's now totally and completely a Vietnamese girl? Has she become one of those smoky sirens of Asia, of Saigon, with no regrets, no secrets she can't forget when her head hits the pillow?

Tuki Aparecio, the one that got away. Has she finally found what she used to call the "peace that passes understanding"? She's the bombshell who sings with the raw soul of Tina Turner. The one who still has an eleven-million-dollar, purloined ruby called the Heat of Warriors to buy her all the safety and love a girl could ever need. Maybe it's a stone big enough to erase her vagabond past lives in Thailand and America. An eighteen-carat miracle the color of red wine. A gem so valuable, so massive, it can make her forget about Wen-Ling. Wen-Ling who will do anything, go anywhere, to get that ruby.

Is the Heart of Warriors so big it has wiped away any tenderness that Tuki once felt for him? Her lawyer, her knight in shining armor. Her lover, too. Once upon a time. The fool who has been adrift, flailing, sinking since she just plain vanished a year and a half ago.

"She's back, isn't she?" Colón drops on her haunches beside him, her Glock in her right hand. Her eyes still wet.

"I got an email … from her half-brother Tran." Michael's so drunk he has to concentrate to form words with his lips, his tongue. "In Ho Chi Minh City. She's … in terrible trouble."

"Tuki didn't write you herself?"

"Tran says … she doesn't want to involve me …"

"That little bitch! How sweet of her."

He stares at the shotgun in his hands, its scratched wooden butt, the oiled barrel.

In little bursts of slurred words he confesses that he hasn't been able to help himself. For months he has been searching the internet for Tuki. He found her in a picture of a band from Saigon, tracked the band to a talent agency's web page. Found an email address. It turned out to belong to her half-brother. And Tran wrote him back … with his fears for his sister.

"You're thinking of going to Vietnam?"

He shrugs.

"*Carajo*! What did I ever see in you?"

He closes his eyes, really wishes he were sober, or drunker. "I feel really awful … about everything. About Chatham Bars Inn …"

"You are … You are actually freaking going to Vietnam, aren't you?"

"I don't know. Maybe."

"She's already broken your heart. Twice."

"You think I don't know that?"

"Give me the shotgun, asshole." She's holding her service weapon like a hatchet, aimed at his head, ready to swing.

Something twists in his gut. His arms seem to have a mind of their own, as if they have better sense than his head, maybe a surer grasp on self-preservation. Slowly, they stretch out before him, offering Colón the weapon.

She grits her teeth, jerks her Glock at him. A swift little chop stopping just short of his left temple, even as she takes the shotgun. For some reason everything about her seems red.

"I'm so done with violence," he says softly.

"You wish."

1

TUKI APARECIO can't believe she's going to sing this particular heart-break song again. Gladys Knight's "Midnight Train to Georgia." She loves it, but she hates it, too. *For all the stinky* plaa *it dredges up in my mind, la.*

And now she's really hating it because the person requesting that she sing is the one person she hoped she would never see again. Wen-Ling. The liar, the self-proclaimed Thai secret agent, the *silab*. The throwing star killer. The ruby hunter. The Dragon Lady. She's the ageless Chinese-looking ho in an expensive crimson suit who has seated herself at the end of the bar in this club. A witch with a long black ponytail trailing down her back. Tuki can almost smell her from up here on the stage ... reeking of cigarettes, jasmine perfume, Johnnie Walker Black.

Just a minute ago Wen-Ling was waving several million-dong notes at Chien, the manager, who's pouring cocktails. Probably mixing threats with her bribe as she lights up her fag.

And now Chien has come up to the stage, his eyes vacant. His little mustache trembling, his voice begging Tuki. "Just sing the song! Do it right. And do it right fucking now! Like *mau. Mau len, nguoi dep* ... if you want any of us to walk out of this bar alive tonight."

She knows that Wen-Ling has requested this song to torture her with memories, wants to see her sweat. And die a little, right now. On stage. In front of the tourists and the local sophisticates.

For a year and a half, Tuki has feared this moment. Another showdown with the Dragon Lady. In the back of her mind she worried that it was just a matter of time before Wen-Ling found her in Saigon and came for her. Still, she has stayed because she has family here that she needs, loves. Because maybe she would rather risk death than exile these days. For thirty-five years she was exiled from this country where she was born, and her life saw misery visited on misery. Now, Vietnam seems the safest place for her to hide, to heal her broken heart.

Her half-brother Tran, who she had only met once, two years before on her first visit to Vietnam, welcomed her to his little flat on one of the alleys off Le Thanh Ton, just a few blocks from her mother's flat and English language bookstore. Even when, at first, her mother—guilt-ridden by having lost Tuki during the chaos of late April 1975 and the fall of Saigon—shied away from anything but a formal relationship with her, Tran embraced her as a full sister. A soul mate, he called her.

He brought her into his band, gave her the chance to fill the space in her broken heart with his three-year-old daughter, Hong Tam. Fill the space in the child's heart, too, left by a mother who drowned swimming against a rip current at Vung Tau. Tuki became family, and little by little, her relationship with her mother has begun to warm as well. Just last week they went shopping on Dong Khoi Street for dresses ... and they laughed.

But five days ago Tran received a threatening note under the door of his apartment. A sealed message addressed to Tuki from Wen-Ling, demanding that she either give up the Heart of Warriors or watch her family die. That's why she has decided to run again, maybe to Indonesia, maybe the Philippines.

The problem is that she has no legal passport. She entered Vietnam on the Thai passport she stole from Wen-Ling back on Cape Cod. Surely, it was reported stolen long ago, flagged by immigration agencies throughout Asia. Unusable.

She has heard that the Vietnamese government won't give people like her real passports. Because her father was an American Marine, because she's what the Vietnamese call, when they are trying to be politically correct, *con lai*, mixed race or *my lai*, Amerasian. On the street folks are not so kind, especially to people like her whose skin is too dark to be Vietnamese, whose father was black. Her kind are called *bui doi*, living dust. The government here, she has heard, would rather send her to America under the Amerasian Repatriation Act than give her a passport. And she can't go back there. She fears that there are open murder cases against her in the U.S., bad guys and cops who would like to wipe her off the face of the earth, too. And a lover—poor, sweet, wonderful Michael—whom she left without so much as a last kiss.

So until she can get a new passport on the black market, she's stuck here, with nothing to protect her against the Dragon Lady who is smoking right now at the far corner of the horseshoe bar. Not even the little Walther pistol that Tran gave her a few days ago. She has been carrying it everywhere. Except on stage.

So ... here she is. Without anything to defend herself. Doing the job she adores. The one she needs right now to make enough money to pay for a fake passport.

She's singing with Tran's band at Saigon, Saigon, the rooftop bar on the tenth floor of the Caravelle Hotel. Its glass walls and terrace overlook the twinkling lights of the city. Outside the steamy haze hangs over the throbbing center of what the government of Vietnam calls Ho Chi Minh City. The locals, though, still refer to it as Sai Gon for the trees that once flourished here—the mangos, the kapocks. She loves the sound of this name, Saigon, so strange and romantic.

Tonight she's wearing a brilliant golden Vietnamese *ao dai*, a traditional long tunic, but without the slacks. The *ao dai* leaves none of her curves to the imagination ... and no room to conceal a weapon. She doesn't even have a nail file to protect her from Wen-Ling.

But that can't be helped. Not here. Not now. So she tells the guys in the band to play "Midnight Train," nods to Tran on the keyboards. He cocks an eyebrow, questioning, knows his half-sister avoids this song. Knows it haunts her for some reason she won't say. But the drummer is already starting the lead-in ... and here comes Tran on the piano. Three bars, the bass is in and she's singing. *Ooooooooo. El Lay* ...

Wen-Ling's watching her, staring like some kind of predator sizing up prey. Sucking on her cigarette until it glows, exhaling a plume of smoke.

Tuki feels heat rising in her belly, her chest. She has this feeling that at any second the whole place is going to blow itself apart in a typhoon of hot winds, flaring sparks. Shrapnel. The spotlights flash silver, gold, red. Her voice seeps from the sound system. Low, raspy. Sultry. Straining. Singing about leaving a life. About going back to a simpler place and time. If only such a thing were possible, such a place existed ...

As the spots catch her, they throw a reflection on the big plate glass window looking downtown toward the river. It's there, in that reflection that the memories rise. She sees her mother. But not really her mother. Not Huong Mei. Not the middle-aged Saigon bookseller of today, not the wife of the communist lawyer who barely acknowledges his *bui doi* stepdaughter, not the fearful, quiet woman who still cannot look her daughter in the eye for more than five seconds. That woman consumed by the guilt of whoring during the American War, of having conceived her with a black man, of having left her toddler in the care of two drag queens fleeing Saigon for Thailand on a shrimp boat the night the city fell in April 1975.

It's not this sad woman Tuki imagines now, singing and dancing in the window. It's Misty. The girl her mother was from 1972 to 1973. The hooker, the singer. The lover of the ex-Marine, the black man, Tuki's father, Marcus Aparecio. There in the window, Tuki can see Misty strutting the runway bar as if it were 1973 again at Marcus's club, the Black Cat, here in central Saigon. She's wearing a silver kimono stitched with little red dragons. Her lips glisten bright crimson. Liner accents the shape of her eyes, her black hair is pinned up in loose geisha folds. A goddess. Pure body heat. Losing herself.

Tuki feels the soul of the music, her call and response with Tran singing backup. Almost forgets the wench watching her from the bar.

But not quite. She smells the danger, feels the sweat beading in the small of her back, behind her ears, between her breasts. Feels Tran's eyes on her, feels his worry as she sashays across the stage in her *ao dai*. Kissing up to the mike, showing some leg. Bringing the night down, the fire up.

Sweet Buddha, help me, la. Saigon's burning again.

2

"DAD, I REALLY NEED your help." Michael Decastro chokes on the fear rising in his throat.

Caesar Decastro, the wiry fisherman in orange, oilskin over alls, blows out a deep lungful of smoke from his Winston and eyes his only child through the tobacco haze. The son, who people used to say reminded them of a swarthy Tom Cruise, has just burst into the wheelhouse of the *Rosa Lee* spouting the tale of his unfortunate encounter with the state police detectives. At the moment, the kid looks less movie idol, more washed-out vagrant or junkie, in those rumpled jeans and the quilted plaid shirt.

"This time the cops actually locked you up, Buddy Boy?"

"Look, I'm sorry ... I should have gone fishing with you and Tio Tommy. I know it. Fishing's the only thing that really works for me around here these days."

"So ... what the hell?"

"After I got that email from Vietnam ... things just kind of got out of ..."

The elder Decastro is kicked back in the worn captain's seat of his steel trawler. He's almost sixty years old, and he's tired. He and Michael's uncle Tio Tommy are just back from a day of dragging for winter flounder in Nantucket Sound, just two men to run an eighty-five-foot boat. Commercial fishing's not what it used to be. So now he's smoking, watching the sun setting, a bright red ball sinking over the western shore of Hyannis Harbor on a November evening.

"You have to stop with this drinking shit, Mo."

"I know. I know." Michael drops into the other swivel chair opposite his father's in the wheelhouse.

"And what was with the gun?"

"I took it off the boat yesterday. I really have no idea what I thought I was going to do with a gun, I hope I never see another one."

"You sure as hell ain't going to see my Remington. The cops probably threw that son-of-a-bitch in Vineyard Sound."

"You want me to buy you a new one?"

"Hell no, screw the gun. Good riddance. What I want is for you to quit trying to hide from your problems by fishing and boozing and terrorizing people."

Michael hangs his head, nods in agreement.

"Why don't you clean your ass up and get back practicing law? Everybody said you were one hell of a public defender."

"All I did was get people hurt. I don't want to hurt anybody. Nobody."

"Seems to me the hurting has happened *since* you quit the law."

A sigh, a gathering of will. "I need your help."

"I am helping. This shit's got to stop, Michael. You're going to kill yourself or someone else."

"*Cristo*, Dad, would you please listen to me? Didn't I already say I was done with all the violence?"

"Hey, okay, but …"

"And I really don't think my problem is the booze."

"Denial is the first sign of trouble."

For a second Michael almost says, *Look who's talking, the king of* saudade *drinkers.* But what he says is, "Will you listen to me for a minute?"

The father stubs out his cigarette on the steel instrument panel, gives his thirty-five-year-old wreck of a son his full attention.

"I got thinking about things after I woke up in the slammer this morning."

"Good."

"Don't take this the wrong way, but you know how sometimes when you get to missing Mom ... you sit around the boat with a bottle and get hammered?"

"I thought we were talking about you."

"Jesus, why do you make this so hard?"

"*Falame.* Just spit it out."

"This is about women for me."

"You miss your mother?"

"Yeah, no shit. Just like you. But ..."

"But?"

"But I *really* miss Tuki."

"You got to move on. She ain't coming back."

"You don't know that."

"She freaking walked out on you. Vanished. Poof. With an eleven million dollar ruby and open court cases hanging over both your heads."

"Her half-brother says she's in trouble."

"Has she ever been in touch with you since she left?"

He shakes his head no.

"I thought you were all done with that skinny little tease. What ever happened to the funky Latina cop who was calling you for a while last year?"

"Don't ask."

"Rebound, huh?"

"She was the one who nearly pistol whipped me last night in Woods Hole."

Caesar Decastro lets out a sad whistle, the note starting loud and high, fading low. "Let me take you out for a big bowl of *sopa verde* ..."

"Dad, *Cristo Salvador*, I don't want kale soup. I want to go to Vietnam."

The father bolts up out of his slouch. "Are you crazy?"

"No. Yes. Maybe. I don't know. But I need you to come with me."

"You *are* crazy."

"Please. Don't you see?"

"See what?"

"This is my only chance. Maybe *our* only chance."

"For what?"

"To put the darkness behind me. The guilt."

"Huh?"

"I let Tuki down. I told her I would protect her. I fucked up ... a bunch of ways."

"You're talking cock."

"We have a chance to try to make things right."

"We?"

"Like you don't carry your own crap around about Vietnam?"

The fisherman reaches into his chest pocket for another Winston and his Zippo. Lights up. His face seems gaunt, dark. "Aw Christ, Mo. Do we have to get into this again?"

The son remembers a confrontation with his father over photos he found hidden behind others in an album from the war. A picture of a Vietnamese girl dancing on a bar in a G-string. And two other pictures of her. One in a red dress standing in some kind of native boat, like a big canoe, waving. In the other picture she's swinging in a hammock, wearing a Red Sox shirt.

*   *   *   *

"Did you have a girl over there, Dad?"

For about thirty seconds his father doesn't answer. When he speaks there's a torn note in his voice.

"Her name was Meng. She was one of the Hmong people, the Montagnards. A refugee from the fighting in the hill country, a nursery school teacher.

*   *   *   *

"I love you, son. You know that. I'd throw myself in front of a train for you ... but wild horses could not drag me back to that freaking country. It's the land of the dead."

Michael hears the pain in his father's voice, maybe even terror.

"What if I told you we could save some lives this time? What if I told you I've already made some calls about getting our visas?"

3

CLUB SAIGON Saigon's blazing.

People are starting to sing along. Tuki struts. Hears the click of her pumps on the wood. Maybe If she can keep this song about a midnight train going, she can buy herself time to think. Time to get away from the Dragon Lady seated at the bar. Time to save her mother, her brother, and her brother's lovely little daughter Hong Tam from Wen-Ling's violence. Maybe even save the ruby, too.

So she thrusts her chest out, swings her hips ... Channeling her mother over there dancing on the plate glass. And now she's Misty, too. A sexy kid from Cholon, a Marine's fantasy. A stroke of lightning. A girl who wears her broken heart for everyone to see ... for the black man who she sent away, sent back to America, Georgia maybe. Far from the war, the threats, the killing. The man who with the nod of his head had rescued her for a while from sin, from whoring. Who left her with a little golden-skin baby, the *bui doi*. That's what Tuki tells people to call her now, *Bui Doi*. No longer is she Aparecio, Dung as it says on her birth certificate. No longer Tuki as the drag queens in Bangkok's Patpong called her, as her beloved Michael called her. For safety, for anonymity she has become this new singer in the new Vietnam. *Like look at me. With my Asian face, my golden skin, my flaming African hair. I'm Bui Doi and proud of it ... but scared as hell the dragon lady's here to kill again, la.*

The humid air shimmers. Smoke rises in the spotlights.

Wen-Ling's still sitting at the bar, sipping her whiskey, smoking with a sad little smile on her face. As if maybe this song, this "Midnight Train to Georgia," carries memories for her, too, of unbearable loss. Of love. And possibly vengeance. The Dragon Lady's hand is on something under the little clutch bag in her lap. Maybe a gun, maybe her signature throwing star. A *tonki*, a *shaken*, like she used to murder Thaksin Kittikachorn two years ago in Bangkok … and, later, to cut down the drag queen Robsulee in Provincetown.

But you can't stop now, la.

Tuki tosses her head back and launches into the second verse. She holds the mike out for Tran as he sings backup from the keyboards. She's smiling. That huge, amazing smile, coming out of the blue night. So full of life, so surprising. It starts with her full lips and straight white teeth, spreads to her chin. Two dimples bloom on her cheeks.

And Tran's smiling back at her. He's so cute in his little straw fedora, his olive t-shirt. This long-lost brother. Not yet thirty years old. Who has loved her from the day he met her. He and his little daughter Hong Tam, Pink Heart, have been the best things about these last eighteen months since she fled Wen-Ling and America to start a new life, to try to hide here in Vietnam.

She shakes her hair out. It falls to her shoulder blades. She's wearing it slightly frizzy and curly, not *rasta*, the way she kept it back in America when she was in her Janet Jackson phase. But anyone can see that she's *bui doi,* with that skin matching the sun streaks in her hair. A perfect girl in her mid-thirties, who looks fresh from a hot beach.

The shoes come off. She weaves among the tables toward the back of the club, half herself, half Misty, looking for the man in her life. The only man. The man she still loves. The one gone on that midnight train. He's her father, Marcus Aparecio. And he's Michael Decastro. Why did she ever leave him? Why did her mother ever let her father go?

Wen-Ling catches her eye, raises her glass of Johnnie Walker in a subtle toast to the singer. Like *gotcha, girl.*

The spotlights flicker across her skin, hot. The air's thick and heavy. Hard to breathe.

I'm so in trouble here, la.

Why did she step off the stage, leave the comfort she felt next to Tran? There's a moist heat fuming through the club. The fetid scents of Saigon. The incense, the *nuoc mam* fish sauce, the charcoal fires, the motorbike exhaust …. the sweat of men … the milk of mothers.

And the acrid scent of the river. The chocolate waters of the Saigon River, this branch of the Mekong twisting into the city. She imagines white mist rising over the water. The current sweeping rafts of flowering water hyacinths downstream along with the flood of the monsoon; egrets hitch rides on bits of broken houses, abandoned rice barges, bodies. Children. *Bui doi. Nguoi dep.* Everything flowing to the South China Sea.

She must work her way back to the stage, to Tran. The room seems incredibly dark now. The lights turning purple, blue. Misty's fading on the window pane, Saigon's melting outside in the flames. Her voice is that midnight train, those broken dreams in the lyrics. Exposing a terrible longing in her soul.

She imagines American soldiers and B-girls staring up at her from their seats, nursing their Budweisers, their fake champagne. The ghosts of GI's faces lost in shadows. Michael's dad, her dad. And Michael, too. Her voice is trying to heal their wounds. Comfort their losses. Put the war behind them. Comfort Misty, herself. Even Wen-Ling.

And buy herself a little more time.

She's back on the stage now, rubbing her hand over Tran's shoulder as he plays, as he's singing along with her. But the song's coming to an end, and Wen-Ling's rising off the barstool, black eyes smiling madly at Tuki.

Just like that terrible night of murder and mayhem at the Provincetown Follies show eighteen months ago. The night she almost died because of the Heart of Warriors. The night she knew she had to run away as far and as fast as she could, change her name, hide herself with this wonderful brother in Vietnam.

Tuki can almost see Michael's sweet face out there among the audience just like that night at the Follies. The shadow of a beard on that fine, but rugged, Portuguese face. She was on stage then, too. Singing this song. And pleading to him with her eyes. Telling him ... as clearly as these lyrics ... that she loves him ... But the world—America, Cape Cod, Provincetown ... it was all too much. Too dangerous. He's got to go. She's got to go.

And so she's pleading to that memory of Michael out there when she realizes that Wen-Ling's fully on her feet. Her right arm's cocking back as if to throw a *tonki*.

This would be the time for Chien to cut the lights.

But everyone in the club seems so focused on the singer, they don't see Wen-Ling. The spots blaze.

Any second the *tonki* will fly.

She's imagining it cutting through her *ao dai*, catching her beside her left breast, nicking her ribs with a sharp sting. Imagining bleeding, falling—the spotlights flaring, wheeling around her as she spins ... when Wen-Leng thrusts out her right arm, towards Tuki's chest.

The Dragon Lady makes the sign of a gun with her right hand, her index finger the barrel. Squeezes her thumb down on the hammer. Winks.

Bang. You're dead, *bui doi*.

4

"SHIT. I SWORE I'd never do this, Mo." The old warrior's face is pale, leaking sweat as he emerges through the fog of air conditioning that fumes from the doorway of the Cathay Pacific 757 into the withering heat of the jetway at Tan Son Nhat Airport. Mid-November. The beginning of the dry season. Ho Chi Minh City. Fucking Saigon.

Michael Decastro feels the tension in his father's voice, wonders if bringing this man back to Vietnam might possibly be the biggest mistake of his life. But then he remembers why he's here. To find Tuki. To help her save herself and her family from the Dragon Lady. To see if she can still love him, forgive him.

"I can't do this without you," he says.

The woman he loves is somewhere out there in this scorching heat. In this teaming, concrete maze on the river. With a predator closing in on her. Who better to guide him into the underbelly of this city than his father? The vet. An MP on these very streets: 1970 to 1972, 716th Military Police Battalion. A man with his own guilt buried in Saigon. His own dragon to face after all these years.

At the immigration desk a young agent, who seems to be wearing a Red Army uniform, glares at Caesar Decastro for a full ten seconds before stamping his passport and visa. The soldier's look is nothing short of toxic.

"*Cho de, thang my,*" he says, mostly to himself, through clenched teeth as he waves the Decastros off toward customs.

"*Cho chet*, Charlie," Caesar Decastro tosses back.

The soldier bristles.

"What the hell was that about?" asks Michael.

"That fellow's from up north."

"How do you know that?"

"Clipped, tight-ass accent."

"And …?"

"He basically called me an American bastard."

Michael's looking at his father, a little in wonder that the guy understands a bit of Vietnamese, can detect an accent.

"Maybe some of my brothers in arms killed his father or bombed his mother."

"What did you say to him?"

"What I always used to say to dinks like him when we had to interrogate them back in the day."

"Which is …?"

"Fuck you, Charlie."

Michael winces at his father's slur for the Vietnamese soldier.

"What's the matter?"

"*Cristo,* Dad. You want to get us shot?"

"Hey, at least I haven't totally forgotten the language, pal."

"That's not the point."

"Something about this place always kind of wound my clock."

*   *   *   *   *

On the cab ride from the airport to the center of the city, Michael has a thousand questions for his father. Does Saigon look the same? Was his base near here? Does he feel something knotting in his stomach, too? *Are we on a fool's errand, Dad?*

But he can't find his voice. And his father obviously doesn't want to talk. He stares out the window. Watches waves of teenagers on motorbikes swirl around the taxi as it plows its way down an urban boulevard lined with shop houses, street vendors, hundreds upon hundreds of billboards and signs heralding deals on flat-screen TVs, diapers, Kentucky Fried Chicken. The air throbs with the constant honking of horns. It's as if all the drivers are signaling each other in some inscrutable code.

He looks at each young woman on her motor bike as if she might be Tuki, wonders whether his father is looking for Meng, too. Or her ghost. Thinks about the day four years ago when Caesar finally talked about his girl in Saigon.

*   *   *   *

"I'm not proud of it. She was just a kid. So was I. It was a different time," his father says.

"The world felt like it was spinning out of control. Any day you could be sitting in a bar or walking down the street and a car bomb or a sniper would take you out. It happened to people all the time. Forty-two people blown to bits at the Mi Canh floating restaurant one night."

"Were you in love, Dad?"

"Not like with your mother … no."

Meng was poor, homeless when she got to Saigon. Not there a week before the pimps were on her like flies, had her trussed up in a bra and G-string, hustling tricks for rent and food money in a bar called Wild Bill's. She had a kid, a toddler by another GI. So it was complicated. But Caesar didn't care. The other guy was long gone.

"I missed your mother so much. I felt so bad about leaving her with you in her belly. I just wanted a woman to make me feel like everything was going to be all right again. And I wanted to take her off the street."

*   *   *   *

"Son of a bitch," says his father. There's surprise in his voice.

"What?"

"Would you just look at this place?"

"What?"

"Same old crazy shit, Mo."

Michael cocks his head as if to say *I'm not following you.*

"Psych-O Gone, we used to call this burg nights when we were out on street patrol."

"It was whacked?"

"*Bookoo* whacked … I thought the Reds claimed to have turned this country into some kind of workers' paradise."

"That's the word."

"Looks to me like business as usual. Everybody out to make a quick buck. Everybody on the go, got his own hustle just like 1972. Freaking boom town."

"So …?"

"So … maybe Uncle Ho's loyal followers won the war, but they have lost all damn control of the people."

"You mean free enterprise lives."

"More than ever, *menino.*"

The last time Caesar was here, almost forty fucking years ago, this had been a two-lane road. Republic Boulevard. Six lanes now. Called Nguyen Van Something-or-other. The MACV Headquarters used to be on that land they passed a click back near the airport. Turned into blocks of apartment buildings now. Motorcycle shops, cell phone stores, beer-and-noodle joints on every corner. Almost everybody looks under thirty.

"I think the war did a pretty good job killing off a generation."

"Well, the survivors have multiplied like a school of pogies."

Michael looks out through the windshield of the cab at the clotted boulevard and the low-rise buildings that stretch for miles ahead, sees a seven-story pagoda towering in the distance. He read somewhere that Vietnam's population has doubled to close to ninety million people since the war. Saigon has become a city of over eight million residents.

"How in God's name are we going to find Tuki?" He should have had more than an email address and cell phone number from Tran before he came. But her brother didn't seem ready to give out an actual street address. His father slaps his cheeks with his hands the way he does when he's just coming up into the wheelhouse after a nap for his watch aboard the *Rosa Lee* … and finds a storm brewing. He's a little twitchy. "You think you can drink a beer without having ten, Kiddo?"

"What do you have in mind?"

"I know a spot down by the river where we should be able to score a couple of cold Tigers and get our game on."

"You mean you're not sorry you came now?"

"I didn't say that."

"Then what?"

"We didn't come all this way to let that poor girl die."

Michael feels something in his chest ease, stifles the sudden urge to hug his dad.

5

SHE STANDS at the entrance to the Xa Loi Pagoda, a small backpack of clothes on her shoulders and the ruby hidden under her tongue. Immense, warm.

The monks have told her that rubies are the sixth treasure in the Buddhist sutras. This particular gem, the Heart of Warriors, is legendary for its powers to ease transitions, provide clarity, inspire loyalty, cultivate courage, engender love.

Love, la. Her dear Michael, two years ago, carried the stone like this under his tongue from Bangkok to Penang to keep it safe for her. It was after he did this that she began to see that she really loved him. And he began to see it, too. See that he loved her.

Now it's her turn to keep it safe ... and leave it once and for all with the Buddha. Before Wen-Ling can steal it back.

So to start ...

No sooner has she entered the temple grounds than the whine—the blaring sirens of Saigon traffic—disappears. She hears the rushing of hot winds through the shade trees and around the tall bell tower of the pagoda, hears vague distant chanting, too. There's a young woman, probably eight months pregnant, taking off her sandals, lighting joss sticks. She holds two or three in each hand, murmurs a prayer as she climbs the right-hand steps, the women's way, to the heart of the temple and the golden Buddha. She's come to beg good fortune for her child. The air drips with the overwhelming scent of incense. Bird songs, too.

Tuki steps from her thongs and lights the half dozen joss sticks that she has brought with her, follows the mother-to-be up the stairs. She watches the fine round belly of the other woman and thinks of the unborn child she lost back on Cape Cod, Michael's child. Suddenly she wants to scream with the pain. Scream. But then she remembers what the Buddha says. Life is suffering, suffer is caused by desire. She must follow the eight-fold path, must erase desire.

Begin with a prayer, la.

She bows her head as she ascends the stairs and lets the words of the Heart Sutra begin to flow from her mouth, wash over her pale blue *ao dai*, her white slacks, her soul.

> *Form is emptiness and emptiness is form.*
> *In emptiness there is no eye, ear, nose, tongue, body, mind.*
> *No forms, sounds, smells, tastes, touches …*

Her heart tells her that these words must have been the same ones flowing through the *bodhisattva* Thich Quang Duc when he burned himself alive in the street not far from here in June 1963. He was protesting the South Vietnamese government's persecution of Buddhists and its slavish affinity for the western colonialism of the Roman Catholic Church. Until it was stolen by the government, his heart, which had never burned, was preserved here as a relic. The thought of Thich Quang Duc's courage makes her shiver. Her own mission to save the Heart of Warriors from Wen-Ling's covetous grasp seems puny indeed.

But it is something, Lord Buddha, is it not, la? A small act to help the world, gone mad with desire, to come back into balance.

＊   ＊   ＊   ＊

When she reaches the altar in the main temple, she props her joss sticks in the sand of a nearby urn, and stares up at the great, golden carving of Gautama as she places a freshly washed apple and orange on a tureen as gifts for the monks. Then she bows her head, closes her eyes. Falls to her knees, begins reciting the Diamond Sutra. Her voice a whisper. The ruby hard beneath her tongue.

"*Evam maya srutam …* " Thus have I heard …

It seems beyond crazy to her how this ruby has controlled her life for more than ten awful years. This eighteen-carat oval stone the size of a playing marble. Had she been able to see the death and heartache it has brought on her, she would never have touched it that night back in Bangkok when her rich-boy Thai lover Prem Kittikachorn came for her with a pistol to take their lives. But he could not kill. He was ashamed that he did not have the will. So he left her and made a loveless marriage with the daughter of a silk merchant. Left her with this wine-red miracle as a symbol of his love unto death. It was as if he had given her his soul for safekeeping, she thought back then. And her heart was loyal.

He told her that the Heart of Warriors was a stone that had vanished during the madness of the American War in Vietnam. A ruby from the crypt of Wat Ratchaburana at Ayutthaya. The ancient royal capital of Siam. Circa 1400. It had come secretly into his father's gem collection back in the chaotic days of the war. And Prem had stolen it from his father the thief—like *fuck that controlling pig*—to give to the princess in his life. The love his father forbid him to marry. The little, half-black orphan from Vietnam. The hermaphrodite. The intersexual. The one who hid her gender ambiguities performing as a drag queen diva in the bars of Bangkok's Patpong.

She fled Bangkok to New York in 2001 to start a new life. But Prem's father and Thai mobsters called *nak-lin* pursued her for the ruby. Now Prem was dead, his father dead, many *nak-lin* dead, a Thai detective dead, her own dear, long-lost father Marcus Aparecio dead. Murdered. During this secret struggle to claim the ruby. The skirmishing that set her running breathless, terrified through New York City, Cape Cod, Thailand, Malaysia, Singapore. Now Vietnam.

And in the middle of this war she met her knight in shining armor, the public defender from Cape Cod. Michael Decastro. She fell in love. She had an operation that made her fully a woman. She was even pregnant for a while. But then she found herself in a fight to the death with the dragon of all dragons, Wen-Ling. She fears Wen-Ling's shadow everywhere. Even here at Xa Loi in Saigon's District Three. Here beyond the Reunification Palace.

For years she told herself that it was her cosmic responsibility to guard the ruby with her life and return the Heart of Warriors to its reputed rightful owners, to the monks at Ayutthaya in Thailand. Believed that to do anything less would be to bring an untold load of bad *karma* down on Prem's soul—and hers, too. But when she fled the Cape, she no longer felt so sure that she wanted to give it back to the Thai monks. After all the misery the Heart has brought her, she wondered if it *is* her karma … and her fortune. The only balm for a heart torn open by typhoons. The symbol of all the men she has loved and lost. Prem. Her father. Sweet Michael. Her lost child, too. The ruby was like their souls for her to hold, keep safe.

Now, with the reappearance of the Dragon Lady, Tuki sees clearly that the stone is not safe with her. Senses that holding onto the Heart of Warriors, holding onto those lost men, has become a consuming desire for her. A suffering that now seems likely to bring Wen-Ling and the dark contest for the ruby to her family here in Saigon. A wrong path. So *not* the way of the Buddha. It's time to find her balance again. *No matter what, la.*

*   *   *   *

Forty minutes of quiet chanting have passed when her lips begin the words of the final *gatha* of the Diamond Sutra and her heart feels the rhythm. The peace.

> *So should one view the fleeting world: a drop of dew,*
> *A bubble in a stream, a flash of lightning in a summer cloud,*
> *A star at dawn, a shadow, a phantom, a dream.*

Her eyes open on a brass incense burner in front of the altar. The burner's about four feet high with ornate dragons cast on the sides and tops. She's alone in the temple except for a monk sleeping on the floor in the corner. Candles flicker on the altar. But it's not with the candlelight or her eyes that she sees the path ahead. It's with her *anja*, her third eye, which has opened during the chanting of the sutra when her eyes on the world were closed.

Her course is clear. She rises to her feet before the incense burner, inhales its pungent fumes. Spits the Heart of Warriors into her right palm. Drops the ruby through one of the vents. Then she takes an unlit joss stick, uses it to bury the gem in the sand at the bottom of the burner … Finally, she tosses a small ball of paper into the sand from a pocket on her backpack. The paper's inscribed with her prayers for the dead, which she recites …

Until she feels her soul levitating.

Surely the monks here will help her if the time comes.

6

"HOLY SHIT." Michael catches his breath after dodging an endless parade of motorbike traffic to cross Le Loi Boulevard from the small hotel where he's staying. "This place looks like New Bedford during the Portuguese feast."

Ahead of him, Ben Thanh Market's sizzling. Literally. The massive French-colonial market building at the heart of Saigon's District One is ringed with cheap outdoor restaurants serving an array of Vietnamese noodles, rice, soup, shrimp, and fish to hordes of families and couples gathered around communal tables. The evening air swirls with the scents of charcoal, roasting peanuts, pepper, garlic, steaming shrimp, scallions, flash-fried rice, beer. Strings of lights cast a yellow glow on diners, crowds of strollers. Motorbikes weave through the sea of people.

One, with two teenage girls in jeans and halter tops, cuts in front of the Decastros and stops.

"Hey guys, you want lady bar? You want good boom-boom?"

Michael hears his father groan. "*Cristo*, here we go again."

"We soooo horny. Hotel very near. Forty dollars."

The girls are pretty, slender. No older than eighteen. The one on the back seat has already gotten off, is putting one arm around Michael's neck. Grinding her body closer.

"*Ngung.*" The father's voice is a sharp bark. "Stop."

He's got the siren by the wrist, grabs something from her hand. It's his son's wallet. "Get lost. *Xeo. Go!*"

Michael has his hands up in the air. Like *what the hell?*

His father waves the wallet in the thief's face. "Better luck next time, *mamasan.*"

"Fuck you, Joe." The girls pivot their motor bike and rocket down Le Loi.

"*Cristo*, she picked my pocket."

"You want me to say welcome to sin city?"

"I'd rather you tell me how the hell I'm going to find Tuki's brother in this carnival."

"Stick with the plan, Kiddo."

*   *   *   *

It's another half an hour of pretending to shop for t-shirts among lines of stalls in an alley opposite the main market before Michael hears someone say his name. He's alone now, his father watching from a stall fifty yards away. It's part of the plan that Caesar and Michael cooked up over beer and steamed dumplings at a riverside canteen this afternoon. Tran's only communication has been by email and cell phone. He still has given no address, no place of employment. No way to help Michael get closer to Tuki without going through him. He's clearly screening the American, and today when Michael called him from a phone in his hotel, Tran told him to come to this vendors' alley at seven PM and pretend to shop until Tran found him.

Michael and his father have decided it could be smart for Tran to think Michael has come to Vietnam alone. This ruse leaves Caesar free to watch Tran from afar, see where he goes after he leaves Michael tonight. "I can do a little surveillance, know what I mean, Mo?" Caesar said. "At best the brother might lead us to Tuki; at worst he could show me that you're being set up for some kind of shakedown."

Now Michael's looking at the slender young Vietnamese man standing in front of him wearing a little straw fedora, a Celtics game shirt that Tuki must have given him. His eyes are large, dark, kind.

But there's a certain skepticism in the way this guy tilts his head a little to the side.

"You're thinner than I imagined," says Tran.

"And you're taller."

*   *   *   *

"Michael, do you really love my sister?"

The younger Decastro nearly chokes on a sip from his tall glass of *so-da chanh*, seltzer mixed with lemon, ice, and sugar. He feels something stab him in his gut. *Cristo.*

"Isn't that obvious?" he asks when he finds his voice.

Tuki's brother stares at him, unblinking, over a steaming plate of *com tay cam*, a blend of rice, mushrooms, chicken, pork, and ginger. He and Michael are seated on plastic chairs at an open-air restaurant called Hai Lua, tucked among a dozen similar eateries beneath awnings stretching from the wall of the Ben Thanh Market building.

"I've come a long way to find her, to help."

Tran pushes his fedora back on his head, leans back in his chair, folds his hands in his lap. Looks down his nose at Michael. "You seem like you feel guilty about something." "No. Why would I feel guilty?" It's an automatic lie.

Colstnĭ on her haunches beside him, her Glock in her right hand, still half-pointed at his head. Her eyes still wet. "What did I ever see in you?"

"Because it's not really Tuki that you're here for, yah?"

"What? Why else would I ...?"

"The ruby."

"Oh, Jesus. If you even suspected that, why did you ever respond to my first email? I ..."

Tran strokes the little goatee on his chin, keeps his eyes fixed on Michael.

"How do I know Tuki's safe and alive?"

"It seems that we don't trust each other."

Michael feels another stab to his guts. "But Tuki's in terrible danger."

"She thinks she's running out of time."

"What do you think?"

"I love my sister. I think she's scared as all hell, yah."

"So what do we do now?"

"Why don't you start by telling me about the guy who has been following us?"

"What guy?"

Tran nods to Michael's father, who has taken a seat at neighboring restaurant and is sucking beer from a bottle of a local brew called Ba Ba Ba—333.

The failed lawyer, the fisherman, feels his belly knotting. "Does *your* father ever think he's Rambo?"

A smile spreads over Tran's face. "That's your father?"

Michael nods. "Take us to Tuki. You can ask her."

"Not so fast."

"*Cristo*, you said she's running out of time."

"Your dad was in the war?"

"He thinks he still is."

Tran nods. "I'm afraid we all are."

"What do you mean?"

"You know Wen-Ling?"

"She's a killer."

"She's stalking Tuki."

"That's what I guessed from your email."

"But did you guess that Wen-Ling's not alone? She's got *bao ke*."

"What?"

"Thugs?"

"How do you know?"

Tran lifts his Celtics jersey. There are a half-dozen burns on his chest. Cindery, red, very recent. Someone ground out cigarettes on his skin.

"Jesus. You better see a doctor."

"It just happened. Trust me. If I wasn't so sure that Tuki's problems can't wait, I wouldn't be here."

"Where's Tuki now?"

"At the Allez Boo. I hope … Waiting."

"Can you call her?"

The brother shakes his head no. "She won't use her cell phone. She's afraid Wen-Ling might be listening."

7

OF ALL THE RAT HOLES in Saigon, she can't believe this is where Chien has sent her to score a fake passport. A dark, little lady bar called the Tiger's Tail on Nguyen Trai Street in Saigon's Cholon district. Chinatown. Twenty-square blocks of street vendors, lethal *can sa* dealers, chicken shit, chaos.

But she's here. In disguise. Dressed like a down-on-her-luck hooker who Wen-Ling would not give a second glance. It's the band's evening off from work. Nine-thirty on a Monday night. The bar's nearly empty except for four young whores dressed in look-alike red vests and minis with gold lamé tops, playing pool to the rhythm of Bruce Springsteen's "Dancing in the Dark."

"I got no job for you, *bui doi.*" A young man eyes her from behind the bar like she's some streetwalker come in here to up her game. He's thick-chested with a buzz cut, wearing wrap-around shades. Kind of hard to see through her sunglasses. But she can tell that he's one of the Viet Hoa, a member of Saigon's indigenous Chinese population.

The guy's filling a bottle of Baileys Irish Cream with a blend of water, coffee and milk. Tuki has grown up in Bangkok's lady bars, strip joints, drag clubs. She knows that if any customers ever come in, the hookers will beg the johns to buy them a "Bailey's" for something like fifty thousand Vietnamese dong, about three dollars a glass.

"I lost my passport." She feels sweat starting to bead on her back even though this little bar is heavily air conditioned.

The young man leaning over the ebony bar smiles, whispers something to her in Vietnamese, most likely indecent.

She shakes her heard, doesn't understand, has only been back in her native country eighteen months. Still doesn't comprehend much more than the Vietnamese of the market place and the home.

"You want a new Vietnamese passport, Doll Baby?"

She nods, presses close to the bar so she can hear his voice better under the Springsteen.

"How much money you got?"

"How much money do you need, la?" She's not toying with him. Not even trying to bargain.

She just wants him to set the price so that she can make the transaction and get out of here. She has a bad feeling about this place. It looks the way she pictures the hooker bar her father ran, the Black Cat, back in the early seventies. It was downtown, not here in Cholon, but still … Her mother was like one of these poor girls.

And now I'm living dust. Maybe soon to be dead dust unless I can get the hell away from Wen-Ling. Get out of Vietnam.

"Passport very expensive today."

She says in Vietnamese that she doesn't have a lot of money.

"You have boyfriend, Girly?"

"Khong." No, she doesn't have a boyfriend.

She thinks of Michael. Her heart's bleeding inside her chest. For all she knows, he could be married or dead by now. Nothing in her life has been harder for her than leaving him. But it was the only way to save him from becoming another one of the Dragon Lady's victims.

"Maybe I be you boyfriend. You can call me Flash. Want to give Flash number one blow job?"

"Cho Chet, Flash," she says. Tells him in English that he can go blow himself.

She's already on the street when he grabs her by the arm. "One thousand two hundred dollars U.S. New price." There's a strange urgency in his voice as if he's more than a little afraid he has pushed her too hard, might not seal the deal. "Pay when passport finished for you."

Chien had told her to expect to pay at least two thousand. Like what's with the discount all of a sudden?

"I'm in a hurry," she says, suddenly feeling as if maybe she has some bargaining power, as if maybe this guy's desperate for her money. "I need this by tomorrow … and let fucking go of my arm, la."

"You come now. Upstairs. We take you passport picture, nguoi dep."

She cringes. Usually, she likes it when people use this flirty little term of endearment with her, when they call her a beautiful kid. But right now it sounds creepy, filthy. She wishes she had stayed at home and waited for Tran to come back from his meeting with some mysterious guy about a new gig for the band. But he was supposed to meet her at a backpackers' bar called the Allez Boo in the Pham Ngu Lao district of the city at eight-thirty, and when he didn't show by nine o'clock, she kind of panicked and came here on her own.

So now she pulls the Walther from her purse and points it at him. "Lead the way, ban toi."

* * * *

"Drop the gun, Tuki." The voice is Wen-Ling's … and the metal pressing against the side of Tuki's head is undoubtedly the barrel of a pistol. "Slowly. Drop it on the sofa."

Tuki has followed the troll called Flash into a dimly lit apartment at the top of the stairs over the Tiger's Tail, has been ambushed by the Dragon Lady, who was hiding behind the door. "Shit, la."

"Yes, shit, la. Indeed."

"Leave me alone."

"You on drugs? You look like hell."

"What makes you think you look so good?" The words are out before she can harness her anger.

"Having this gun at your head."

"Excuse me?"

"Drop the fucking pistol, girl."

Tuki lets the gun fall from her right hand onto a dirty maroon sofa, grits her teeth. Calls herself ten times a monkey for not realizing that she was being set up with the promise of scoring a fake passport at the Tiger's Tail. She wonders how much Wen-Ling had to pay Chien to send her here. Wonders whether Flash works for Wen-Ling, whether this bar is the dragon's lair, or whether Wen-Ling is just using Flash and the Tiger's Tail to spring her trap. Wonders whether there is even a chance that she will leave this place alive.

Wen-Ling picks up Tuki's Walther, waves at her with a gun in each hand to sit on the sofa. "You know you have caused me no end of trouble and time?"

Tuki looks at Wen-Ling standing over her with both guns leveled on her chest. The woman is probably in her fifties, Tuki's mother's age, but she could pass for a young thirty-five in that tight little blouse, silk slacks, sandals. Her skin is so white, smooth. Her long hair silky in that ponytail flowing from beneath a straw hat. She's elegant, too, with the string of black-blue pearls around her neck, the burnished gold bracelet, diamond and sapphire earrings, matching finger rings.

How does she do it, la? Does the killing keep her young? Or is it the hunt that she lives for? This moment when she has her prey backed into a corner, when she can smell my fear? Is this what the ho craves even more than the Heart of Warriors? Or is there something more driving her I can't even imagine? Something more personal?

"The people of Thailand want their ruby back. It belongs to them, not you. I come as their servant. Do the right thing."

Tuki feels a tightening in her loins. "I know you don't work for the Thais."

"How can you be so sure,?"

"I've been doing some research about the Heart of Warriors, la."

She says that, yes, it has been an important antiquity in the collection of a Thai temple in Ayutthaya for centuries. A stone cut in the fifteenth century. But the ruby originally came from Vietnam mines, resided for hundreds of years in Saigon. It was a gift to the Thai monks from Vietnam's Prince Nguyen Anh for their help pushing back the Tay Son rebels and the Chinese, for assisting him to unite Vietnam under the Nguyen dynasty in 1802.

"So who really owns the ruby? The Thais or the Vietnamese?"

Wen-Ling's upper lip is beginning to curl.

"And if the Thais really want the Heart of Warriors, they would send a real Thai, maybe even a monk, instead of you."

"Just give me the ruby, Honey."

"I don't have it."

"I saw you take it. It was lying on the floor in the drag club back on Cape Cod, and you picked it up. The night that katoey wench Robsulee had her unfortunate accident."

"You mean the night you killed her with the throwing star?"

"I saved your life. She was going to torture you to death with that stun gun. And she was going to take off with the Heart of Warriors."

"You would have killed me next ... and Michael."

"Why would I do that? Hadn't I helped you to escape from jail in Singapore, escape from the police and jao pho in Bangkok?"

"Sometimes I see the future."

Wen-Ling growls. "Do you see that I'm going to let Flash rip out your heart and eat it for dinner after he fucks your dead body?"

"You wish." Tuki feels flames rising in her neck, plays her only ace. Hopes it will buy her some time to think what to do, what to say next. "With me dead, the ruby's lost, la."

The dragon racks Tuki's Walther, points it at her nose. "You think you're so smart, *bui doi.*"

It seems odd to Tuki that this Thai-Chinese vampire would use a Vietnamese slur like *bui doi*, instead of the Thai luk sod. But she doesn't have even a second to examine that thought as Flash throttles her with a chokehold from behind.

"If you're so smart, why haven't you considered this? If you don't tell me where the ruby is, your beloved half-brother or Michael Decastro will."

Michael? The name alone is a lightning bolt through her heart.

Lord Buddha, she can't let him get mixed up in this mess again.

"Michael?" She can barely get the name out. Flash's forearm's crushing her throat. He has a knife blade poised just inches from her right cheek.

Wen-Ling smiles. Like victory. "You didn't know he was here? With your brother at Ben Thanh Market tonight? Tell me you didn't know that Prince Charming has come for you once again ... with his father?"

"No ... I ... Michael? His father? They don't know ... Tran doesn't know ..."

Wen-Ling nods to Flash. "Cut off her fucking ear. We'll see if her boys know that when they see it."

8

"ARE YOU SURE Tuki was meeting you here?" Michael stands on the sidewalk next to his father and Tran, peering into what looks like a bamboo beach bar plopped down at a busy corner in central Saigon on Pham Ngu Lau Street.

The place is throbbing with twenty-something backpackers. Australians, Germans, Dutch, Swedes, French. A couple of Americans. The blond, blue-eyed, unwashed crowd in grungy shorts and tank tops. A lot of females who seem to be traveling together are seated at the tables, eating, drinking, taking cell phone pictures of each other. Male backpackers and Vietnamese Don Juans weave among the tables—among the little, twinkling white lights—cruising the girls. A couple of tired young hookers are flirting with the boys.

Lady Gaga's "Bad Romance" pulses from the sound system. A four-year-old Vietnamese street kid is freak dancing on the curb, humping the rear wheel of a parked motorbike, while the clientele toss coins at his feet. The air stinks of cheeseburgers and Heinekens. Michael can't imagine Tuki even stopping here for a minute. Definitely not the style of the girl he loves. Too white, too young, too touristy.

"You don't like this place?" Tran has an impish grin on his face.

"We have bars like this on Cape Cod."

"And …?"

"Tuki used to call them meat markets."

"She still does."

"So then why would she …"

"Because Wen-Ling probably would not think to look for her here. She used to be a drag queen, yah?"

Michael is starting to get the picture. "You mean she's not dressed like herself tonight?"

Tran nods. "You remember Halle Berry in Jungle Fever?"

"With Spike Lee?"

"Of course."

"The crack-head girl with nothing but a bra under her open denim jacket?"

"That would be who you're looking for."

"Is she on drugs?"

"Not that I know."

*   *   *   *

"Have you seen her?" Tran's standing at the bar, talking to the bartender in English. She looks like a former backpacker, from England by the sound of her accent, who has settled down in Saigon for awhile to make some money before heading on to some place farther east.

"We're talking about a half-caste?"

"Yeah." Michael swallows hard. Hates the superior racist tone of this term. Half-caste.

"Dressed like a bleeding hooker?"

"I already said that, yah?" There's anger, frustration in Tran's voice.

A waitress gives him a look like lighten up, mate.

"Look, sweetheart," says Michael's father, sliding a twenty-dollar bill to the bartender. "It's really important that we find this girl."

The bartender smiles. "She was here earlier. Sat at table three and nursed an ice coffee. Fidgeted with her coffee stirrer a lot. Kept checking her watch. Seemed pretty nervous. I thought she was waiting on a john."

A little part of him wonders. Could it be true? What if she has moved on? Is this total madness that he's even come here? He hears Colón's voice in his head. She's already broken your heart. Twice.

"She had this strange way of flicking back her hair over her shoulder with her index finger."

The image catches Michael by surprise, a tender memory. It's as if for the first time since he arrived in Saigon he actually feels that Tuki's really here, he'll really see her. And, Cristo, he forgives her everything she has ever done, will ever do. I only hope that she can forgive me.

"When did she leave?" Tran.

The bartender shrugs. "Think I bloody know? A while ago, mate."

Caesar Decastro slides another twenty-dollar bill her way.

Another smile. "She didn't say anything about three guys looking for her."

"You talked to her?" Michael.

"She came up to the bar. Said if a cute Vietnamese guy with a straw fedora came in here I should give him this." She reaches under the bar, pulls out a drink napkin.

There's a note written in lipstick.

9:15—went to Tiger's Tail

"What's that?" Michael's already feeling something starting to boil in his belly.

"A bar, no doubt," says his father.

"It's in Cholon, I think." Tran heaves a heavy sigh.

"What?"

"Chinatown, Ace," says his old man.

"Wasn't that where you were with the 716th MPs?"

"The Liberty Hotel. It was our barracks."

"I don't know Cholon very well," says Tran.

"Afraid I do ... but ..." Caesar's voice sounds suddenly faint, froggy. His eyes look moist.

"But what, Dad?"

"But nothing. I lost someone there a long time ago."

Michael feels himself cringe, thinks of Tuki. Thinks, too, about the pictures he found of Meng in his father's photo album from Saigon.

*   *   *   *

"You lived together?"

"Just a few months, Mo."

She had a one-room flat in Cholon. The army didn't feature that sort of thing. But they knew what was happening. There were a lot of GIs shacking up in Chinatown. It had been going on for so long when Caesar got there, you could see many Amerasian kids in the streets. They spoke English.

"What happened?"

Caesar says that he got new orders. To the Philippines. The war was going badly. There was hell to stop it back home. Someone up top decided that the GIs fraternizing with the locals was out of control. The press had started to write about it (the hooch girls), and the army didn't like the heat. They decided to pull the plug on all the love nests. Coming off duty one night, a sergeant major grabbed Caesar and a bunch of MPs who were shacking up. Sent them to pack up their gear, get on the bus to the airport. Just like that, they were history. Cholon—history. Meng—history. No chance to even say goodbye.

"One hell of a heartbreaker, losing a girl like that. You know what I mean, Kid?"

9

"TAKE A SHOWER and put these on, *bui doi*." Wen-Ling crosses her arms, leans against the door into the penthouse on the roof of a well-worn hotel. She nods with her head, gives a dreamy roll of her eyes, points with the black mug of tea in her hand to a pair of white vinyl fashion boots with four inch heels tossed on the seat of an armchair. Draped over the back of the chair is a skimpy, cotton jersey dress with long sleeves. It's red with a big yellow star on it like the Vietnamese flag. The star's on the belly of the dress.

Tuki doesn't move. She's lying on a queen bed, the covers pulled up around her, hands pressing a washcloth to what's left of her right ear. It has been two hours since Flash sliced off her earlobe with the little golden sand dollar stud that Michael gave her back in America on Nantucket Island. An hour and a half since the bleeding more or less stopped. An hour since Wen-Ling brought her to this suite on the top floor of a short-time hotel on a side street off Phan Van Khoe Street near the market district of Cholon.

If she hadn't been so sick with pain and shock, she might have laughed at the name of this place. Just about the perfect name for a whore house in both Vietnamese and English. The Luc Phuc, the Fragrant Moment. The name must be a leftover from the American War.

"Get out of bed. Time to work, girlfriend. It's the midnight hour. Plenty of boys waiting downstairs for a special party."

"I'm no whore."

Wen-Ling puts a pistol to Tuki's head. "You're anything I want you to be until you decide to give up what doesn't belong to you."

"Go away."

"You want me to get Flash in here with his knife?"

Tuki imagines his dry fingers on her earlobe again, the sharp tug on the sand dollar stud. The terrible hiss as he slices a half-inch of flesh off the bottom of her ear, the hot blood splattering on her neck, her shoulder, her chest. Soaking her denim jacket, her bra. Sudden death, she thinks, she can handle. But being carved up, fading away little by little? This is definitely not how she wants to go. If Michael ever sees her again, dead or alive, she wants him to know her. To still love her.

"What will it be? Flash's knife … or a shower?"

Tuki rolls out from under the covers. Sits up on the edge of the bed in her bra and panties. "Shower."

"What?" Wen-Ling's still leaning against the exit door, still flashing her piece. Still looking like some glamorous society babe. Freaking Dragon Lady.

"Just let me take a shower."

"Fifteen minutes. Clean yourself up good. When you come out of that bathroom, you better have covered that ear with your hair … and look like a million bucks in that dress."

Just as Tuki is about to close the bathroom door behind her, Wen-Ling springs three steps across the room, grabs the door by the edge.

"This stays open, Love. And when you put on that dress—no underwear."

*   *   *   *

Surprisingly, considering the general sleaziness of the Luc Phuc, it's a great shower. Brilliant water pressure and a massage shower head that dynamites away a mountain of fear locked in her neck, shoulders, back. As the water streams off her body, she tries to think about what she must do next to save herself, to keep Tran, Hong Tam, her mother safe. And Michael. Sweet Michael.

If Wen-Ling's telling the truth, he came for her. Again. As he came for her when she had all the trouble in Bangkok two years ago. And this time he has his father with him. They are in danger. She never would have asked him to come. Not in a million years. But they have, and her heart sings with uneasy hope.

Lord Buddha, the cavalry's coming, la. But where? When? And can they escape what her favorite Clint Eastwood movies call an ambush?

She feels that water massaging her forehead, her cheeks, burning her wound a little, too. Wonders if Tran got the message that she left with the bartender at Allez Boo. Wishes she had never left it. She might be leading Tran into a trap. Leading Michael and his father, too, if they have already found Tran. Surely, it was Tran who got in touch with Michael somehow, urged him to come to Saigon, even though she begged him to leave Michael out of this mess. She could not help but tell her half-brother about Michael and the terrible things he has saved her from in the past. She told him, too, how much she still loves the lawyer with the big Portuguese heart, the fisherman's son.

Tran felt her heartache when she arrived in Vietnam eighteen months ago looking to start a new life. He knew that she was still in love with an American. After some months living with her half-brother, she confessed to him the sad and glorious story of how Michael had saved her from conviction and prison on Cape Cod when she was framed for the murder of Al Costelano in Provincetown. That was four years ago, when she was still an intersexual person and working as a drag queen, singing the songs of Janet Jackson and Whitney Houston on stage.

And she told Tran how Michael had come to her rescue in Bangkok two years ago after the operation that made her fully a woman. After the Thai police wanted her for the murder of her ex-lover's father, Bruno Kittikachorn. After the Thai mob, the nak-lin, started chasing her for the Heart of Warriors.

She turns her back to the shower, lets the water beat on her shoulders again. Feels deep in her chest that even during all of that madness with the nak-lin, she never felt like she was in anything close to the danger that she's in now. She's seen Wen-Ling kill for the ruby before. In Bangkok, in Provincetown. And she has seen how relentless a hunter the witch is. The Dragon Lady doesn't give up. What else does a girl need besides a missing piece of her ear to prove that? How long before the ho goes after Tran, the rest of her family? Or after Michael and his father? They'd barely guess the brutality Wen-Ling may visit on all of them. To have a prayer of keeping the people she loves safe, and keeping the ruby safe, she needs to come up with a plan. She needs to get her gun back. Needs get out of here and find her boys. Must put Wen-Ling off balance.

So as they say back in Thailand, la, ao kung foi pai tok plaa kaphong, she says to herself. Use shrimp to bait a perch. But ... first things first, get out of the shower, dry yourself, nguoi dep.

She will put on the tight little jersey dress, the disco boots, some bright red lipstick. Let the johns looking for love downstairs in the bar of the Luc Phuc see her body smoldering. Let them wonder if at any minute Saigon might go up in flames ... While Wen-Ling runs to consult her mirror, like Snow White's bitch stepmother, wondering who's really the fairest of them all. Wondering if the phoenix has risen yet again from her own *bui doi* ashes to kick some ass.

10

"CRISTO, WHAT THE hell's this guy talking about?" It's after midnight now. Michael Decastro's jet-lagged, sick of drinking the can of 333 in front of him. He sees that his father's looking ready to kill the thick-chested bartender called Flash, who's polishing a glass at the Tiger's Tail.

"He says Tuki left something for us." Tran has been talking nonstop with the bartender in Vietnamese for two minutes.

"What? Are we on some kind of treasure hunt here?" Caesar.

"He wants a hundred dollars," says Tran.

The older Decastro screws up his face as if he's in actual pain. Then Caesar looks around the bar. He eyes three of the young hookers fondling a trio of Japanese businessmen on couches in an alcove. One other girl's playing pool with herself, bending over the table and flashing her booty, in a way that someone has obviously told her looks provocative. The vet's mind seems to be drifting as he listens to the stereo filling the room with riffs from Jimmy Hendrix's "Purple Haze."

"Dad?"

"Yeah?"

"I think we have to give this guy the money."

"A hundred goddamn dollars?"

"I don't think we're in a position to bargain," says Tran. He nods to a trio of young thugs stationed as bouncers at the front door.

Michael's dad has not stopped staring at the girl playing pool.
"Dad?"

"Ask him how much for that girl."

"One hour, fifty dollars," Flash says in English.

"How much for the night, Charlie?"

"One hundred."

The girl must have been listening, must understand English, because she has put down her cue stick and has come over to the bar. She's already pressing a hand on the fisherman's thigh, sliding an arm behind his neck.

Michael and Tan look at each other. Like where the hell's this going?

"Uh uh, khong, nguoi dep," says Caesar to the girl. "No. Okay?" He slides her hand off his thigh, lifts his arm off his shoulder. "What's your name?"

She can't be more than seventeen years old. Gives him a shy look, says something that sounds to Michael like, "Wing."

"You aren't from Saigon, are you?"

She says the name of a town, holds the older Decastro's hand in both of hers.

"Where's that?"

"Dad. What the hell are you …?"

"It's up the coast," says Tran.

"Not too far from our old navy base at Cam Ranh Bay." Caesar gets that faraway look in his eyes again.

"She give you good loving," says Flash. "Fresh from the country."

Caesar spins away from the girl. "Nobody fucking asked you, Charlie."

The thugs at the door are watching, one has his hand in a jacket pocket, maybe fishing for his cannon.

Michael grabs his father's elbow. "Come on, Dad. Let's give this guy the money, get whatever it is that Tuki left for us and blow this pop shop."

Caesar shakes off Michael's hand and reaches into the pocket of his jeans, comes out with a wad of cash. He peels off two one-hundred dollar bills, throws them down on the bar, one after the other. "I want the girl ... and I want to see what you got from Tuki."

Flash swipes up the money, then reaches under the bar.

"I'm supposed to give you little present, if I see you," he says and hands Caesar a plastic sandwich bag with something in it that looks like a sparkly, little red jelly bean.

"What the fuck's this?"

Michael grabs the bag, shows it to Tran. "Jesus H. Christ. That's Tuki's earring ... and ..."

Tran's face has turned pale. He mutters something in Vietnamese.

Caesar still has the girl's hand. "What'd he say?"

"Please ... please, take me out of here." She has begun to sob.

The bartender sneers at Caesar and the girl. Says something harsh to her in Vietnamese. "You go now, Old Man."

The three thugs at the door are starting to move in on Michael, Tran, Caesar, the girl.

"We've got to get out of here." Michael's feeling something like a scream or a cry rising in his throat.

"Go now, American Pig."

"Cho chet, Charlie."

"Go."

The thugs have them surrounded. Tran's still looking shell shocked. Michael's eyes are filling with water. The girl's wiping tears from her cheeks.

"Dad, come on." Michael has never wanted so much to just bolt from a place.

But the fisherman, the ex-MP, won't let up. He points a finger into the bartender's face. "This girl, she's just a child. Someone ought to cut off your balls and stuff them down your throat for what you're doing to these children, fucking pimp."

"Please," the girl's pulling Caesar toward the door.

"She stays here." One of the thugs pulls a .45.

"Not on your life." Michael's father looks at the weapon for a second, smiles, pushes it aside with the back of his free hand. Then he shoulders past the thugs and leads his little posse out the door.

"This isn't over, American." Flash shouts. Then he adds something threatening in Vietnamese.

*   *   *   *

"Have you gone crazy, Dad? You could have gotten us shot in there." There's a shrill note to Michael's voice as the four of them hail a cab.

"Relax, Buddy Boy, nobody was going to get hurt."

"That guy had a gun in your face."

"It wasn't loaded."

"What?"

"The thug was trying to cover the bottom of the grip with his hand, but I could see his piece had no clip in it."

"Cristo."

"Old lady bar trick."

"From back in the day?"

"These whoremongers know that if they really were to light up one of their cannons, no amount of bribes could stop the cops from shutting them down.

"The hell of it is the police ought to drown these rats in the river for what they're doing to the girls." Caesar looks at the girl beside him in the red vest and mini. She's still holding his hand. "The question is what the hell are we going to do with you, Little Red Riding Hood?"

She's looking like she's going to break into tears again when a cab rolls up.

*   *   *   *

"Why the hell is everybody acting like someone died?" Caesar's in the front with the driver and looking back at three miserable faces. The four of them are heading toward District One in the cab.

"That's a part of Tuki's ear in the baggie," says Michael. "I gave her that earring."

"What?" His father's voice sounds startled. It's like he's just now rising from some memory of the war.

"They cut off a piece of my sister's ear." Tran's words come out shaky.

"Jesus H. Christ, you think they killed her?"

"Not yet," says the girl softly. She says she knows that Tuki's still alive. She saw Flash and a rich-looking Chinese lady take Tuki away from the Tiger's Tail sometime earlier, around ten o'clock maybe.

"You saw my sister? In a denim jacket?"

"She is very beautiful. Con lai."

"But where in hell have they taken her?" Michael's feeling like his father looked back in that bar … as if he wants to break something.

"That bartender, Flash," says Tran. "He told me she's going to die, piece by piece … unless someone comes up with a ruby, fast."

"Now what do we do?" Michael switches his gaze between Tran and his father.

"Maybe I can help," says the girl sandwiched between Michael and Tran.

"Not a chance," says Caesar. "I didn't pay all that money just to get you killed. We're sending you back to be a kid and fall in love and have babies in whatever that little place is called up the coast."

"Vinh Hao," she says and starts to cry.

Tran says something to her in Vietnamese. His voice is soothing, tender.

She chokes out words in her native language between her sobs.

"She can't go back," Tran says. Her parents promised her to the head of their village in exchange for a small vineyard of table grapes. If she goes back, her parents will lose face with the head man. They will lose the grapes, maybe a lot more."

Michael has read stories about people like this girl, but he never believed it. "You mean her parents sold her?"

"She says, please, she hopes one of us could use a strong, young wife."

"You've really done it this time, Dad."

Caesar Decastro curls his lower lip, casts his eyes down at his hands folded together on his lap.

"It wouldn't be the first time," he says quietly. "I guess now you know where you got your urge to save the world, Mo."

Michael leans his head back and stares at the ceiling of the cab. "Can you help us find my girlfriend, Wing?"

"Her name is Nguyet," says Tran. "Like new we, accent on the we. It means moon." There's an edge to his voice. Seems he's had way too much of bumbling Americans for one night.

11

TUKI FEELS someone rustling her shoulder, waking her. It's late afternoon. She opens her eyes and recognizes the bright pink walls of the
top-floor suite at the Luc Phuc. Sees Wen-Ling, standing over her
looking like some kind of movie star again. Fit, firm, glossy hair. A
pink business suit showing off her legs. Gold on her wrists, fingers,
neck. Bitch.

"Why don't we put an end to all this pain and make a deal,
Tuki?"

The right side of her head's on fire. She feels instinctively for the
burning, remembers the amputation as her fingers touch the scab
on the bottom of her ear, the crusty blood on her neck. Remembers
now how last night ended downstairs at Wen-Ling's private party in
the little hotel bar. Three drunken Dutch oil contractors were trying
to force her into a gang bang … until one of them grabbed her in
a headlock and her ear started bleeding all over his silk shirt. That's
when he hit her. Three times. The abuse was even too much for Wen-
Ling, who seemed to be enjoying the show up to this point from her
station behind the bar. After the contractor's third blow, the Dragon
Lady zapped the bastard with a blast of mace to the eyes and chased
him and his friends out of the bar, shrieking in several languages.

"I really didn't want you to get hurt last night, Sweetheart.
Really."

Tuki eyes her captor. She's just waiting for the next bashing, not sure if she can ever find her balance again amid these mixed signals from the dragon.

"Sit up and drink some of this." Wen-Ling hands her a frothy glass of durian fruit blended with crushed ice, sugar, condensed milk.

What she wants to say is leave me alone. What she wants to do is finish this amazing drink and pray to Buddha, recite the Heart Sutra about thirty times. But her mind has already begun to race. It's telling her she can't take many more beatings, wonders whether Tran and Michael and his father are being beaten like this, too, somewhere. Wonders if maybe Wen-Ling may actually be offering her a different way out of this misery. Like why am I so ready to die for a piece of red rock, la?

"You want another drink?"

"You want to stop killing me?"

Wen-Ling sits down beside Tuki on the edge of the bed. She has a wet washcloth in her hand. "Close your eyes. This may sting a little."

Tuki feels a gentle hand brushing back her hair from her wounded ear, a warm cloth cleansing her forehead, eyelids, nose, cheeks, lips, chin, neck. Finally, ever-so-softly, squeezing water on her wounded ear.

"I know you won't believe this," says Wen-Ling. "But I've always liked you, admired your courage and your talent, actually. I wish we could be friends."

Tuki doesn't say anything. She's telling herself that she's *bui doi*, dust. All living dust can do is listen.

"How about I get you a doctor, Tuki?"

She feels the warm water, lifting the sting from her ear and the right side of her head. Tells herself this too will pass, even the phony kindness. Whatever is form, that is emptiness. Whatever is emptiness, that is form.

"And then, when you feel ready to travel, we'll go on a little vacation?"

"What about the deal?"

"Why don't we just wait on that, Honey?"

She imagines what it must have been like to be the bodhisattva Thich Quang Duc when his body was going up in flames.

*   *   *   *

It's almost too cold in Wen-Ling's limo, a nineties-era Benz. Black. Very shiny. Tuki and Wen-Ling have been riding together in the back for more than two hours since leaving Saigon. The sun's setting as they approach the arching bridge over a boat canal separating the heart of Cai Be town from the mainland. Ahead, to the left, Tuki can see a canal stretching to a broad branch of the Mekong. In this light the rim of sky to the west and the water beneath are bronze streaked with tongues of red and gold. Between the sky and water lie the islands of the Mekong Delta looking like a black line of land. Sampans of all sizes move over the water. Dark creatures, their red and green running lights glowing eyes.

Tuki rolls down a window in the limo, breathes in the night air, catches the burnt scent of coconut candy factories and the sweet smell of fish and shrimp rising from the canal.

"They call this place Song Cuu Long," says Wen-Ling.

"The River of Nine Dragons." Tuki translates the Vietnamese words, feels her heart starting to hammer against her ribs.

In her eighteen months in Vietnam, she has never been to the Mekong, and yet she knows it. She has a long attachment to terrain like this. The Mekong reminds her of Bangkok where she grew up and the muddy waters of the Chao Prya. The canals here look like the klongs of Thonburi, like Klong Thuey where Prem's family had their escape. The River House. Where she fell in love with Prem so many years ago. The house that she set afire, burned to ashes, when he left her for his heroin and marriage to that innocent girl.

She has pictured the Mekong so often in her mind as the home of her mother. Stood here on its banks a thousand times in her mind as she danced, as she sang, feeling the Delta's moist heat. The air growing thick as river fog, incense, opium … ginger and charcoal fires … water buffalo and rice paddies. Bangkok. Saigon. A midnight

train. Georgia. Georgia must be like this, too. On the edge of a vast
flowing darkness.

An old conversation about her mother with her long, lost father
replays in her head. "Misty was a whore?" "She was just a kid from
up the river, Sugar. Eighteen years old."

The car twists off the main road after crossing the bridge, makes a
sharp right turn down a narrow street leading to a wharf. The night's
coming. The first stars are in the sky. Tied to the dock is a sampan of
about sixty feet in length. But this is no rice freighter. This is a yacht.
The front three-quarters of the boat's a teak cabin, low lights burning in the windows. Mood music, Lena Horn, plays softly within. A
crew of men and women in white, nautical uniforms line the wharf
in greeting.

Wen-Ling claps her hands. A little act of joy. "Let the adventure
begin."

Tuki feels the pain in her right ear flare, reaches for it uncon-
sciously. Feels the three stitches the doctor sewed in before she left
the city.

"No one's ever going to find us here, la," she says before she
remembers that she's not alone.

"Isn't that the point of a vacation, Sweetie?"

Am I going to die on this river of nine dragons?

12

"THIS IS HONG Tam," says Tran.

Michael feels the shrimp that he just ate for dinner at Ben Thanh Market rising in his throat. The little girl standing in front of him looks like a miniature Tuki. It's not the jet hair pulled back in twin ponytails that marks the resemblance, nor the beige cotton jumpsuit adorned with images of the cartoon dinosaur Barney. It's that grin, that huge, amazing smile, coming out of this blue evening the way it does. Tuki's grin. The full lips and straight white teeth. Two dimples bloom on her cheeks. Catlike ... and, yet, so vulnerable. What's not to love? If Tuki had not lost their baby two years ago in an attack by Wen-Ling's thugs, the child would be almost this age. Tuki must be head-over-heels for this kid.

Seven-thirty in the evening. The Decastros, son and father, are back on the hunt for Tuki again after ten hours of sleep, after Tran has met them at the market and invited them to his home. Now they're standing in the small living room of Tran's third-floor flat above an alley off Le Thanh Ton in a neighborhood apartment building on the northeast edge of District One.

"And this is my mother," says Tran, motioning to the middle-age woman standing behind the smiling little girl, hands on the child's shoulders.

"Ten toi la Huong Mei." She stares hard at Michael, squints as Tuki does when she's trying to read someone's character. Then her gaze settles on his father. Her face is a mask of no expression, but something's softening in her eyes. "You old GI Joe, yes?"

Caesar looks startled, ambushed. He tries to speak. Nothing but a stuttering sound comes out. The man who was all bravura last night seems beyond flustered, ready to bolt or cry, when Huong Mei steps from behind her granddaughter and reaches for the veteran, draws him into a hug.

His lower lip trembles. "I'm so sorry ... for what we did to your country ... I ..."

She hugs him tighter. Caesar is weeping now.

"It long time ago," she says. "And we all poor lost children then."

Michael can hardly comprehend what he's witnessing. Has never seen his father cry, except at his mother's funeral. And after all the years of hearing Tuki talk about her mother, the legendary bar hostess Misty ... The myth, the real thing, a middle-aged lady, stands before him, giving comfort to his wilting father.

She's not like Brandy and Delta, Tuki's surrogate mothers, the drag queens who raised her in Bangkok after the fall of Saigon in '75. Not an aging beauty trying to dress like someone in the movies. Huong Mei's face is smooth, open, white. Her hair's dark brown, full, a little wavy. Parted a bit to her left side, hanging to the shoulders. Pushed behind her ears, held in place with a green headband. Little ebony pendants hang from her ears. A simple brown cotton jersey—almost like her granddaughter's, without the images of Barney—shows the broad shoulders, high breasts, and narrow waist of a woman who is still a size four. Her brown skirt comes to the knees. Her calves slender, athletic.

Michael, Tran and Hong Tam are looking on awkwardly as the war survivors continue their embrace, when Huong Mei abruptly breaks the hug.

"Now we in new war, GI. The Dragon Lady steal Tuki."

"We're going to find her," says Michael.

"I thinking hard," says a shadowy figure, emerging from the bathroom. "Maybe I know where Chinese gai diem took your Tuki."

It's the girl Caesar rescued from the Tiger's Tail last night. Nguyet has a towel wrapped around her wet hair. She has just emerged from a shower ... wearing what seems to be one of Tran's t-shirts. Nothing else.

*   *   *   *

Maybe it's the peculiar hotel smell that's getting to Michael, that scent of freshly laundered linens, recently vacuumed carpets, bathroom cleansers. But he hasn't even been in the lobby of the Luc Phuc for more than two minutes this evening, waiting while Nguyet and Tran quiz a chambermaid about Tuki, before the scents start taking him back to his monumental mistake that ended at the Chatham Bars Inn on Cape Cod a little over a year ago.

And now he can't help it. He's not thinking about Tuki, except for the guilt he's feeling with regard to her. He's thinking about the day in October when his rendezvous with State Police Detective Yemanjá Colón took a turn.

For five months after Tuki had vanished from Cape Cod, Michael met Colón once a week or so at the remains of an Indian mound hidden in a marshy thicket called the Whispers overlooking Chatham's Stage Harbor.

*   *   *   *

He's seated beside Colón in a small, sandy clearing. In the center is a hillock of black, greasy sand mixed with shells. Scallops, quahogs, sea clams, soft shell clams, razor clams, mussels. Stone chips. The mound is perhaps twenty-five feet across, three feet high near its center. The perimeter is marked by the stubs of thick stakes, charred and nearly petrified by the salty winds and sea.

The leaves on the vines, the trees, the brush, the marsh grass surrounding the trail into the Whispers have turned brown, yellow, a rusty red. The southwest wind gusts in off Nantucket Sound, churning the water of Stage Harbor to foam in the crystal light. The only noises are the melodies of songbirds in the high brush at their backs. The whir of the wind across the marsh.

"Are we here for another pity party, Michael?" asks Colón.

He can't answer. Sometimes this detective can be so blunt. But it's true. Meeting here has been a little like visiting a cemetery, each pilgrimage to this spiritual place is a chance for both of them to talk about all the people in their lives who they have lost. Their ghosts. Her mother asphyxiated during sex with her drunken father, his mother lost to cancer. Her lost loves. His, like the Wampanoag Indian Awasha Patterson who showed him this place. And Tuki. Especially Tuki.

"It's okay," she says. "If that's what you want."

Her words draw his eyes away from the lines of tiny waves melting against the salt hay shore, draw him back to her. Colón's black hair whips in the wind. There's something penetrating and steady, scary, in the way she's looking at him now. The way the setting sun catches on her cheekbones, her thin nose. She could almost be Tuki's sister. His sister … if he had one. Is that what this woman has become?

"I can't stop thinking about Tuki."

"Mira … I know you've been hiding out there on your papa's boat." She nods to the sea. "But you can't just fish forever, Michael. You can't hide from your grief."

"You think she still loves me?"

She takes her eyes off him, stares out to sea. An odd look on her face. She seems to be brushing back tears with both hands. "How could she not?"

Tremors start rising in his chest as he realizes what she's telling him. He reaches for her hand. Feels its strength, fine fingers, soft skin.

"I'm sorry. I didn't want this to happen," she says, still looking out to sea, "between us."

The ground is shaking. Everything is swaying inside of him, around him. Nothing's firm or steady anymore. Tuki seems gone for good.

"Can I hold you?" he asks. Jesus Cristo.

*   *   *   *

"She was here," says Tran. He and Nguyet have just passed a handful of money to the chambermaid at the Luc Phuc and are steering Michael toward the door leading out of the hotel to the cab where his father's waiting.

"But now she gone," Nguyet says.

"Tuki?" Michael feels himself rising from a dream, picturing a sliced ear.

"Who else?"

"Where is she?"

"I hope you like boats, white boy."

He thinks about Tuki and the fishing trip south of Nantucket that he took her on aboard the Rosa Lee. The one when they scattered her father's ashes, the one where he stood with her in the bow of the trawler and held her like a scene from Titanic. She smelled of jasmine and some kind of sweet citrus blossom.

"Let's go." Michael's on a mission once more.

"Not now. We must wait for daylight," says Tran.

"Why?"

"Song Cuu Long very dangerous at night." Tran's voice is faint. "Boats go out, never come back," says Nguyet.

13

TUKI HAS NEVER liked tight places. And right here, right now, she tells herself, feels like the worst of the worst, la. But it's so mysterious, magical.

It's her first morning in the Delta, and sometime during the previous night the yacht-like sampan carrying her and Wen-Ling came to rest with a thud on a mud bank. Now, having wakened and emerged from her berth beneath a cocoon of mosquito netting, she sees that the boat is in a canal only a few feet wider than itself. Thick foliage drapes overhead.

When she looks forward from the bow of the sampan she sees the canal has come to a dead end just ahead, facing a teak house ashore. It's built on stilts, not like Prem's River House back in Bangkok that stood above the flowing water of the klong, but more like a Cape Cod cottage set amid an orchard of jack fruit. The air is thick with river mist, bird songs, the sweet scent of longan trees. When she looks astern, she sees that the narrow canal has been totally blocked by a sampan overburdened with sacks of rice. Its bow painted red like a dragon's head, big black eyes leering from white pupils.

Cold fingers slide across the back of her neck, right shoulder.

"We get off here," says Wen-Ling. "I have a surprise waiting."

*　　*　　*　　*

"Put this on your shoulders, Sweetie." Wen-Ling has been talking softly on her cell phone. She's standing over Tuki, who has been seated at a breakfast table in a little outdoor pavilion beside the teak house. She's sipping tea and eating with chop sticks from a bowl of bun rieu, crab soup and noodles, brought to her by a shriveled old man who seems to be the owner of this orchard and house.

The Dragon Lady has an immense python slung around her waist, holding its tail in one hand, head in the other. The snake's head is inches from Tuki's face, and its forked tongue is flicking rapidly toward her as if demanding a kiss.

"This is the surprise?"

"Take her. Take the snake."

Tuki wants to recoil. She doesn't like snakes, doesn't like creatures in general. But if she ever hopes to get away from Wen-Ling, she has to save face, show absolutely no weakness, no vulnerability, no fear. So she stretches out her arm, supports the python's head with her hand. Makes a bridge for the python to cross to her.

"Come, my beauty," she says, feeling the smooth, cool strength of the animal as it slithers up her arm, across her shoulders, down her other arm.

Wen-Ling flashes a fake smile, playing a game of "dare you" with Tuki. "Isn't she magnificent? The queen of the jungle."

"First cousin of a bitch dragon." Tuki can hardly believe she said this. She's taunting Wen-Ling. But surely the wench knows that a lot of victims and witnesses of her mischief and murder in Thailand, Malaysia, Singapore, and Cape Cod call her the Dragon Lady. She wallows in the role.

Wen-Ling drops into a chair opposite Tuki, takes a sip of tea from a cup handed to her by the shriveled man. "We'll see about that won't we, *bui doi?*"

Tuki does not take her eyes off Wen-Ling's, squints a little. Like *I'm still the only one who knows where your precious ruby is, la.*

"Do you feel the dragon's cousin starting to squeeze you yet?"

Tuki does, indeed, feel the snake tightening its muscles, trying subtly to coil back around her chest. "I think it's more like a hug."

"She'll keep applying pressure, until you can no longer breathe."

"Only if I let her get the best of me."

"I'm afraid that's inevitable."

"Is that a threat? Did you bring me out here to Buddha knows where, la, to threaten me again?"

"I told you we are on vacation."

"I'd rather go back to Cape Cod."

"I bet you would. Go back to a love nest for another tumble in the sheets with Michael Decastro. The guy's hot."

"That's none of your business." Tuki feels the snake squeezing her now. "I'm just saying …"

"Do me a favor, la."

"What?"

"I've told you before. Leave Michael out of this."

"But I can't. Michael, his father, your half-brother. They're all part of the deal."

The python's strength is becoming almost too much for her to resist. "So … now you want to talk about a deal?"

"Just a little."

"I thought we were on vacation."

"Something's come up, Sweetie."

"I should have guessed."

"Vang," says Wen-Ling. It's the expression people in northern Vietnam, not here in the south, use for "yes."

Once again Tuki finds herself puzzling over the Dragon Lady's word choice, her knowledge of Vietnamese. But once again, she doesn't have time to reflect. The snake's pinching her around the ribs.

"Do you want me to take the snake?"

"Whenever you wish." She can't back down now.

"Well, then how about you charm the dragon's cousin a little longer, Sweetie …?" Wen-Ling sets down her tea cup and stands up. "I should be back in a day or two."

"Hey, la …" She's got the snake by the neck with both her hands how. I want this bloody thing off me.

"Your boyfriend's looking for me. Want me to give him a message?"

14

AN HOUR AGO this seemed like such a good idea, meeting Tuki's mother over coffee to beg her help.

Tran had suggested it, said his mother would not listen to his own pleas for help. She's too afraid that his father will come unglued if she drops her daily responsibilities to her bookstore, her husband, and Hong Tam to dash off to the Delta to find Tuki. Tran's father is a kind man, but a morally rigid one. An old-school communist, a government lawyer, a party member. He has never really accepted Tuki back into the family, can't help seeing Tuki as a reminder of his wife's life during the war, her life as a prostitute and mistress to an American. Maybe Michael and his father would have more luck if they talked to Huong Mei on their own, said Tran.

So ... they have asked her to meet them during her lunch break from her second-hand, foreign-language bookshop on Nguyen Hue Boulevard. But now, five minutes into the meeting, everything's going to hell.

"I know you're terrified, but I don't think we can find Tuki without you." Michael's face is pale, sweating, unshaven. He's seated next to his father, facing Tuki's mother across a table in the restaurant at the Rex Hotel.

"You Americans ask too much." Huong Mei's voice is a whisper.

"Please ... help us. We're running out of time."

Noon in Saigon. Day Three in-country, as Caesar says. A day and a half since Wen-Ling snatched Tuki, since someone cut off a piece of her ear. What will they cut next? It's hard for Michael to discern Wen-Ling's game. Did she leave them the ear to draw them into a trap? To spur them head-long into a dangerous chase? She has made no contact with them, hasn't asked for the ruby in exchange for Tuki. But, of course, they don't have the ruby. Does Wen-Ling know that? What if she left the ear just to taunt them, to show them who has all the power? To show them that she's a sadist who's taking a peculiar pleasure in disfiguring a goddess, that she likes seeing others suffer because she has?

Michael remembers the first time he met Wen-Ling two years ago ... before he knew she was the Dragon Lady, that she was stalking him in search of the ruby. They were on the night express from Bangkok to Penang. He had the Heart of Warriors hidden beneath his tongue, was sneaking it out of Thailand to Tuki in Penang. Wen-Ling sat in the facing seat on the train. A magnificent Asian woman, offering him her bottle. Him lonely and confused because Tuki had left him in Bangkok ... getting drunk on the Mekong whiskey and the lazy song of Wen-Ling's words, her story. Was any of it true?

She said she had been a bar girl once. Bangkok, Singapore, other places in Indochina. Long time ago, Honey. She found love. But she lost her man. Very sad. Nothing is forever. Know what I mean? She called herself a refugee of love ... then she tried to persuade him to get off the train with her. Had she intended to screw him or kill him for the ruby? Or both? Who knew? He didn't go, was suspicious even then. Fucking inscrutable Dragon Lady ... "I cannot be involved, la." Tuki's mother stares at her cup of coffee as if she's expecting it to explode.

"Last night you hugged me. You said that we were in a new war," says Caesar. "You made me think that we had ..."

"I not soldier like you. I get much misery because I love American, because I have American's baby. Con lai baby."

"Tuki," says Caesar. He seems like he needs to connect the dots of the story this woman is telling him in order to move the conversation forward.

"Not Tuki, Dung."

"Dung?" Caesar is confused.

Michael feels beads of sweat sprouting on his forehead. He has explained to his father more than once that Tuki was born intersexual, with a dick as well as a vagina. But he never got into the details because he could tell that his father's uncomfortable thinking about Tuki as anything but wholly female, which she surely has been for the three years since her surgery.

Michael has never told his dad that Tuki's mother had named her child Dung. Courage. A boy's name. It made as much sense as anything did to her back in 1973 … when the Americans who were still left in Saigon called her Misty. When communist forces of the Viet Cong and the army of the North were overrunning the Mekong Delta, taking aim on Hue. When she sent her beloved Boo away from Vietnam for fear her countrymen, maybe even his former Vietnamese partners in the bar, would kill this ex-Marine whose real name was Marcus Aparecio. This ex-Marine who was the whoremaster of the Black Cat bar. This man who had saved her … for awhile.

"Dung?" Caesar asks again.

"Yes, la. Dung. Tuki. I lose that baby April 30, 1975, when NVA soldiers come into Saigon."

"I'm so sorry," says Michael.

He knows the story. Knows how Misty put her baby in the care of the two Saigonese drag queens named Brandy and Delta while she went to the bank to get money amid the chaos in the streets as Saigon capitulated to a swarm of Northern troops rolling down Highway One. Knows how the queens were waiting with the baby on a shrimp boat that day to escape the city with many of the other citizens who had been friendly to Americans. Knows how the shrimp boat steamed for Thailand before Misty could return.

"I cry for that little, lost baby, and baby's father, every day for many, many years … My heart broken."

"I can't even imagine."

"One day I meet new man. Good man. From Hanoi. I start new life. New baby. Tran. The Buddha give me second chance."

"But surely …" Caesar's pleading.

Michael can tell from the ache in his father's voice that there's something new and very personal for his father about this mission to find Tuki.

"No but," says Huong Mei, still staring at her glass of ice tea. Her face its nearly habitual porcelain mask with no expression. Michael has seen the look on Tuki when she gets petrified by pain or fear. "Now it somebody else turn to cry for that baby."

"What ….?"

"I already tell Tran, ya? Americans turn to cry. You turn cry. I love Tuki. I fear for Tuki. But no more cry."

"Wen-Ling has taken her somewhere in the Delta, but we don't know where. Huong Mei, you know the Delta. You know the people there. They are your people."

"That other life. All gone now."

"Please … come with us." Michael voice is starting to crack. He feels as if he hasn't slept for a year. His very soul is torn and jagged. He wants to tell her about the piece of ear. But what good would that do?

Tuki's mother stands up. "I so sorry. I forget something at bookshop."

Michael's on the edge of shouting, Jesus Cristo, lady, your daughter is probably going to die if you don't find a little dung yourself. He's on the verge of screaming, begging, grabbing this frozen woman and shaking her back to life … when he sees his father reach out and take Huong Mei's hand and wave him away from the table with a nod from his head.

"Go," says Caesar. "Cut me a little slack, Mo. Go!"

Even before Michael can fully rise from his seat and head for the bar at the far end of the room, his father has dropped onto one knee in front of Tuki's mother and started murmuring in flowing, plaintive phrases. The language is Vietnamese. This is the first time he's ever heard his father speak more than a phrase or two of this language. It's like he's seeing and hearing a man he has never known.

God Almighty.

*   *   *   *

"She said we must get Tran at his place, leave Nguyet to look after Hong Tam, meet her at the bookshop in forty-five minutes," says Caesar when he sits down next to his son at the bar.

"Huong Mei's coming with us?"

"She has family in Ben Tre who can help us find anything and anyone in the Delta."

"But how did you get her to change her mind? I saw ... You ... you were talking to her in Vietnamese. How ...?"

Michael sees that there are tears in his father's eyes.

"I don't want to get into this right now, Buddy Boy."

15

SHE HAS TO GET out of here ... soon. If there's one thing she knows, it's this. Escape or suffer. Unto death.

But escape to where, la? Escape how?

She doesn't have the slightest idea where she is. Ever since Wen-Ling left aboard the sampan late this morning she has been searching for clues about her location and the nearest town to flee to. But luck has not been with her. No sooner had the rice freighter and the sampan backed out of the canal, no sooner had she put the python back in its cage, than two young men emerged from the teak house carrying automatic rifles of some sort. They said they were here to keep her safe. She must stay in the orchard. She should tell the old man if she wants drink or food.

All afternoon, almost until sunset, she has been walking through this orchard no bigger than the club she played in Provincetown on Cape Cod. Meandering among the trees of longan and jack fruit. Picking and eaten dragon fruit, searching for signs of where she is in this vast delta, trying to invent an escape plan. But coming up with nothing but thoughts of Michael. Not Michael here in Vietnam—she still can't picture it. Maybe Wen-Ling is lying and he's not even here. Rather it's Michael, her Cape Cod hero, whom she's picturing. Her Cape Cod prince.

*   *   *   *

"Close your eyes, la."

He's spread out beside her. Nude, except for his shorts on the bed in the Jared Coffin House on Nantucket Island this early summer night.

The street light filters through the trees, the curtain. A soft glow, casting the shadows of leaves and a tall bedpost across his silvery thighs.

Her fingers glide along the skin, feel the curls of leg hair.

He shivers a little.

She kisses the vee at the base of his neck.

He makes a humming sound. "I love you."

"I love you too." She feels the urge to sing something. Kisses his lips. Tries to taste their fullness. The sweet, wet hardness of longans.

His hand slides up the back of her neck, cups her head. Fingers probing her thick, tight hair.

Her tongue meets his, is starting to explore his mouth when she feels something stirring in her hips. The old urge to die in a tangle of limbs. To explode into a thousand bright bits.

She wants this, la. Wants to give herself to him. Wants him. Michael. The father of her child. Once more. Merciful Buddha.

And now she can feel his body wanting this too. The perfection of it all. His muscles tightening one-by-one. They wrap her. Pull her beneath him. Fill her with something there is no word for. Only the melting away of pain, the sweet surging, the slow dancing of paired hips. The making of a new life together. The no flight that is flight.

She curls an arm around his waist, closes her eyes. Smells the scent of coconut soap on his shoulders again, feels the warm wind blowing in off the ocean. The night birds fussing in the trees, the waves combing the beach.

*   *   *   *

From somewhere in the gathering dark of the orchard come sounds she can't identify. Dragons maybe. Or her own voice.

Pleading. Baying for her lost child … and the father of her lost child. For Michael who she must find, if he really is in Vietnam, before Wen-Ling does.

She can't help herself. She's drawn to the screeching, hears the laughter of her guards. They have tossed a small monkey into the python's cage. They're betting on how long it will take the snake to catch, kill, eat the primate. They're seated in plastic chairs at a little outdoor table, drinking rice whiskey in the glow of a tiki torch whose citronella fumes drive the mosquitoes away.

"You next, nguoi dep," one says, nodding to the cage, when he sees her.

The other snickers, pats his rifle.

The snake's cage is near the edge of the canal. She can see it clearly, a box of chicken wire the size of a small car. There's one short, thick tree within. The little monkey has clambered to the top. The creature's got one arm and leg on the branch of the tree, the other hand and foot clinging to the chicken wire overhead, trying to get as far from the serpent as possible. The python has started its slow, deliberate climb up the tree. The monkey's shrieking.

"Nam phut," says the one guard. He's betting, throws down a collection of Vietnamese dong bills on the table next to his whiskey glass. Five minutes before the snake strikes.

"Muoi phut," says the other guard, adding cash to the pile in front of him. He's betting ten minutes.

"Ngay mai." One of the guards points at Tuki and laughs. She understands. He's saying tomorrow it will be her turn in the cage.

"Cho chet," she says under her breath. By then I'll be long gone, la …

Maybe the guards have not noticed but she has discovered many things in her orchard walk this evening. Just before dark the old man came back from some mission in his woven bamboo canoe, pulling it up in the bushes on the canal bank near the house. There's a paddle in it. And now that it's dark, Tuki can see the glow of lights in the western sky. There must be a town over there. She's going to slip away. Follow the water to those lights.

As soon as she can lather her skin again to ward off mosquitoes with the peppery-feeling lemon grass oil she stole from the sampan crew this morning.

As soon as she can change out of this pants suit that Wen-Ling made her wear into a pair of the old man's black pajamas hanging on the clothesline. As soon as she disguises herself beneath a non la, the conical hat discarded on the front porch.

As soon as the python attacks the monkey and launches the guards into a delirium of blood lust and final wagers, she's off. Looking for her Prince Charming.

Wan phra mai mi hon dieo, they used to say to her back in Thailand. Every dog has her day. She can't let herself believe that hers is behind her.

16

"BOAT VERY CHEAP. You pay only one million dong, GI, for two days." Huong Mei waves at a sampan tied to the wharf. She has been talking to its captain.

Even though it is dangerous to go out on the river at night, Michael, his father, Tran, and Houng Mei have decide that they must take the risk if they can get a boat. Every minute that they delay, Tuki slips further away. Soon her tracks will be too cold to follow.

"Jesus Cristo. A million what?" Caesar doesn't understand the money in this country anymore. During the war the South Vietnamese currency was called piastres, peez.

"Dong. Vietnamese dong, Dad … like twenty thousand dong equal a dollar. One mil is about fifty bucks."

"Damn, Mo, look at that thing. I wouldn't buy that hulk for twenty dollars. You have some kind of death wish? There are crocs in this river."

Caesar points to the thirty-foot-long sampan. Even with the sun nearly down and the sky growing dark, Michael can see that this boat is devoid of paint; its diesel smokes, fumes. A bilge pump's gushing a nearly constant stream of water from a hose hung over the side. If the pump fails the vessel will surely sink … in minutes if not seconds.

"My dad's a fisherman in America," Michael tries to explain to Huong Mei and Tran. "He's kind of picky about boats."

The two Vietnamese shrug. They don't know anything about watercraft. They just know that by standing here on the waterfront of Cai Be next to a mom-and-pop coconut candy manufactory and staring out at the twinkling kerosene lamps going on aboard hundreds of boats in the town's floating market, they're wasting time. It's already nightfall on the eastern edge of the Mekong Delta. Almost two full days since Tuki disappeared.

"How about that boat over there?" Caesar points to a yachty-looking sampan tied to a dock near the bridge over a canal. There are soft lights burning in the windows. Bluesy love songs drifting from within.

Huong Mei mumbles something in Vietnamese.

"She says that kind of boat probably carries French tourists," says Tran.

Michael feels his shoulders flinch.

"Then, that one." Caesar points to a sturdy sampan moored at a dock near a very French-looking Catholic church.

The boat is probably seventy feet long, almost as long as the Decastros' fishing trawler Rosa Lee back on Cape Cod. But unlike the trawler, this boat is built of some kind of dark tropical hardwood, not steel. It has a wheelhouse back aft, mounted up high for better visibility looking forward. The main and foredecks are enclosed by what looks like a long shed with windows.

Huong Mei is speaking Vietnamese again with her son.

"We want to go to your people right?" asks Michael. "In Ben Tre? To see if they can help us find Tuki?"

"My mother says Ben Tre's that way." Tran points out across the black stream lit by the pale running lights of river craft. "Maybe three or four kilometers."

Tran's mother, Tuki's mother, turns to the Decastros, points to the sampan in question. "That bia hoi boat," she says.

"You mean it's loaded with draft beer?" Caesar has a smile on his face, maybe considering his fatigue and parched throat.

"Hundreds and hundreds of small kegs to carry around to the villages," says Tran. "The captain's family sleeps in the back."

"We can sleep in front," says Michael. He has a backpack on his shoulder, a bundle of blankets and mosquito netting under his arm.

"They no carry passengers," says Huong Mei.

"Want to bet on that?" Caesar's pulls a thick wad of twenty-dollar bills out of his jeans pocket.

Michael understands that the wad is not for betting. It's for persuading the beer boat's captain to get underway tonight for Ben Tre. To carry a party of four. To crack open one of those kegs for a little refreshment.

Huong Mei says something urgent in Vietnamese to her son and Caesar.

"Is something wrong?" Michael's getting bad vibes.

"We have to hurry. Like di di mau." Caesar is already striding toward the beer boat. "She thinks someone is watching us."

*   *   *   *

"We may have just had a bit of luck." Tran and his mother have come forward to the bow of the sampan where Michael and his father are sitting on plastic beer kegs sipping bia hoi from tea cups. The boat's charging out across the black river, a satisfying beat rising from the bow wave against the sides of the hull.

"I talk with captain family," says Huong Mei. She has a cardigan sweater pulled over her shoulders to hold off the damp.

Tran explains. Last night the beer boat captain's little boys saw two beautiful women go on the sampan yacht in Cai Be and sail away into dark. One woman was con lai.

"Tuki and Wen-Ling." Michael feels like he wants to shout.

"Do we have any idea where they went?"

"Bin Hoa Phuc."

"What?"

"A large island in the Delta. Not too far from here."

"But we should stop and see your family, first. Huong Mei," says Caesar.

Something in the tone of his father's voice sounds consoling … like advocacy. A tone Michael hasn't heard his father use with anyone except his mother before. A tone that suggests some kind of understanding about the absolute pre-eminence of extended family in Vietnam.

"No time," says Huong Mei. She looks at her son with sad, tired eyes. Maybe he has told her about the piece of Tuki's ear.

"The boys told us one of the pretty women came back to Cai Be this afternoon on that yacht," says Tran. "She was not Tuki."

Caesar gulps the last of his beer. "Why am I really starting to get a bad feeling about this country again?"

Huong Mei says something to him in Vietnamese.

Michael looks at Tran. Like what gives?

"She says everyone here is carrying ghosts."

Cristo Salvador.

17

SHE HAS BEEN CHASING the glow in the sky all night, paddling her canoe through a maze of canals until she's on a wide river. At last the thick night air has turned into a silvery mist. It's heavy with the scents of mud and crabs. The broad surface of the Mekong's just starting to flare a coppery red with the sunrise at her back when she reaches the town.

Tuki hears a bell clang, then a horn bleat. Ahead, a medium-size ferry inches free of its loading quay on the waterfront of a large river town and heads toward the islands from which she has come. As the ferry passes, she reads a sign. Vinh Long-Binh Hoa Phuoc. The names bring clarity after a long, terrifying night in the bamboo canoe. Probably the name of the island that she has escaped from is Binh Hoa Phuoc. The town ahead is Vinh Long, a legendary river port in the central Delta.

Lights on a microwave tower twinkle in the early morning sky. Near the tower she sees the distinctive roof of a pagoda with its curled-up corners. Blessed be the Buddha, la, she thinks, who has led me out of the dragon's lair and darkness.

Her heart has begun to soar like the flocks of white birds rising over the river when the mosquito bites on the back of her neck begin a fearsome itching. For some reason her mind leaps from this beautiful morning to Wen-Ling's parting words yesterday. Your boyfriend's looking for me. Want me to give him a message?

She dips her paddle, gives a sharp tug. Pulls with the last of the strength in her shoulders for a canal leading off the river into the town, toward the pagoda. Somehow she has to find her dear Michael before the Dragon Lady does. She can only hope that the monks will help her.

*   *   *   *

It's nine o'clock in the morning when she drags her canoe up on the muddy edge of a trash-laden canal. Nine-fifteen when her bare feet pass through the outer gate to the temple and start across the cool flagstones toward the pagoda. Nine-sixteen when she finds herself face-to-face with two young monks who are filing out toward the street in their saffron robes, empty rice bowls in hand to beg for their breakfast. They stop and look carefully at her.

"Come, quickly, con lai," says one of the monks. He takes her hand, pulls her toward the temple sanctuary. "You must not be seen."

Because of these beggar monks, she knows that this pagoda must be a monastery dedicated to the teachings of Minh Dang Quang, founder of the Tang Gia Khat Si. The mendicant Buddhist order is one of the largest Buddhist sects in Vietnam. They take their origins from the mixing of Viet and Khmer traditions here in the Delta, and the monks are known for their kindness, austere habits, vegetarian diets, independence, and inclusion of women in their order.

When they have drawn her into a small shrine room, she smells the overwhelming scent of burning joss sticks, sees a photograph of crew-cut Minh Dang Quong, who disappeared mysteriously in the late 1950s, possibly a victim of South Vietnam's Diem government, which feared the power of the Buddhists. He's smiling gently at her from an altar. Behind the image of the bodhisattva there's an image painted on rice paper of a large burning torch rising from an open lotus blossom. Enlightenment.

Tuki pulls off her non la, holds her conical hat in both hands, drops on her knees to pray, to give thanks. She has learned the words in Vietnamese.

Be grateful to those who make us stumble
Because they make us strong.
Be grateful to those who abandoned us
For they have taught us independence.
Be grateful to ...

"No time pray," says one of the monks. "You hide now."

His friend says that word reached the monks here at Tinh Xa Ngoc Vien monastery late last night. They were told to watch for a special con lai spirit who's being chased by a cruel and powerful Chinese woman. The monks must try to keep the con lai safe until her mother and brother ... and two Americans can come for her.

Tuki smiles to think of what the monks call the Darhma Telegraph. It's a secret and almost instantaneous communication network between bhikkhu all over the country who have taken a vow to become sangha and enter into the holy life of the monastery. During the American War in Vietnam the Darhma Telegraph helped the Viet Cong freedom fighters stay one jump ahead of the Americans and South Vietnamese Army. Now, the bhikkhu have broadcast an all-points bulletin for Tuki's protection. Praise Buddha. Long live the spirit of Minh Dang Quang.

The tightness in her chest eases a little, her breath's slowing. She's starting to feel a little warmth from the spiritual hug she's getting from these monks, this monastery. And she's imagining Michael standing side-by-side with her mother and Tran on one of the flimsy monkey bridges over a canal off the River of Nine Dragons, searching the shores for her. Picturing the shadow of a beard on his dark cheeks, his soft brown eyes, his full lips. She's thinking that her knight in shining armor is coming for her again, when she senses that something's wrong. The song birds, all astir just seconds ago, have gone quiet. The faces of the two monks freeze. Shouting erupts in the main sanctuary beyond the small shrine room.

There's a low popping sound like a muffled explosion, and the air fills with gray, acrid smoke. Tear gas maybe.

Tuki's dropping to her knees, coughing, to find air for breathing when she feels a wire tightening on her neck, feels herself being dragged somewhere.

"Nice try, *bui doi*." The voice is Wen-Ling's. "You almost got away."

"Cho chet." Tuki's throat aches from the smoke and the wire.

"Maybe, Sweetie, but first there's someone on the sampan you might like to see."

18

"RISE YOUR ASS, Buddy Boy." Michael feels his father shaking his left arm. "We have a problem."

The former public defender and fisherman rubs his eyes. They sting with sweat, and he realizes that the sun must have been up for several hours, the heat already soaring well over ninety degrees here in the Delta. He casts off the mosquito netting and rises from his blanket on the foredeck, looks around bleary-eyed. Sees that the beer boat is still in the place where they tied it off late last night at a canal side wharf. It's under a monkey bridge that spans a canal on Bin Hoa Phuoc island.

"What's going on?"

"Tuki's mother thinks Tran's missing."

"What? How?"

"I don't know, Mo. She just woke me up about five minutes ago."

According to Huong Mei, Tran went ashore to talk to the locals about Tuki early this morning. He said he would be back in an half an hour. That was two hours ago.

"Jesus Cristo."

"The lady's pretty much in a panic," says Caesar. For the last fifteen minutes she has done nothing but curse herself, the Decastros, and Tuki in Vietnamese. Now she's on the phone to her husband. He wants to call the police, the army, to look for Tran. And Tuki.

Michael feels the all too familiar twisting in his guts that comes along with the awareness that despite his noble intentions he has brought a shit storm down on everyone around him. He imagines Yemanjá Colón looking into his eyes and asking him why she didn't just shoot him and get it over with last October.

"Why did I ever fucking come here?"

"That's what I've been asking myself for several days, Kid."

"And …?"

"And what? I got to stand by you no matter what. That's what dads do."

"We've walked into a hell we can't even begin to fathom."

"Now you know how I felt when I was here forty years ago."

"But you didn't have a choice. You got drafted."

"So did you. By love and something else that you're carrying in your chest. You want to talk about it?"

Michael thinks about that October night with Colón. "Probably not any more than you want to tell me what you were talking about to Huong Mei in Vietnamese yesterday afternoon."

Caesar looks away, the muscles knotting at the corner of his jaws, in his cheeks. "That poor woman."

"You think Tran's in deep shit?"

"I think we need to get our butts in gear before Huong Mei's husband calls in the cavalry and all hell breaks loose. We have to find that boy."

"How are we going to do that?"

"We've got to chat up the locals, Buddy Boy. Somebody knows something about where Tran is." Caesar seems to have slipped back forty years into his old role as a military policeman in this country.

Michael looks at Tran and Tuki's mother. She's sitting on a bench near the back of the boat with the captain's wife beside her, weeping into her cell phone. She's clearly in no shape to go ashore and start interviewing islanders and translating for Americans.

Caesar nods to the gang plank. "Come on, Mo. Let's go talk to Charlie?"

Michael winces at his father's wartime slur. "You think your Vietnamese is up to this?"

Caesar pulls his roll of twenties from the pockets of his shorts. "Maybe this will help."

*　　*　　*　　*

The Decastros stand next to a canal where it passes a restaurant for tourists, surrounded by a throng of jabbering women with baskets of wet laundry. The clothes on their backs are wet, too.

"What are they saying, Dad?"

Caesar seems not to hear. He's passing out twenties, pressing his hands together in prayer, bowing. Saying, "Cam on ... cam on, em." Thank you, ladies.

"Why are they all wet, Dad?"

"They got soaked by a sampan that blasted through here about an hour and a half ago."

"I don't understand."

Caesar says that the women were doing their morning laundry alongside the canal, using the restaurant's wharf for spreading out their wet clothes to dry a little before folding them and taking them home to hang on clotheslines. A yacht-like sampan came bombing through the canal at full speed pulling a four-foot wake that rolled right up and over the wharf, these women, their clothes. They have spent more than the last hour fishing their clothes out of the canal with poles.

"The same boat those kids in Cai Be said took Tuki?"

"I've got a feeling she wasn't on it."

"What?"

"One of the women is complaining that someone stole her uncle's canoe last night. A pretty *bui doi*."

"Then Wen-Ling's on that sampan ... and she's after Tuki?"

"And she probably kidnapped Tran for insurance."

"It could just as easily have been us."

"You think we're being followed right now?"

Caesar nods to a couple of young men in shorts who are lingering about fifty yards down the village road. One of them has a huge python draped over his shoulders.

"Shit. What next?"

"Back to the boat, Buddy Boy. Regroup."

"And?"

"We could pull the plug on this freaking fiasco right now and go home. Know what I mean? Blow Dodge before the sheriff's posse gets here?"

"Not a chance."

"Then I hope you still have a big pocket full of dollars, not just the local bongo bucks. Because I'm running low on cash and I guess we've got to unload bookoo scratch on that beer boat driver."

"Where we going?"

"After that canoe and the sampan, right?"

"Where's that?"

"The ladies say the sampan looked like it was headed for a town called Vinh Long."

"Oh."

"Just one thing you ought to know before we decide to make this leap."

"What's that?"

"Some of the washer women know the sampan that drenched them."

"It's some kind of yacht that tourists like to charter, right?"

"Maybe not."

"What do you mean?"

"The boat has a rep."

"For?"

"Some of the women say it belongs to a drug dealer ... Some of them say it belongs to an agency called Tong Cuc Hai."

"What's that?"

"Secret police. Like the Vietnamese version of the CIA."

Michael thinks about the time two years ago in Bangkok and on Cape Cod when everybody seemed to think that Wen-Ling was an agent for the Thai Secret Service. But, whether the truth or a lie, the Thai government denied it.

Here we goddamn go again.

19

"I KNOW WHERE we are." Tran's voice hits a high note of discovery.

He's sitting in a deck chair, his hands bound together behind the back of the seat ... and bound to it, too. His eyes are peering out the side window from the saloon in the sampan. He has just worked the cloth gag way from his mouth. A thread of dried blood clots at the corner of his lips. Tuki sits facing him, tied to her chair in a similar fashion, still gagged. She no longer has the non la on her head, but she's still wearing the wrinkled black pajamas she stole from the clothesline on the island. Her hair's pulled back in a ponytail. She and Tran are, at the moment, alone. Wen-Ling and her thugs are eating pho back aft with the crew in the sampan's wheelhouse.

"We're in Sadec," he says, nodding out the window.

Tuki follows his gaze. Another sunset on the Mekong. The broad river's a violet ribbon in the haze. The town off to the left looks like a pastel painting of wharves, stilt houses, the umbrellas and awnings of a quayside market. People seem wavy silhouettes or nothing at all.

"Ma and my father brought me here for the Tet holiday one year when I was about ten, to see the flowers."

Tuki is only half-listening at the moment, her mind's drifting. She's been tied in this chair all day, nodding in and out of sleep. Maybe there was some kind of sedative in the lychee nectar the boat crew has been giving her to drink. She rubs her mouth and chin on her shoulder the way Tran has done and scrapes the gag—little by little—away from her mouth so that she can talk. Her throat aches from the wire garrote that Wen-Ling used on her at the pagoda in Vinh Long. All she can think about is Michael and whether Wen-Ling or her thugs have gotten to him, too. Whether her knight in shining armor is even still alive.

"There are huge nurseries here. Fields and fields of all kinds of flowers and bonsai trees. I remember a rose garden ..."

"Michael and Ma were with you on the beer boat?" This is the question she has wanted to ask since she first saw her brother.

"And his father."

"How were they?"

"What do you want me to say?"

"I don't know, I ..."

"They were tired. They were worried about you. They looked like ... like what the Americans call shell-shocked."

"You should have never gotten them involved."

Tran shakes his head. "Maybe you're right. But at the time ..."

"I'm so sorry I ever told you about the ruby, la."

"Maybe you should just give it to that dragon whore."

"It doesn't belong to her, Brother. But ..."

"But after all this, Wen-Ling may never let any of us live ... even if she has the ruby, right?" Tran's still looking out the window, watching the lights flicker on in the houses of Sadec.

She nods. Yes.

There's no turning back. Part of her has known this for some time. She has been avoiding the facts. She got herself into this battle two years ago when she chose not to give back the ruby to Wen-Ling in Thailand. Calling a truce now will work about as well as the Paris Peace Accords did in ending the American War in Vietnam. The accords simply guaranteed the American withdrawal from South Vietnam. The civil war continued for two more years. Many Vietnamese died before Saigon fell, before reunification of the country. Before she was exiled from her mother for more than thirty years.

Chances are that the Dragon Lady would kill them all to cover her tracks if she gets the ruby. Tuki has seen Wen-Ling kill multiple times, and without the slightest hesitation, in her quest for the Heart of Warriors. Prem's father, Thai mafia, the Provincetown drag queen Robsulee. All dead by Wen-Ling's hand because of a stone. Police and Tuki's own father dead, too. As ... what did the American government call it during their war here? Collateral damage? For the Chinese gai diem, that filthy whore, life is cheap.

Tran contorts his shoulders, grits his teeth, growls. He's swearing under his breath in Vietnamese when he snaps a rung off the back of his wicker deck chair. His left hand pulls free of its binding.

"We've got to get out of here," he says.

Tuki nods to the cell phone that Wen-Ling left on a little end table. "We have to call Ma and Michael."

Tran has the phone in his hand. He's calling his mother, when the sampan suddenly lurches into a sharp left turn. Toward the shore. Toward the nurseries, the street markets of Sadec. The lights.

It's only after the boat has settled on its new course into a canal that Wen-Ling appears in the saloon.

Tran's standing near the front entrance to the cabin, cell phone to his ear. He has just started speaking rapidly in Vietnamese into the phone, when he sees the throwing star in Wen-Ling's hand. The color's draining from his face even before she cocks her arm and throws. Before the phone falls to the floor with Huong Mei's voice still buzzing from the speaker.

"Why can't we be friends, Tuki?" asks Wen-Ling in Vietnamese. Her accent is clipped, as if she learned to speak the language in Hanoi. But her vowel tones are a little off ... as if she did not grow up there. "Why must I always be the dragon?"

Tuki can't answer. Her mind's shrieking Tran's name. Again and again.

20

THE DECASTROS have been combing the streets for much of the afternoon and evening, especially the market area along the riverbanks of Vinh Long. An area that makes the busy fishmongers' wharves back home in New Bedford and on Cape Cod, the Vineyard, Nantucket seem organized, tranquil. But they've found no clues. No Tuki nor Tran, even though Caesar has tried to strike up dozens of conversations in his crude Vietnamese with the fish sellers and fishers about thuyen, boats, and ca, fish.

There has been much hand shaking and embracing as the Vietnamese recognize the seasoned fisherman in Caesar's wiry frame, leathery skin, rough hands. They recognize the war veteran, too, in those sad eyes, the hesitant speech. But when Michael's father turns his conversation to questions about whether anyone has seen a yacht sampan coming from the islands, a beautiful con lai, a young Saigonese man with smiling eyes, the locals look away, stop their conversations with abrupt denials.

"Khong," Michael hears the Vietnamese saying over and over again. No. Like we don't know anything, have seen nothing. Xin phep, please excuse. Don't ask, ban toi.

It's after dark now, and Huong Mei has still not emerged from hours of prayers with the monks at Tinh Xa Ngoc Vien monastery. The air's humming with insects, heavy with the scent of burning incense from the temple.

Michael and his father have been waiting here in the courtyard outside the pagoda for what seems eternity.

At last Huong Mei exits the temple. She's surrounded by monks and nuns, and she looks different. Transformed. She's no longer the grief-stricken Saigonese bookseller who entered the pagoda this afternoon, wilting in a typhoon of tears. Not the fearful woman who can barely let herself look Tuki in the eye. Not the buttoned-up and distant grandmother.

The monks have given her a white robe to wear. Her hair's pulled back in a tight queue. Her skin, so pale and white just hours ago, glows. As she walks, chants with the sangha, her body no longer shuffles, but glides like a dancer. And for just an instant or two Michael sees Tuki in this gliding. The same lightness, the joy in movement, the unconscious sensuality in the swinging shoulders and hips that used to bring the house down when Tuki sashayed across the stage singing about love back in the drag theaters of Cape Cod. Jesus Cristo.

"Tuki no here," she says when the chant ends and she approaches the Decastros. "Tran no here … But they here before. In morning."

Michael's not quite processing Huong Mei's words. He's lost in an ocean of worry and fatigue. Lost in memories of the woman he loves, who he's seeing for the first time through her mother. Lost in this reflection of youth, this ghost of an innocent young girl from the Mekong Delta in 1970, before she was Misty. Before she came face to face with the Black Cat bar and Marcus Aparecio. Michael's lost, too, in the new way that she looks at him with warm and steady eyes.

"No be sad, Michael." She reaches out and touches his cheek with the fingers of her right hand. "Buddha teaches … sea that rises, falls, rises again."

This sounds like something Tuki would say, has said. He wonders if Jesus would offer this same counsel. The tides change. Now. Always.

"Tuki love you very much."

"I don't know."

"She lucky girl. Find brave, tender American boy."

"I think my coming here … it's just made a mess of things."

"We do what we must do. You have noble heart, loyal heart."

Not exactly, he thinks. Not one hundred percent.

Maybe she sees the guilt in his eyes, the doubt. Maybe she fears how Wen-Ling or her crew have mutilated Tuki and her son. Because she turns away, to hide the pain rising in her cheeks. She turns to Caesar, draws him into a hug.

"My husband coming." Her voice seems to be fading. "He take me home. Police start look for Tran and Tuki. They very good, la. They find."

"Don't go," Caesar's voice is thick with emotion. "Not now. Not yet."

"Granddaughter need me … I need granddaughter."

Caesar says something to her in Vietnamese. It sounds like he's reciting a poem. Plaintive, tender.

Her arms tighten around his shoulders. Her body molds to his as she speaks softly in her language. In the shadows of this moment, Michael's father looks like a much younger man.

Michael turns away. He can't watch. Something most strange and terribly private is taking place here between this phantom of a woman and his dad. Something beyond reason and feelings. Something he can't begin to understand. So he settles his stare on the column of monks and nuns as they file away in the dark to their beds at the monastery. Watches them until the courtyard is empty of everything but the persistent humming of insects and the calls of night birds.

When he hears Caesar clear his throat, he turns back to look at his father. Huong Mei's gone, and his dad's wiping tears from his eyes.

"Let it be, okay, Mo? Just let it be."

"Can I say that this really bites?"

"Yeah … you can say that."

Michael remembers something his father always says when things are going to hell while they're out fishing. It's an old army thing. "Situation normal. All fucked up."

"Yeah." A sad little laugh.

"So what do we do now?"

"I'm betting the beer boat is long gone."

"And we're running low on cash," says Michael.

"But heading home with a busted trip's not an option, right?"

Michael feels the stab of guilt in his gut, remembers that stupid, stupid night with Colón in Chatham again. Remembers, too, the love that bloomed between him and Awasha Patterson after the first time Tuki left him lonely and broken on Cape Cod. "I can't go home."

"Well, Buddy Boy, we're mariners and fishermen. I guess we got to borrow a boat and go fishing for Huong Mei's kids."

"You mean steal a boat? Tonight?"

"You think if we wait until tomorrow, or for the police to take seriously a missing persons report on a half-breed and minor league musician, we have a prayer of seeing these people alive again?"

"Shit. Where would we even start?"

"The monks know where Tuki is."

"They told Huong Mei?"

"Up the river. Town called Sadec. Wen-Ling's sampan's tied up in the town's main canal right now."

"You think we have a chance?" Michael's a little boy again, looking for a shot of confidence from his old man. The master mariner, the war vet. The hero.

"We grab one of those long-tail boats, I figure we can be there by midnight." He's referring to one of the sleek, narrow boats, almost like very large slippers, that the river men use. The boats have inboard engines that turn propeller shafts stretching back ten or more feet behind their sterns. They make a terrible racket with their un-muffled auto engines and go like rockets.

"Then let's roll."

"Wait a minute."

"What?"

"We're in a holy place. Get down on your knees, Kid." Caesar kneels.

"Oh."

"Yeah, you better get going on the best prayer you can think of."

21

TUKI HAS BEEN sitting with her brother's body in the saloon of the sampan all night, wishing she had the monks here to help share her vigil. The boat has been tied to a wharf in Sadec since Wen-Ling threw a screaming tantrum then went ashore for hours. Now the sampan rocks with the current. The misty night swirls around it. One of Wen-Ling's thugs sits in a chair with a rifle pointed at Tuki as she prays.

As rivers full of water
Fill the ocean,
Even so does what is given here
Benefit the dead.

Like all Buddhists she believes that the soul leaves the body immediately after death but hovers around for three days and sometimes decides to reunite with the body to complete unfinished business. So she's praying that Tran will come back to this torn corpse … if only for a second. The killing gash over his heart is now a dark scar amid a field of scabs from burns of some sort. She guesses that tonight was not his first encounter with Wen-Ling. She saw him without his shirt the day before her abduction and his skin was clear, so these wounds are only a few days old. It seems like it must have taken more than a year before Wen-Leng found her and Tran in Saigon. That night the Dragon Lady showed up in the bar in the Caravelle Hotel was the ho's signal that Tuki's days of freedom were numbered, that suffering was about to descend like a plague on Tuki and the people she loves. Looking at Tran's wounds, she can feel his pain … and his release from pain, as she washes the flesh, combs the hair. Then she puts her remaining gold earring and some pieces of rice in the mouth so that he will not be lonely or hungry in the afterlife until his day of reincarnation.

Finally, she spreads out her brother's body on a mat and places a chopstick between his teeth according to custom, so that he may breathe and speak in that moment when he comes back to life to bid her farewell. It's then, in the instant when he speaks to her, that she will tell him he's the best brother a girl could ever want. That he gave her a family, gave her Hong Tam. That he must go now in peace and carry the name Trung, which means faithfulness, into the next life.

Until then she sits … a lotus on the cabin sole, rocking, chanting softly.

> *Impermanent are formations,*
> *Subject to rise and fall.*
> *Having arisen, they cease,*
> *But their subsiding is bliss.*

*　　*　　*　　*

"Let me ask you again, Tuki, why must I always be the dragon? Why not you?" Wen-Ling has returned to the sampan in her white pantsuit. She has her black tea mug in one hand, a pistol in the other as she dismisses the guard.

The grieving sister pretends not to hear.

"You think you are better than me?"

No response.

"You think you're not a thief?" Wen-Ling keeps the pistol vaguely pointed at Tuki, settles into a chair where she can stare at Tuki over the dead body.

"I'm not a killer."

Wen-Ling laughs.

"What's that supposed to mean, la?"

"Don't you see that if you had given me the real ruby two years ago in Singapore, not a glass fake, your father, your half-brother and all those others who died would still be alive?"

"That doesn't make me a killer. A dragon."

"Doesn't it, Sweetie? You and me, there's no difference."

Tuki feels her grief starting to catch fire, sadness turning to anger. "Except that you have the boat and the gun."

"And you have a ruby that does not belong to you."

"Eat your heart out, la."

"We could be sisters." Wen-Ling takes a long drink of her tea. Closes her eyes, savors the drink.

"Cho chet," she says.

She hates it when Wen-Ling plays this let's-be-friends, let's-be-sisters game the way she did back at the Luc Phoc in Saigon, and this proposed vacation here in the Delta. Some freaking vaction, la! The dragon ho is a queen of mixed signals, relentlessly trying to get Tuki to drop her guard by alternating violence, intimidation, and tenderness. She has heard that this is how the most successful prisoner interrogators work. Well, she thinks she can resist such ploys ... And yet the tenderness sometimes seems so genuine. You have to wonder if the bitch is truly lonely, truly looking for someone to understand her, to share her life. There are layers and layers to this wench. She's like an onion. You never quite know what you'll find when you peel a layer away.

It's scary as hell.

"Come on. Don't be like that."

Tuki strokes her dead brother's arm, feels its cold, stiff muscles to remind herself on the most basic level why she's never going to back off from this battle, why the entire core of her body is beginning to boil. This thing will not be over until either she or the gai diem has left the planet. There's no turning back now.

"Michael's going to make you pay." She likes the sound of this threat, likes the way it makes her nose tingle. As if she smells blood.

"How's that going to happen?"

"He's going to find us."

"You think?"

"Michael's father knows this country, la. He was a soldier. And the Decastros are fishers. They know more about catching things … and boats, rivers like this, than you can even dream of." As soon as Tuki says this, she knows she has made a mistake, overplayed her hand.

Wen-Ling sits silently for a half-minute as if thinking over what she has just heard. Sips from her black mug. Then she laughs. A strange, vacant laugh. "Americans. They never learn do they?"

"What?"

"That dragons like us, like this country, Japan, China, Korea. All of Asia. We have more snares set for those poor long-noses that they can even imagine."

"The Buddha preaches against the evils of arrogance and over-confidence."

Wen-Ling stands up. Walks over to Tuki, bends down and kisses her on the forehead. "Exactly, Sweetie. That's why we're moving the sampan again in five minutes. Careful dragons always have backup plans. Don't we?"

"Cho chet, gai diem."

Wen-Ling shrugs off the curse. Kisses Tuki on the forehead again. "I'm sorry your brother had to die. Tomorrow we will take him to some monks and give him a proper funeral."

"Fuck you," says Tuki.

She's getting a vibe that maybe Wen-Ling regrets killing Tran, that whacking him with a *tonki* was an impulsive reaction. An explosion triggered by something hidden deep behind that calm and controlled mask. Possibly Wen-Ling had not foreseen murdering Tuki's loved ones, at least not until now, as a means to persuading the *bui doi* to give up the ruby. But seeing Tran on the phone touched off an overwhelming fear, and the dragon's first urge was to protect herself by silencing Tran. Maybe she had hoped to torture Tran. Cut off pieces of his body, like cutting off Tuki's ear, as a way of intimidating Tuki into giving up the Heart of Warriors. With Tran dead, the Dragon Lady has to change her game. It's grown deadly and just plain weird, la. Like she wants more than the ruby.

Lord Buddha, help me.

22

SADEC. Another sunrise on the Mekong. Still no sign of Tuki. The mosquitoes are coming in swarms.

Since midnight Michael and his father have been scouring the wharves and canals along the Sadec River, a side channel of the Mekong. Their stolen long-tail boat is running low on gas, and they have not found Wen-Ling's yacht sampan. Michael feels his eyes going blurry with fatigue, stress. He's worried that the noise of their boat is going to attract attention. Two white guys in a local boat cruising the shoreline of Sadec all night? How long before some local person alerts the police or the army, who may already have been contacted by Huong Mei's husband? How long until word comes from Vinh Long about the stolen boat? How long could the Vietnamese put them in prison? How long before Wen-Ling mutilates Tuki again, or her brother? Or all three of them just totally vanish?

Part of Michael wishes he could find the ruby and use it to negotiate for Tuki and Tran's freedom, but he hasn't the faintest idea where to start looking for the stone. And his gut tells him that Tuki would never forgive him for trading it for her life. At least in her mind, her suffering has given her the right to decide the stone's fate.

"We have to park this boat." Caesar seems to be channeling his son's thoughts as he bats the air to keep the insects away.

Michael steers to a vacant patch of wharf on a small canal, cuts the engine. "Maybe we could locate some monks. Maybe they know something."

Caesar leaps onto the wharf, ties off the boat. "I should have thought of that earlier."

"How do we find a pagoda?"

"Look for the tallest building."

*   *   *   *

"Beautiful con lai you seek? She no here," says a monk. He's wearing a deep red robe, has his rice bowl in hand as he stands outside the gate in front of an immense yellow temple. It looks something like a Western cathedral with a three-story pagoda rising over its roof.

"The monks in Vinh Long told us we could find her in Sadec."

"Many pagodas in Sadec. Maybe other temple. Maybe she there."

"This is very important. The con lai is in terrible danger, you understand?" Michael's voice wobbles with weariness, worry.

"Kidnapped, yes?"

"Then you've heard about her."

"Oh yes, the sangha know. Powerful lady take girl from Saigon."

"And now her brother, too."

The monk's gaze follow a flight of doves rising from the temple roof. "You try Chua Co Huong Tu. Not far from here. But maybe better you not go right now."

"Why?"

"Everybody busy preparing funeral. Someone left them body in the night."

"What kind of body?"

"Young man … killed with throwing star. He what you Americans call gangster, maybe."

"Maybe not," says Caesar Decastro.

Michael feels his blood freezing.

*   *   *   *

Caesar Decastro is out of breath and wheezing when they reach the Huong Tu Pagoda. His son has led him on a sprint around a city block from the first temple. This pagoda is much smaller, one story, very ornately decorated with pale blue walls and lots of gold leaf paint. More like temples in China that Michael has seen in pictures than the towering ones here in Vietnam.

In the courtyard beyond the walls separating the temple from the street a dozen monks are chanting, ringing little bells, lighting hundreds of joss sticks, carrying wreaths as they file into the main sanctuary of the pagoda. Michael removes his shoes and follows them, a man drawn into the temple by invisible wires. He sees the monks arriving from a back room, carrying a simple wooden casket. They rotate it until the head is facing west, while one of the sangha lights an oil lamp beside the coffin. Another lifts and pours water over the hand of the dead . Still other monks drape a white cloth around the coffin while chanting the sutras.

Michael draws closer. Peering into the coffin, he's not surprised to see Tran's face. But he's shocked to see Tran looking like a little boy wrapped in a winding sheet. To see him almost for the first time without a smile, looking vaguely angry about the chopstick clinched in his teeth.

"Jesus Savior, forgive us our sins," he says under his breath. Perdoai as nossas ofensas ...

He's fading back from the circle of mourners, sliding away toward the front door of the temple, toward the courtyard, when he feels more than sees his father beside him.

"They got that poor boy in there, don't they?"

"Somebody has to tell his mother."

"We're really in the shit, Kid."

"Now what are we supposed to do?"

"Run like hell, I think."

"Where?"

"This place has to have a back gate." Caesar has his son by the arm, his son's shoes in his other hand. He's guiding him around to the side of the pagoda.

"What do you mean?" Michael doesn't understand his father's urgency, secrecy.

"Don't look now, Buddy, but there's a cyclo stopped by the front gate. It's been following us all morning."

Michael can't help himself. He twists, looks over his shoulder, sees two figures in black pajamas and conical non las sitting in the bicycle rickshaw. He's thinking that something about them looks familiar ... realizing that they are women and that one of them has her wrists bound together on her lap ... when the monks start shouting some kind of warning. Maybe to him and his father, maybe to the women in the cyclo. Maybe to someone else. Maybe the dead.

*   *   *   *

Lord Buddha, it's him. After an hour of following Michael and his father from a distance to tease Tuki, to kindle the flames of love and desire for Michael, Wen-Ling has finally let her see his face clearly. This is flat-out emotional torture. The olive skin, the shadow of his dark beard, full lips, the razor-cut hair. Michael, la. Most-wonderful Michael. Michael, whose arms can wrap her in a cocoon of shiny dreams, warm her against the furnace of his chest. She can almost smell the fresh fishiness of his body, taste the saltiness of his mouth.

And she wants to scream. Wants to tell him to run.

But it's too late. Wen-Ling's six thugs have already surrounded her beloved and his father alongside the temple. Michael's staring at her, reaching out to her with those large, black eyes. She can feel him calling her name.

"You can still stop this, Sweetie." Wen-Ling's voice is unnaturally soft. "Where's the ruby?"

She's on the edge of telling everything about where she hid the stone when she hears a whistle, sees police running from a van toward the pagoda.

"Beat it," says Wen-Ling to the cyclo driver. "Ngay bay gio."

23

MIDNIGHT … and an all-black plane whispers in for a landing with no lights at the abandoned U.S. airbase on the outskirts of Vinh Long. The aircraft looks to Tuki like something out of an old war movie about this country.

A minute later a hired Toyota sedan rolls out of hiding in the shadows of an abandoned building along the runway. Forty seconds after that Wen-Ling tosses back the last of her tea, stashes her black mug in her large purse, and shepherds Tuki, hands still bound, from the car into the high-winged, single-engine, turbo prop aircraft.

In less than another minute the Porter PC-6 is whining north through the black night. Wen-Ling has ditched her thugs. Just she, Tuki and the pilot sit in the aging canvas seats. The sky and the land below are all darkness save a few lights winking from towns. Tuki's thinking of Tran's spirit, hoping that the monks will release it to soar up here with her. Thinking that her soul, too, may soon be here forever with Tran and her father. She remembers scattering his ashes with Michael on the Rosa Lee. Remembers another flight when she left her knight behind. Boston. Eighteen months ago.

She continues peering out the window of this aircraft, a survivor from the American war. Inhales fumes of jet exhaust through the leaky windows, notes a parachute stuffed under the seat in front of her stamped PROPERTY OF U.S. AIR FORCE. And now, as on that other flight, her lips begin to move without sound, the words of the Heart Sutra stuttering behind her lungs.

> *There's no decay, no death*
> *No extinction of decay, of death either …*
> *No suffering, no origination, no cognition.*
> *No attainment and non-attainment …*
> *No stopping … no path.*

The last time she was flying away from the man she loves, she was hoping to save his life. Running away from the American police and Wen-Ling. Running in baggy jeans, a tank top, cardigan, and sandals she had stolen from a Cape Cod department store. Running with $823 in cash, a Thai passport, and a Visa card she lifted from Wen-Ling's purse. Running with an overseas airline ticket to Saigon. And an immense stolen ruby wrapped in a condom, pressed deep in her cervix. Back then she thought that this stone was the only balm for a heart torn open by greed and the Americans' war in Vietnam. But tonight, in this black airplane, she's thinking it's her ticket to nirvana. And maybe Michael's and his father's, too. Trouble is, la, she doesn't think any of them are quite ready to leave planet Earth just yet.

"Say, the word, Sweetie, and the pilot will have us safe and sound back in Saigon in less than an hour."

"What word?"

"Say, I give up, Wen-Ling." The dragon has a dreamy look in her eyes. Her speech is the slow, lilting way of talking that Tuki has noticed a couple other times before coming from her captor. Like last night when Wen-Ling came back aboard the sampan in Sadec after hours ashore. Odd.

"Give up? What's that supposed to mean?"

"It means you're going to take me to the ruby."

"And what do I get back, la?"

"Your life, Michael's life, his father's life, your mother's life, that cute little girl's life."

"You're threatening Hong Tam now?"

"I'm not threatening anybody."

Tuki feels a chill rising in her chest.

"I'm just saying that if you give me the ruby, everybody can be happy."

She pictures Tran's gray, frozen face with the chopstick clinched between his teeth.

"What can you hope for by keeping that stone hidden?"

"Maybe I want to protect it from people like you."

"But can't you see that's not possible?"

Tuki shrugs.

"It doesn't belong to you. It belongs to the people of Thailand."

"You don't fool me anymore. You don't work for the people of Thailand."

"How can you be so sure?"

"Thais are very Buddhist people, la. Buddhist and patient."

"Haven't I been more than patient with you ... for the last two years?" Wen-Ling tilts her head back in the canvas seat. Stares at the bare aluminum ceiling in the plane. She seems weary or dreaming.

"Buddhist people do not kill, do not threaten."

"They hire people for that."

"Not the sangha. They pray. They do not hire."

Wen-Ling's still staring at the ceiling. "So ... the smart *bui doi* thinks she has everything figured out."

"Enough."

"Enough for what?"

"Enough to see your greed."

Wen-Ling rolls her eyes again. "You have no idea, Sweetie."

Tuki feels the urge to push back. "Why would you make a whore of yourself for a stone?"

"I told you. You have no idea."

"Then give me some help, la. Why you want the Heart of Warriors?"

"I told you it's not for me."

"And not for Thai people."

Wen-Ling, still staring at the ceiling, waves her hand, like whatever. Then suddenly she jerks to attention, thrusts a pistol under Tuki's chin. "None of your business!"

"Then just shoot me, la."

Wen-Ling sighs. "I really hope that day's not coming."

Because maybe I kill you first, gai diem, thinks Tuki. It's a very un-Buddhist thing to think, harming someone. But she sees how this fight is going to end, with everybody dead, unless she gets up off her butt and finds a way to drive a stake through this slut's twisted and mysterious heart.

24

SOBS TUMBLE FROM Huong Mei's throat as she clutches Caesar Decastro. He and Michael are back in Saigon after fleeing Sadec by taxi when the police and Wen-Ling's thugs went toe-to-toe. She's squeezing him so hard that sweat shadows bloom on their clothes where their bodies touch.

Unnerved by the display of grief, the customers in this second-hand, foreign-language bookshop withdraw from their browsing nooks and bolt out into the late afternoon heat of Nguyen Hue Boulevard in central Saigon. Michael stands in a corner of the store, near the American mystery novels, and tries to make himself invisible. His father's attempting to comfort this woman over the news that her only son has been murdered in Sadec, and her daughter is still missing.

Everything about Huong Mei seems wrong now. The little jade triangles dangling from her ears. The reading glasses, the pink cotton jersey, the fashionable maroon skirt, even the athletic curve of her calves. None of it matches the shrill keening of her voice. The fractured, red face.

"I worry you all dead," she says in English.

"Maybe we should be," Michael hears his father say.

"When my husband finds out Tran dead, find out that monks now waiting for us to come claim body, he have you arrested."

"For what?"

Huong Mei tosses her hands in the air as if to say whatever. Like you know, this is Vietnam, GI? Things just happen.

Michael has never actually met Huong Mei's husband, Tuki's stepfather. The woman keeps her husband at arms' length from Tuki, most likely on account of shame. Shame that she was once a consort of the Americans. Once called Misty. Once a working girl at the Black Cat, once the mistress of an American, once and forever the mother of a *bui doi*.

Michael only knows what he has gathered in bits and pieces. Cao Ho Trung, the mysterious husband, is a government lawyer working for the Ministry of Industry. He's from Hanoi, five years younger than Huong Mei. He met her when she was assigned to a re-education camp where he worked after the American War. Cao Ho Trung is a devoted husband and father, a committed civil servant. A man obsessed with justice. And now a man whose heart is about to be broken by the death of his only son. A man who will be sure that his son would still be alive if it were not for his con lai stepdaughter and her decadent America friends.

"We are so screwed," says Michael to nobody in particular.

Caesar Decastro breaks from his hug with Huong Mei, looks around with wild eyes. "This country. We have no business … I have no goddamn business …"

She takes his hand, says something tender to him in Vietnamese and pulls him back into an embrace.

His eyes start to tear as he squeezes them shut.

Michael turns away, tries to study the title of the romance novels on a nearby shelf. Has grabbed a worn copy of Pride and Prejudice, and has started reading the first page. He's trying to distract himself from the drama playing out between these war survivors, from their unfathomable whispers in Vietnamese, when he sees his father finally pulling back from Tuki's mother and look her in the eyes.

"That's what you really want? You still want us … to stay? To find Tuki?"

"Please. She my only child now. Americans very brave, very

strong. Maybe you have good luck. I get you help." Huong Mei draws Caesar into another hug and starts in with the Vietnamese again.

"I can't do it," he says. "Not this." He seems to be talking about something other than continuing the search for Tuki.

"For the dead," she says. "Please." She presses a folded scrap of paper into Caesar's hands, gives him a last squeeze and flees through a back door to a stockroom. Michael can hear her bolt the door behind her.

*   *   *   *

"Jesus Cristo, Dad. What the hell just happened in here?" The strident tone in Michael's voice surprises him. It's not just the voice of the public defender that he thought he had lost forever, his voice is almost prosecutorial.

"Un-fucking-believable."

"What?"

"She gave me an address."

"I don't understand."

"She found Meng."

"Meng?" Michael says the name as if he has never heard it before. As if he has not been imagining his father's wartime Vietnamese girl friend for more than half of his life. Since he was just a kid and found those photos of her tucked behind others in his dad's photo album from those days in 1970 and 1971 with the 716th Military Police Battalion here in Saigon.

"Yeah, Kid, Meng."

An old conversation stings him. One he had with his father in the wheelhouse of the Rosa Lee a few years back.

*   *   *   *

"You ever see her again, Dad?"

The fisherman gets a damp look in his eyes, says that he and Meng always knew it wouldn't last forever. After the Army shipped him abruptly out of Saigon to the Philippines, he sent her his checks for a few months. She never wrote. But he didn't expect her to. Writing English was hard for her. He felt the loss, unbelievable saudade. He hoped she had found someone new. Someone from her own country who could cherish her forever, take care of her and her child by another soldier . He worried about her a lot. Then Michael was born back in Massachusetts. Caesar felt he had been given a new life. A chance to start over.

"But sometimes you remember?"

"I'm not proud of myself for what happened ... I should have been loyal to your mother. And honest with Meng ... But it's over ... a long time ago."

*   *   *   *

"I can't believe such a thing could even happen, Mo. Finding someone after ..."

"But how ... ?"

"Dem dem lam nho khong gian ..."

"What?"

"It's from a Vietnamese poem called 'Buon Dem Mua,' 'Sad Rainy Night.'" Caesar closes his eyes, recites, "Night after night do you not remember the time ..."

"Jesus, Dad, you're really losing me here."

"Remember those times when I talked with Huong Mei in Vietnamese?"

"You told me not to ask."

"Yeah. Well. On that first time I met her she reminded me of this poem that Meng taught me. It just came into my voice. I was reciting it ... then she was reciting it, too."

"What?"

"We both knew the same love poem, see? It was a poem from the war."

"What?"

"And then I just found other words in my mouth. Found myself telling her about Meng."

Michael looks at his father once again like this is someone he doesn't even know.

"She asked me if I wanted her to help me find Meng. I said that I didn't know."

"And?"

"I guess she took that as a yes. She persuaded her husband that if he helped me find Meng, and you found Tuki, we would go away and leave his family in peace."

"Now what, Dad?"

"I think this comes under the heading of one of those things I never thought I could do."

"You mean like come back here to Vietnam?"

"We have to meet Nguyet at the Hotel Rex in an hour after she drops off Tran's daughter with Huong Mei. Nguyet's taking us …"

"To see Meng?"

"Huong Mei thinks Meng will know something about Wen-Ling … can help us find Tuki."

25

IT'S SUNRISE when the pilot of the one-time CIA spy plane, the PC-6, cuts the power on his engine and starts a swooping bank through the mist. He's aiming his bird toward the red dusty ruins of what used to be an airfield.

"Wake up," says the pilot in Vietnamese. "We're here. Khe Sanh."

Khe Sanh. Tuki has heard the Vietnamese people talk about this place. It's halfway between Hanoi and Saigon, poised at the narrow waist of the nation. Situated just south of what was called the DMZ during the American War, the Demilitarized Zone dividing Communist-ruled North Vietnam and capitalist South Vietnam on either side of the Ben Hai river. The Seventeenth Parallel. Khe San—the site of the bloodiest battle in the war. About five hundred Americans and ten thousand North Vietnamese soldiers died. Countless civilians. American B-52s dropped the equivalent of five Hiroshima-sized bombs here.

Tuki has raised both her hands to shield her eyes against the bright sunrise turning the mist that clots over the hills below into a blinding veil. The three nylon electrical ties binding her wrists pinch her skin so tightly that the discomfort and her fear has kept her from sleeping all night. With each beat of the propeller, she has been thinking on murder.

Her intended victim, sitting beside her, is waking up. Tuki could do it now. Throw her arms over Wen-Ling's head while she's rubbing her eyelids and cheeks, trying to rise from her strange grogginess. Squeeze her throat until the filthy bitch turns blue, her larynx cracks beneath hot *bui doi* fingers.

Wen-Ling fishes around at her feet for her tea cup and mutters something to the pilot in a tonal language that Tuki has never heard before, and looks around. Seeing Tuki, as if for the first time, she shifts to English.

"Welcome to the wild side," she says.

Tuki tries not to show any concern.

"The pilot needs to refuel in Dong Hoi … but we will wait here … you can commune with your comrades for a while."

Tuki thinks of Michael, his father. "My comrades, la?"

"Yes, Sweetie. The dead. The Americans killed them here by the thousands … And you are going to them."

Not without you, gai diem.

*   *   *   *

Within a minute of the Porter's landing on the rutted former runway, an old U.S. jeep appears. An ancient woman's driving. It whisks Tuki and Wen-Ling down a dusty road amid coffee plantations, through the ground fog. They descend into a valley. As the sound of the plane's departure fades beneath the rumbling of the jeep, the vehicle makes a sharp left turn and lurches to a stop.

"Mau … mau," the old lady driving shouts. Some kind of self-appointed drill sergeant. She motions to a tunnel entrance cut into a steep lime stone hill.

"Don't just sit there," Wen-Ling says, pushing Tuki out of the jeep. "Make like a mole, Girl."

Tuki stumbles to the low hole cut in the hill, half hidden by brush, stoops, steps into the tunnel behind the old woman who's shining her flashlight on the neatly carved limestone walls and muttering away in a broken mix of Vietnamese and what must be a hill tribe language. The cool, damp air of the tunnel hits Tuki first, then the scents of rich earth, burning kerosene, and something else, something organic like vinegar.

By Tuki's count, she has traveled two hundred and thirty-nine paces through the cramped tunnel when it opens into a gallery the size of the interior of a Saigon transit bus. In the center of the room a large kerosene camp light hangs from the ceiling, bathing the walls with a yellow glow. There's a dining table set with a tablecloth, breakfast fruits, toast, jam, china plates, silverware, a tea service. Several cushioned litters sit against the stone walls, covered with cushions, fabric, pillows to function as makeshift couches. An iPod is playing sentimental Vietnamese music from its speaker dock powered by a car battery.

Against the far wall there's some kind of chemical lab—beakers, flasks, connecting pipes, Bunsen burners—set up on a line of benches. Ringing the rest of the room are deep alcoves. Some are stuffed with irregularly shaped bricks tightly bound in black garbage bags. One alcove has stacks of two-liter-sized baggies filled with white powder.

"Oh, shit." Tuki can't help herself.

"No," says Wen-Ling. "Just business."

That strange vinegary smell. "This is an opium laboratory, la?"

"It used to be where the Viet Cong and the North Vietnamese Army staged their ambushes on the Americans."

"So this is what you really do? You make heroin?"

"What I really do is try to recover a stolen ruby." Wen-Ling cocks an eyebrow. "Have you forgotten, Sweetie?"

"This place is evil."

"Why don't you try to get over it? We could have a nice time until the plane comes back."

Tuki thinks about all the death she has seen from drugs in Bangkok, New York City, Cape Cod. Thinks about Prem, ruined by his addiction. Thinks too, that the Dragon Lady would never show her this place if there were even a remote chance that she might escape to tell anyone.

"Sit down. Let's have a good breakfast." Wen-Ling motions to table. The old woman jerks back a chair for Tuki to take her place at the feast.

Tuki doesn't move. She looks around. Wonders what she could use to kill these two vipers. Fast.

Wen-Ling looks at Tuki's wrists bound with the wire ties. "Let me make this easier for you." She grabs a paring knife from the table, slices off the bonds.

"Lethal mistake, gai diem," thinks Tuki, settling into the chair and watching precisely where the Dragon Lady sets the knife.

"Try some of this tea." Wen-Ling's gaze doesn't leave Tuki while pouring a cup of the dark liquid.

Tuki's mind's fixed on the knife. And deep into pondering where the nearest temple might be that she can flee to after the dirty deed. Lost in wondering if the Buddha will ever forgive her when she has fresh blood on her hands … She barely notices the huge smile on Wen-Ling's face as her captive takes her first swallow of the strange-tasting tea. Its bitterness nearly hidden beneath the scent of fresh oranges, the taste of honey, ginger. Its wetness such a relief to her dry and aching throat.

Only when she feels the numbness creeping through her lips, her cheeks, her chest, does she realize she's in trouble here. She probably won't be killing anyone today.

26

NGUYET STOPS WITH a jerk beneath the huge portrait of Ho Chi Minh and spins abruptly to face her followers. Michael and his father almost tumble into her, Michael grabbing onto her shoulders for balance. Inhaling the scent of her freshly bathed skin ... and lavender. She has been borrowing Tuki's perfume.

Almost everything about Nguyet this afternoon reminds him of Tuki. This young Vietnamese woman, rescued from the Tiger's Tail five days ago, has filled the space left by Tuki in the city. She has been sleeping in Tuki's bed, caring for Hong Tam, wearing Tuki's clothes. All with Huong Mei's blessing and encouragement. And, just a moment ago, following her through the vaulted mezzanine of Saigon's central post office on Nguyen Du Blvd, Michael thought Nguyet even walks like Tuki. Could be Tuki in those golden pumps, red mini, black cotton blouse cinched at the waist by a thick gold belt. Medium-length black hair bounces off the shoulders like Tuki's. It's strange, almost as if Tuki has been cloned. Until he sees this face. Pretty, to be sure. But young. Very young. Still a girl's face. Whiter than Tuki's, with more Asian eyes, a smaller nose, thinner lips ... That right now are trembling.

"Cristo," he says, "please don't cry. Not now."

She stretches her arms behind his back, holds him in a hug, lets out a sob.

It's truly an awkward moment here in this lovely French-colonial post office. Another in a series over the last hour with Nguyet. Since meeting her at the Rex, Michael has been distinctly aware that she's struggling with all her soul to keep it together. Struggling to be useful to these Americans to whom she owes her freedom from Flash's evil empire at the Tiger's Tail.

But the news of Tran's death has blown a hole in her chest that she can't hide. She and Tran seemed to have had an instant affinity for each other during just that one day when they were together at Tran's apartment. Caring for Hong Tam for the last four days must have ignited all sorts of emotions in both the little girl and her caregiver. And now Nguyet is struggling with the secret that Huong Mei is still keeping from the little girl. The terrible news that her father is never coming home again.

"Sorry. So sorry," says Michael, stepping back from the embrace. He feels like his life has become an endless apology.

Nguyet wipes her eyes, smiles through tears at Michael, then his father. "Lady you want, she work here … somewhere," she says. "Wait, please. I find."

Caesar's swarthy Portuguese face has lost all color, streams of sweat trickle from his brow. "May your mother forgive me, Mo." He seizes his son by the forearm.

Michael pictures his dead mother, feels the warmth of the smile that always bloomed on her face when she looked at her husband. "I think she already has, Dad … a long time ago."

*   *   *   *

"Holy Mary Mother of God," says Caesar Decastro. He and his son have been sitting on a bench in the post office for more than a half an hour. And now he bolts to his feet, a bouquet of roses in his hands.

Two women have emerged from a doorway leading to the administrative offices. One is Nguyet. The other looks like she could be Nguyet's older sister. Just as much style, vigor, primal good looks. But much darker skin. Both women approach with poise and confidence, though it's clear that they've been crying … their hands brushing their cheeks as smiles begin to spread on their faces.

Still ten yards away the older woman is stretching out her arms to Caesar. And he's doing the same to her, offering her the roses, catching her smile, dropping his jaw like a teenager welcoming his prom date as she sails into his life, a dream made flesh.

"Holy Mary," he says again.

"Holy goddamn Mary," she says, still smiling, as if this phrase is some kind of secret code between them. "Holy goddamn Mary, Joe."

And then she's taking the flowers. Smelling them even as she folds herself into his arms. They are hugging. Not like Michael and Nguyet were hugging thirty minutes ago. Not that desperate, fearful, embarrassed clutching. This is a waltzing, twirling ecstasy of an embrace. Complete with screaming and shrieking and howling joy. Patrons are stopping, staring. And suddenly someone starts clapping. And then, it seems hundreds of people are clapping. A few Westerners and many Vietnamese. Because here, now, they believe that they are finally witnessing a happy ending to the heart-ripping story of Miss Saigon.

"She still love him," says Nguyet. "She always waiting. Forty year."

Michael knows he should be having mixed feelings, should be thinking about his mother. About Caesar's faithlessness to the saint named Maria who was carrying his child back home during the war. Carrying baby boy Michael Francis Decastro. But all he can do is feel some awful shadow rising off that tough, old, Portagee fisherman. And he prays to the Espiritu Santo that his time with Tuki is coming, too. That this long-lost woman in his father's arms is the angel who can help him save the woman he loves, help him escape his own shadows, too. Help him put the death of Awasha Patterson behind him. But, even more … help him put his awful mistake with Yemanjá Colón to rest. It was a betrayal to both her and Tuki, to the woman he supremely respects and to the woman he hopelessly loves.

"Isn't there a church next door?" Michael asks.

"Notre Dame Cathedral," says Nguyet.

"I think I need to pray."

"Maybe more than that."

*   *   *   *

Forty-five minutes later. Michael hears his name being spoken, feels his father's hand on his shoulder.

"You make your peace, Kid?"

"Starting." Michael rises off the knee-board. Beside him Nguyet is still praying, eyes shut, forehead pressed against her folded hands on the pew in front of her.

"How you doing, Dad?" He's trying to keep his voice at a whisper as he looks at his father and the ex-lover by his side.

"Let's get out of here. I really need a smoke."

"I'm sorry."

"Don't be. I'm sorry enough for both of us ... sorry for a thousand things."

"That bad?" Michael has a dozen questions he's afraid to ask, starting with whether this angel from the past can really offer any help in finding Tuki.

His father shakes his head no, not bad. "Not bad at all. Just ... just un-freaking-believable ... She ..." Caesar clears his throat. "She ... Meng. She never married ... She lost her baby at the end of the war. She wants to help us ..."

"Find Tuki?" Michael leads the two women and his father down the aisle and out the front door of the church.

"She's Hmong. You know, Montagnard?"

Michael knows. Cape Cod, the south coast of Massachusetts and Rhode Island have a fairly large population of Hmong refugees who came to the U.S. after the fall of Saigon. Michael had Hmong clients when he was a public defender on the Cape. The Hmongs are one of the hill tribes whose culture covers northwestern Vietnam, parts of Laos, Thailand, China. Many of them migrated south from China in the nineteenth century into the so-called Golden Triangle region of Southeast Asia. They are one of the largest ethnic minorities in Vietnam. Nearly a million strong.

During the American War they created an army of thirty thousand warriors to fight the communists. A secret war, staged out of Laos under General Vang Pao. The Hmong are largely farmers, opium being one of their traditional crops. Air America, the CIA's puppet company, used their aircraft to smuggle guns to Vang Pao's soldiers in Laos and carry opium/heroin out. Michael has seen the Mel Gibson movie called Air America about this secret operation. Wicked.

"Where's Tuki?"

Caesar says Huong Mei was right. Meng can help Michael find his girl. Tuki's mother knew from the first time she heard Meng's name that Caesar's old lover was Hmong, and she knew from Wen-Ling's name that she was Hmong as well. The Hmongs are a tight community within Vietnam, despite their various clans. Huong Mei hoped that by uncovering Meng's address and workplace for Caesar, she would not only bring the old lovers back together again, but also give the Decastros a way to network through the Hmongs to find Wen-Ling. A villain of her stature had to be known to them, even if she had moved away from the traditional Hmong homelands years ago. "Really?" Michael's starting to connect the dots. Being Hmong would explain Wen-Ling's Chinese-like name, her looks, her facility with Thai—and probably Vietnamese. Her ability to slither around Southeast Asia without anyone taking much notice.

"Shit, huh, Kid?" Caesar pulls a pack of Winstons from his shirt pocket, taps one out, lights up. Inhales deeply.

"Yeah, no shit."

"It seems Wen-Ling's a bit of a legend among what they call the Flower Hmong up north along the border between Vietnam, Laos, and China."

"They call her the Dragon Lady, too?"

"No. They call her Robin Hood."

"You're saying Tuki's gone to some sort of Sherwood Forest?"

"It's way the hell up north, Buddy. Where no police will ever look."

"When's the next plane?"

"This beautiful woman," Caesar nods to Meng. "She wants to come with."

"For real?"

27

TUKI'S STILL DREAMING

Even after leaving the tunnel at Khe Sanh, after another four hours of flying north to the Golden Triangle. After landing on a road in a narrow mountain valley where the air is damp and cool and the poppies are just starting to bloom. After being shepherded through terraced fields by a troupe of little girls with immense hoop earrings and brilliant rose-and-indigo dresses. After crossing a swaying suspension bridge to a teak stilt house on the crest of a steep hill ... After listening all the while to Wen-Ling's voice, like a distant, alluring music, twining in and out of itself, promising Tuki love and peace and plenty forever.

After all of this she's still dreaming.

It's the same dream over and over again. Everything tangled together.

*   *   *   *

Saigon, 1968. Bangkok in the 1990s. August 2006 on Cape Cod. Winter 2010 in Ho Chi Min City, too. The clubs are smoking. The heavy beat of bass guitars oozes from the bars up and down Tu Do, Bangkok's Patpong, Commercial St. in Provincetown. And she's in the mix, la. A little club. On stage. The song's "This Old Heart of Mine." Classic Motown. It winds up like a carousel ride.

She's wearing a gold kimono. Her lips glistening bright crimson. Liner accents the Asian shape of her eyes, her hair pinned up in loose geisha folds. And she's in on the downbeat, her body burning to the pain of the lyrics, a kind of lazy shimmy in her hips. Her voice gaining strength with each step, an approaching train. The audience is whistling and cheering, so loud that the sound and light kid has to amp up the volume on the speakers.

Singing, sweet Buddha, singing. Feeling the words. Telling the crowd how her heart's been broken a thousand times. Voguing— chin high, turning, smiling, posing. She's a stroke of lightning. A girl who wears her bloodied chest for all to see ... For the beautiful Portuguese lawyer she still yearns to see before she dies. Who may yet rescue her ... or she rescue him.

She wishes the dream would end here. Her vocal chords are sizzling at the roots. But she can't stop. Even though she suddenly feels as heavy as a river. The music and the sound of her own voice cut her. Her skin's burning in the reddish glow of the spotlight. The air's growing thick as smoke. She smells incense and opium ... the ginger and the flames ... the water buffalo and the rice paddies ... the river and the fish ... the desire of men, the misery of women.

And then there he is, watching from a table near the back wall of the club. It's Michael, and she's not certain what to feel. She just knows he looks glad to see her. She struts, singing about lonely nights, tender memories. She holds the mic to her lips, weaves among the tables toward the strong, dark, Portuguese face of the man who saved her life ... more than once. The face that erases everything from her mind except the tart scent of the South China Sea, the prick of his unshaved whiskers against her cheek.

He slides his lips along the rim of her jaw, reaches her mouth. Lips brushing hers, soft, sweet. And just like that, with a kiss, they are alone ... lying on a beach in nothing but their skins. She puts her hands beneath his shoulders, pulls him to her. Tears at his back with soft claws.

"Never let me go."

He tells her without ever speaking that tigers are loose on the beach. And she feels them. Charging in, out of the surf. Fishing. The spray soaking their bellies, flanks. Tails flying in the wind. Eyes not seeing the tsunami rushing toward them.

Until it's catching them. Sweeps them into these fields of red poppy blossoms. These steep, green hills. Wave upon wave tumbling them ... Flesh and fur. Mouths. Roaring back at this hot, roiling sea ... Even as it sucks them down into the flowers, the planet's blood.

*　　*　　*　　*

"You drugged me, la."

"Tell me you didn't love it." Wen-Ling has an exhausted, satisfied, slow-eyed look as she lies on a dais, wrapped in a blanket, propped up by an elbow.

"It was the tea. Opium tea."

"Of course."

"I was having the most vivid dream."

"And you forgot that you wanted to kill me."

Tuki feels hot, parched, possibly baking to death ... even with the chilling, black wind whistling through the open windows of this mountain house.

"Not really," she says. Finds herself staring at the tea mug sitting on the floor next to Wen Ling's dais. It's the same black and gold mug she has had near her so often lately.

Does it always have a little opium tea? Is the Dragon Lady an addict? Will the tea open a door for me to slay her? Then let us drink again.

"Where's the ruby, sweetie?"

28

"I DON'T THINK we can go into those hills above Dien Bien Phu by ourselves, Mo," says Caesar Decastro. "The police and the army won't even go there."

"But that's probably where they have Tuki."

"Meng says we'll be killed."

"She brought us all the way up here to Hanoi, to tell us that?" Michael still can't believe that he's now traveling with his father's ex. The only good news is that they finally persuaded the ever-eager Nguyet that she would be most useful remaining in Saigon and caring for Hong Tam.

"The Hmongs make a living growing opium up there, Kid. It's a secret world. They aim to keep it that way." Caesar throws up his hands as if to say he imagined that things were going to be easier before he, Michael, and Meng boarded the noon flight from Saigon to Hanoi.

Now it's late afternoon in the capital of Vietnam, and Meng, the woman Michael had once thought of as Madame Butterfly, has disappeared. The two men are sitting beneath a fuming, gray sky at an outdoor table in a café on the edge of Hanoi's Hoan Kiem Lake, a place that legend says is enchanted by a giant, sword-swallowing golden turtle.

"Are we out of tricks, Dad?"

"Meng has a plan. She's looking for someone who can drive us."

They are in the heart of the city's Old Quarter, sipping from overpriced glasses of Tiger beer amid groups of French and German tourists.

"I get this feeling that we're being watched?"

Caesar looks around, surveys the wait staff in the café. The place is loaded with young Vietnamese women with serving trays in their hands, staring at the foreigners with absolutely no affect on their faces. "You think some of these waiters are mat vu?"

"What?"

"Plainclothes cops."

"More like Tong Cuc Hai," says Michael.

"The CIA types?"

"I don't know, Dad. I just feel creeped out by this city."

Caesar shrugs, "You got to wonder about any place that sets aside a dozen blocks of real estate at the center of its business district for a fortified military citadel."

"You noticed that, too?" Michael thought he was the only one looking out the window during the cab ride from the airport. He was in the front seat with the cabbie. His father and Meng in the backseat whispering and laughing in Vietnamese and English.

"Didn't Tran say that Wen-Ling might work for the Tong Cu Whatever?"

Michael says that she claimed to work for the Thai Secret Service.

"Come on, Mo. We've been over this before."

Caesar says that after Wen-Ling vanished from the U.S. with a murder rap for the death of the drag queen Robsulee on her head, the Thai government swore that it never heard of Wen-Ling. "I'm just saying …"

"What?"

Michael feels himself sweating despite the cool, overcast day. Must be the high humidity. "I don't know."

"You mean things are never what they seem in this country?"

"Tell me Meng's not leading us into a trap."

"I can't say that for sure … yet."

"Jesus. Yet?"

"Yeah yet."

"Are you talking about having sex with that woman?"

The older Decastro reaches to his breast pocket for his pack of butts. "Do I really have to get into this? Some things are too god-damn personal."

"Nothing's more personal than betrayal."

"Are you pissed that I brought Meng along, that I'm having feelings I thought that I would never ..."

Something's locking up in his chest. "Cristo, Dad. It's just that Tuki's in danger, and I'm feeling powerless, you know?"

"Yeah."

"Yeah. Well, now on top of that we end up in this city that's giving me really fucking creepy vibes   and along for the ride, of all the people in the world, the woman you cheated on Mom with."

"Shit, I knew ... I just knew sooner or later you were going to freaking guilt me over all of this."

. Michael can't help himself. Some dark anger he's been pushing way deep in his guts has begun to vent. "I'm sorry, Dad, but Jesus Christ—"

"Hey, can you just give me a little bit of a break here, Buddy Boy? I didn't ever want to come to this fucking country again in my life. I'm only here because—"

"Aw hell, Dad. It's just that I wasn't expecting to have to deal with ..." Michael sees Meng standing by his left shoulder, has no idea how long she has been here, what she has heard. But it's obviously enough. Her eyes are swelling with tears.

"Maybe it better I go away," she says.

The words seem to drive a rail through Caesar's heart. He chokes on his cigarette. And now, Michael feels the pain, the loss. Like the death of his mother all over again. Like after that October night with Yemanjá Colón. Like the day Tuki disappeared from Cape Cod eighteen months ago.

"Please," he hears himself say. "Don't go ... I couldn't stand missing one more person."

*   *   *   *

"Just pretend that you are going on a tour with me," says Meng. She opens the sliding back door to a Nissan minivan with the words TurViNam in large red and yellow letters painted on the side. "And keep hats and sunglasses on."

It's seven in the morning, barely light outside, and the minivan's parked in front of a small tourist hotel in Hanoi's Old Quarter where the Decastros and Meng took rooms the previous night. It's annoying to Michael to see his father's ex dressed like a woman half her age ... and looking the part of one of Hanoi's chic tour guides in her skinny jeans, tight pink bodice, golden fashion belt, mini clutch purse, wrap-around sunglasses, and binder full of travel brochures.

"Where exactly are we going?" Michael's climbing into the back of the minivan and pulling the Red Sox ball cap low on his forehead. Adjusting his shades.

"To find your girlfriend." Meng avoids a direct answer. Her voice sounds tired like his father's. They shared a room last night.

"This is going to be a journey isn't it?" Caesar tumbles into the van, drops in the seat so hard that the driver, a withered old man, turns around and glares at the stupid long nose. Like chill out, Joe.

"Driver bring sandwiches for this part of trip."

"This part?"

"We change cars first time in Mai Chau."

"First time?" Michael doesn't like the sound of this.

"No want anyone follow us," says Meng. "Besides. Roads in mountains not so good. Better stop for night in Son La then hire four-wheel."

"She has this all figured out, Kid." Caesar takes her hand.

"Unless someone starts shooting," she says. Then she tells the driver to get going, stick to the alleys. Lays her head on her lover's shoulder as if she always knew somehow that Caesar would come back to her.

Women? Go figure. Michael looks away. Sees it's starting to rain, wonders if a monsoon season is beginning ... and whether Tuki's thinking about doing something crazy. Wherever the hell she is.

29

THE SAD TRUTH IS, she thinks, she could really get to like Wen-Ling's tea. The dreams it brings are so sumptuous, so relaxing. And Michael's always there in the mist, holding her close in the swirling storm ... like there will be no tomorrow. If only, la.

Tuki has just awakened from a long opium fantasy to the sound of gales of rain whipping across the roof of this hilltop hideaway. It's some time in their second afternoon here in the mountains beyond the town of Lai Chau. None of the young Hmong women who tend the house seem to be around. Usually they are here keeping the fire going for warmth against the damp and the cold, cooking the food, brewing the tea. Wen-Ling's in the hammock next to Tuki, bundled in a blanket, still lost in a dream. Her dark hair tangled across her face, a sad little smile on her lips. They look so pale, the lipstick washed away by too many sips of poppy-stem tea. The gray light brings out a web of tiny lines around the corners of the dragon's eyes, and Tuki sees that this woman is considerably older than she had imagined. Maybe her mother's age. But when she looks at Wen-Ling, she doesn't picture Huong Mei, she pictures Misty. A bar hostess. A bombshell. Like the most dangerous kind, la.

If ever there were a moment to kill this dragon bitch and run, it's now. Tuki shifts her eyes around the one-room house, looking for a weapon.

She sees nothing at first glance. Not even a table knife, a fire poker, a frying pan. Wonders whether she could do it with bare hands as she has imagined. Just squeeze the dragon's neck until, finally, her tongue pops right out of her head … squeeze while she stares into the wench's surprised and desperate eyes. Telling her that Tuki always gets even, la. You can ask Prem Kittikachorn or his father when you get to hell.

The Buddha would never forgive her for such killing. But the Buddha never had a father and half-brother die because of this smug and evil reptile. Never lost the love of his life because of this monster with the pretty face. Never felt that the sixth treasure in the holy sutras depended on saving the Heart of Warriors. Never worried either that with the ruby in the hands of the Dragon Lady, the gem's legendary powers to ease transitions, provide clarity, inspire loyalty, cultivate courage, engender love … all those gifts could be lost to the world.

And yet … Wen-Ling saved her life by killing Robsulee. Sometimes she wonders why Wen-Ling let her live. For this? For torture? To witness the death of more people she loves? Or something else even crazier? No matter, la. Karmic debt to the dragon for her life not withstanding, Tuki must do it, choke the beast.

And then she must find a way off this mountain top and back to her mother and Hong Tam in Saigon. Back to Michael, wherever he is. Even if she can only find him in opium dreams. At least the Heart of Warriors will be out of danger. Maybe there's a motorbike that she can steal while the Hmongs in the settlement down in the valley hide in their houses from the rain. There will be no tending to the poppy fields today.

*　　*　　*　　*

Tuki has lain motionless, eyes closed, in her hammock for at least another half an hour, picturing exactly how she will slide out of her panties. How she will push those pink panties in Wen-Ling's mouth to muffle any cries an instant before she seizes the dragon by the throat. She has decided that taking Wen-Ling face to face, standing beside her hammock, would be too hard. She would be within range of the dragon's flailing arms, claws, legs. And no matter how certain she is of her goal, killing would be difficult when you're close enough to smell the woman's breath, almost taste her tears.

No, la, she cannot not kill like that.

Her best chance will be to come at Wen-Ling from behind, approaching the top of her head as she lies in her hammock. Viewed like this, upside down, Wen-Ling will look like the monster she is, not human. Easier to hate, kill.

And you will be almost totally out of range of Wen-Ling's arms. You can reach down over the beast's face to stuff her mouth. Then you can clamp hands around her neck, fingers pressing against the voice box, hands squeezing not just to cut off the wind, but to crush the cartilage and bone. It's a plan, la.

Tuki opens her eyes, watches Wen-Ling for two minutes to make certain she's still lost in sleep, listens to the dragon's snuffled breathing, soft moans, groans. Sees the subtle flickering of dreams twitching across eyelids.

Deep breath ... Ready, go.

She pushes aside her blanket, slips off her panties, balls them in her right hand, slides from her hammock. In three nearly noiseless steps she's behind the dragon. She's taking one last slow breath for energy before she pounces ...

... when Wen-Ling opens her eyes and smiles a wicked grin. She tosses aside a light blanket to show Tuki the little pistol in her hand.

"Did your father ever tell you, *bui doi*, that he knew me ... a long time ago?"

"Say what, la?"

"Maybe I'll tell you later."

Ouch.

30

MICHAEL'S NOT SURE whether it's rain or sweat running down his chest in streams. Probably both, even though the air seems too cool for sweating. For four hours they have been hiking on a winding trail through the hills of Northwest Vietnam, somewhere near the border with Laos and China.

During the two-day trip up here from Hanoi, Meng has changed her look completely three times. From chic tour guide, to Vietnamese peasant, to Hmong tribal woman. Now she's leading him and his father along a muddy path through a bamboo forest wearing a blue and pink embroidered skirt, black leggings, a dark linen jacket. She's carrying a wicker basket full of fruit on her back, gifts for the Hmong.

And she has the Decastros dressing a part, too—olive-drab Chinese paratrooper fatigues, complete with jungle hats and counterfeit Doc Martens that she purchased in Hanoi. "Now everybody think maybe you CIA finally come back," she said when she gave them the gear and told them to suit up. "Maybe nobody shoot you right off bat."

She says that some of the Hmong in this area who fought for General Vang Pao's secret army against the North Vietnamese forty years ago are still hoping that their CIA sponsors will return with guns and money to help them maintain their independent life, including poppy farming, free from genocide and relocation schemes aimed at them by the governments of Laos and Vietnam.

"Village not far now," she says, pointing through a cut in the trees.

Michael can see smoke rising from a field that's being cleared for planting on the edge of a hamlet about a quarter mile ahead and lower in the valley. He has heard that in just a few years, a new hydroelectric dam that the Vietnamese have built farther south on the River Da will submerge all this area beneath a mammoth lake. There is more than one way to drive out these free people.

Meng has explained that there are five different groups of Hmongs in these hills—Black, White, Red, Green, Flower. She comes from the Black Hmongs. Wen-Ling is a Flower Hmong. The two groups don't get along. The village ahead has been traditionally a Black Hmong settlement, and Meng has high hopes that villagers will have some knowledge of a beautiful con lai held captive by the Flower Hmongs. But with the dam project nearing completion and government resettlement of the hill tribes progressing quickly, there's a chance that the passive Black Hmongs in this area have already been persuaded to leave. More aggressive Flower Hmongs may have taken over the village.

In which case our little search party is, to use my father's words, in the shit, Michael's thinking.

A strange whistling sound echoes from the forest ahead.

Meng stops. Cocks her head, listens.

The whistle again.

She puckers up her lips and whistles back.

Within two beats of the heart, Michael sees six teenage boys with automatic weapons fill the path in front of him. The guns are shouldered and pointing at the intruders.

"Jesus Cristo, I haven't seen freaking Kalashnikovs for forty years." Caesar sounds more surprised than scared.

Michael starts to reach for the field knife that Meng bought for him back in Son La. It's tucked in a leg pocket of his fatigue pants.

"Don't move." Meng's voice is a whisper as she turns away from the Americans to gunman, hands raised and bows. "Ti nau."

"Cao cu." They bow in return. And when they rise from their bow, they lower the weapons and smile.

Meng smiles back. "Black Hmong," she says to the Americans. "My People. Our lucky day."

"I feel like it's all happening again," says Caesar. "That stupid, fucking war."

*   *   *   *

The one-room house with its steeply pitched thatched roof is hot and shadowy. Michael, his father, and Meng are meeting with the local clan's headman. The four of them sit on low stools arranged in a circle on the dirt floor. In front of them sits a small shrine altar covered with an old white quilt and decorated with urns, pots, cups. Out of respect for the spirits of the house, they have left their shoes at the front door.

The songs of caged birds punctuated by the baa, baa of goats filter around and behind the quiet conversation in the tribal language between Meng and the headman, a well-muscled man Caesar's age who's wearing a handmade black hoodie. She seems to be explaining to him her origins, clan, sub-clan, family. There's nodding, a smile, finally the headman places both his hands on top of hers.

"Can you ask him? Once we find Tuki, what do we do to get her away from Wen-Ling?" Michael's thinking he might suffocate in this dark heat.

"First we must smoke with him," says Meng. She nods to a water pipe being prepared by a young woman in a corner of the house.

"Dope?" Caesar doesn't sound enthusiastic.

Meng takes his hand. "Just a puff, maybe two. Out of respect."

"We're dead if we don't, right?" Michael has the feeling Meng is saying less than she knows.

"Better not to find out."

31

"WE'RE LEAVING, Sweetie." Wen-Ling jabs Tuki in the side with her pistol.

She opens her eyes, moves to stretch her arms. But then she remembers that last night after she tried to kill Wen-Ling, the Dragon Lady made her get back in this hammock, bound her hands together and tied them to the hammock knot over her head. She has been lying like this, covered with a scratchy blanket, all night.

"What's going on, la?"

"You ready to behave, Girl?"

"Behave," says Tuki. Her voice is heavy with affirmation. Her shoulders, back, and the sides of her chest ache from the way she has been tied into this hammock.

Wen-Ling stands over her. She seems to be thinking about whether to trust Tuki. Two young Hmong women are at her side, the housekeeper and the cook. She says something to them in Hmong, her tone a question.

The cook pulls a knife from her apron and cuts Tuki's bonds.

"Leaving?" Tuki's still in a bit of an opium fog. When she asked for water last night, she was told it was poppy tea or nothing.

"It seems your boyfriend doesn't give up so easily. He must really love you."

"Michael's here?"

"Coming."

She wants to shout, wants to say this is what she dreamed last night.

"These Americans are better at tracking than one might expect." The Buddha still smiles on me.

"They dress like old-time CIA, and they have a Hmong partisan with them. What do you think of that, Sweetie? Does it make you feel all gooey inside? Like Rambo to the rescue?"

"I …" Tuki's afraid to speak. Anything she says can only make matters worse.

"Maybe these Decastro boys have big balls, eh, *bui doi*?"

Shut up.

"Big balls … just like your Daddy? Saigon 1972?"

"What are you talking about?"

"Wouldn't you like to know the real story?"

"What story?"

Wen-Ling takes a bundle of clothing from the housekeeper and shoves it toward Tuki. "How about you just go pee, brush teeth, put on these new clothes. The helo will be here for us soon."

"What story?" Tuki asks again. She accepts the new clothes tentatively.

"You make up your mind to show me where you hid the ruby. Could be I'll tell you why your daddy really left Misty behind."

Tuki feels her skin turn clammy. It was on a Cathay Pacific flight three years ago from L.A. to Ho Chi Minh City with her newly found father Marcus when she asked him the same question. They were on their way to make peace with their ghosts here in Vietnam. Or at least to try. Fat chance, la.

*   *   *   *

"You think it was my choice to leave her?" asks her father. "There was a war. Nineteen seventy-two. Things were crazy."

"Misty was pregnant with me," she says.

He tells her that Vietnam was madness. The US couldn't pull troops out of the country fast enough. The NVA and Viet Cong were kicking American ass all over the country. Everything was coming apart in Saigon. People spitting on soldiers. Bombs going off in District One and Cholon. New rumors every day that the government was going to collapse. Legions of South Vietnamese troops were throwing down their guns and going home ... or crossing over to the Viet Cong.

"But didn't you love her?"

He rubs his eyes with his fingers, strokes his beard.

"Hell yeah," he says, closing his eyes. "I fell in love with her the moment I saw her ..."

"Then why did you leave us?"

"She made me go."

"What? Why?"

"Somebody wanted to kill me."

*   *   *   *

The helicopter's racing east down the Red River toward the coast as Wen-Ling nudges Tuki in the seat beside her.

"You decide to tell where the ruby is yet?"

"Maybe." Part of Tuki is hedging her bets, trying to stay alive until she can find a place and time and way to kill this wench. But another part of her is so exhausted—so deep in an opium daze—that it's just about ready to give up the ruby if relinquishing the gem will buy the people she loves safety.

Wen-Ling grunts softly. She's heard this waffling, these pseudo promises, too many times. "I think you are going to see very soon that the time for games is ending, *bui doi.*"

Tuki frowns, stares out the window. Sees the hotels, towers, and lakes of Hanoi sliding by off to the right.

"And when the games end, when you're feeling very sorry for all this trouble that you've caused ... then maybe I will tell you something about your daddy and me in 1972."

"Like what?"

"Those hot and steamy nights on Dong Khoi. They called it Tu Do Street back in the day." There's a wistful tone in the dragon's voice. "When we used to smoke together."

"Cigarettes?"

"Don't be silly."

32

"SHE NOT HERE anymore," says Meng.

"But she was here?" Michael has been guzzling from a pitcher of water, trying to shake off the deadening lavender taste of the opium he smoked two hours ago.

"At Flower Hmong hill camp beyond next valley … yesterday."

"With Wen-Ling?"

"Robin Hood, yes. She bring whole suitcase of U.S. dollars to hill people, pass money out like New Year's gifts for Tet. People think your Tuki some kind sign of good fortune."

"Tuki's okay?"

"Yes, looking fine. But maybe little dreamy from too much yaj yeeb."

"Where did they go?"

"Fly east this morning … shiny, blue helicopter. Headman say maybe Cat Ba."

"What's Cat Ba?" Caesar's waving his hand in front of his face as if pushing away the cobwebs from his mind.

"Island. Gulf of Tonkin. Little bit vacation place. Big fishing place."

"Good spot for pirates?"

She nods. "Very far from here. Maybe better we fly from Dien Bien Phu."

"I hope they take credit cards," says Caesar.

No shit, thinks Michael. He and his father have already spent over five thousand dollars in-country on this search for Tuki. They are almost out of cash.

"Pardon, but headman have question for boss CIA," says Meng. She looks at Michael's father like don't screw this up.

The older Decastro tries to nod cryptically as if he's some kind of government spook.

"He want know if pretty *bui doi* is same clan as Tiger Woods and Barack Obama."

"Cousins." The word roll from Caesar's mouth.

*   *   *   *

As it turns out, there's no plane to Cat Ba from Dien Bien Phu … or from anywhere else. So the Decastros and Meng have to fly to Hanoi, take a hired car to Haiphong on the coast and wait overnight in a hotel for the next ferry to Cat Ba.

Eight-thirty in the morning. After a visit to replenish their cash at an ATM, they're standing in line in a little ferry terminal on Haiphong Harbor, waiting to board an antique Soviet-era hydrofoil for Cat Ba island.

"No wonder the Russian empire fell apart." Caesar Decastro's scratching his head as he checks out the silver ferry. "That thing looks more like a freaking flying saucer than a boat."

"You no want go?" Meng looks confused.

"Do I have any choice if I want to get to the mysterious Cat Ba, darlin'?"

Darlin'? Michael's not loving how in only five days or so his father has begun acting like the nearly forty-year break that he and Meng took never existed, that his marriage to Michael's mother never existed. He's starting to picture his father and this pretty, ageless woman tangled in the sheets of their hotel room last night … when Meng's cell phone chimes.

Everybody in this packed little terminal gives her the evil eye, no one wanting an electronic intrusion on his or her world yet this muggy, gray morning. Least of all Michael, who's really wishing he had a proper American breakfast of eggs, bacon, hash browns, not the bowl of pho offered him back at the hotel.

"Da," says Meng into her phone.

She draws more annoyed looks from the other people in the terminal. Michael has learned that da means yes in southern Vietnam, but here in the north people say vang. Meng has marked herself as an outsider with these people.

"Da," she says again. More softly, but stressed. Her face is turning pale as she wheels around, pushes her way through all the people waiting in the ferry queue and bolts out in the street.

"Something's wrong," says Michael.

"I better go after her." Caesar's cheeks look frozen.

There's the creaking of a door opening onto the wharf. The ferry's about to board. People in the queue are pushing toward it.

"Dad!"

"Save our places. I'll be back."

The queue surges forward again. Caesar is already bulling his way through the crowd, heading the other direction. Heading toward the street where Meng holds her phone to her ear with one hand, covers her mouth as if to stifle a sob with the other.

"Dad?"

A space opens between Michael and the passenger in the queue ahead of him. People start shouting at him in Vietnamese. They clearly are having no patience with him or his traveling companions. They're pushing him toward the wharf, the ferry.

"Mau, nguoi my," says someone making a movement with his hands like shove it along, American.

Michael, almost at the gangway onto the ferry, sees that his father has caught up with Meng out on the street. He's holding her in his arms. She seems to be crying, and Caesar has his eyes squeezed closed.

"Dad ... hurry."

Caesar hears his son's urgency. He opens his eyes, steps back from his hug with Meng, throws his hands in the air. He's waving.

Frantically. Like a man in the water waving for help.

"Mo!"

Michael feels his shoulders starting to shiver as he steps out of line, jumps a railing that's meant to keep passengers in queue and sprints to his dad and Meng. Until now, until seeing his father and this strange woman clutching and crying, he has not fully realized how much like a stranger in a strange land he feels. How dependent he has been on his father and others like Meng and Tran and Nguyet to help him navigate this country and find Tuki. How like a lost little boy he feels.

It's the same thing he was feeling that night he got so drunk back in Woods Hole on the Cape and the cops had to coax him off the jetty. The same feeling that October night when he sat in the cocktail lounge of the Chatham Bars Inn, pushed his glass of merlot aside and reached out for Yemanjá Colón's hand across the table.

*   *   *   *

"Are you sure this is what you want to do?" she asks as his fingers tighten around hers.

He feels the silky smoothness of her skin, the strength of her muscles as she squeezes back. "Yes."

She looks deep into his eyes, asking question after question without saying a word. And telling him things, too. Confessing the way only eyes can confess.

"You have to know … I'm the kind of girl who could drown on a night like this and never come up for air."

He's not sure what she means, but he finds the idea of drowning with her as fetching as the sweep of her long black hair over her shoulders, her pink lips.

"I don't want to be your rebound, Michael," she says. "And I'm not that girl who left you standing."

"I love the way you look in the candlelight." It sounds sappy, but he means it.

"You're still hurting … I can't change the past for you."

"I've had enough of the past." Even as he says this, he knows that what he's saying is more wish than fact. That just hearing Tuki's name is enough to make him feel stabbed through the lungs with icicles.

She lifts his hand and rubs it against her cheek, closes her eyes as if to say that she has had a crush on him for one hell of a long time.

* * * *

"What's going on?" He's feeling dizzy when he reaches the street. Meng's still crying.

"We're in bookoo shit, Kid."

"What happened?"

"That was Tuki's mother calling. I gave her Meng's number in case of an emergency." "And?"

"Someone broke into Tran's apartment ... Nguyet's dead. Strangled."

It's as if he has just taken a punch to the solar plexus.

"And Hong Tam has been kidnapped."

Michael hears his soul scream. "That poor girl."

When he catches his breath, when he can finally think again, he asks if Huong Mei has told the police about the little girl going missing.

"She fears telling the police will only make things worse."

"I don't understand, Dad."

"Meng says Huong Mei's totally terrified. Claims that Wen-Ling sicced her thugs on Tran's household."

"Cristo."

"Probably that Chinese fellow we met at the bar in Cholon is behind this."

"Flash?"

"He said he would get even."

"You think Wen-Ling put him up to this because Tuki's not giving her what she wants? She's taking another hostage?"

"I don't even want to think of any other reason why that whore-monger would grab that little girl."

33

"WANT TO SEE some pictures I downloaded?" Wen-Ling's holding a compact laptop computer in one hand and her tea mug in the other as she comes in off the balcony of a top-end suite overlooking the Gulf of Tonkin.

It's late morning and for the third day at this little resort hotel just over the hill from Cat Ba Town, Wen-Ling has had a masseuse come to the room to give herself and Tuki massages. The Dragon Lady is trying to pamper Tuki into submission again. And right now the former diva of Provincetown Follies is lying on her belly in her queen bed, wrapped in a towel. The young male masseuse is working on her feet, kneading them with his thumbs until all the stress begins to vanish in twitches of ecstasy. The last two and a half days on this island have passed in a blur of these little orgasms, sunbathing, swimming in the pool, opium tea. She keeps her eyes closed. To hell with pictures.

"Don't you want to look at these?"

Tuki groans. What's left of her mind is more or less lost to these little explosions in her feet that are sending waves of pleasure right up the backs of her legs to her brain.

"I just thought you would like to see your niece."

Tuki opens up her eyes slightly, "Hong Tam?"

"Do you have any other?"

"Why do you …?"

Wen-Ling hands the masseuse forty U.S. dollars and tells him to go away.

"What kind of pictures?"

"You know my friend Flash?" asks Wen-Ling after the masseuse closes the door behind him.

The Tiger's Tail. Cholon, Bruce Springsteen's "Dancing in the Dark" weeping from the sound system.

A young man eyes her from behind the bar. Thick-chested with a buzz cut, wearing wrap-around shades. He's filling a bottle of Baileys Irish Cream with a blend of water, coffee, and milk …

"Want to give Flash number one blow job?"

"He's Hong Tam's daddy now." Wen-Ling sets the laptop down on the bed beside Tuki's face and heads across the room for the teapot to refill her mug and Tuki's.

More dream juice. She's sort of, kind of, thinking that after five days of being given nothing but poppy tea to drink, this stuff is really starting to get ahead of her. Thinking what the hell … when her gaze settles on the slideshow of images scrolling across the laptop screen.

There's a photo of the inside of the Tiger's Tail. The same young whores who were there when Tuki visited are in the picture, dressed like clones in their red vests, minis, gold lamé tops. They're gathered around one end of the pool table holding cue sticks. And with them, seated on the pool table, dressed just like the hookers—with lipstick, eye shadow, rouge—is Hong Tam. Her eyes glisten with excitement.

"What's she doing?"

The picture scrolls. In the next photo the hookers have their backs to the camera. They are bent double, looking back over their right shoulders at the photographer, smiling and, it seems, shaking their booty. Red thongs in full view. And with them, mimicking them, is Hong Tam.

"How …?"

Another picture pops up. In this one Flash is standing behind his bar holding the little girl. She's wearing nothing but a tiny black bra and thong. She has her arms around his neck as he kisses her on the belly. The expression on her face is not playful as in the first two images. Her eyes bulge with terror. It strikes Tuki like some kind of high-voltage shock, and she rises out of her euphoria and confusion. Bolts up on the bed, holding her bath towel wrap against her chest.

"You wouldn't ..."

Wen-Ling's lips curl into a self-satisfied smile.

"Why would you ...?"

"Her father's dead. Her Auntie Tuki's disappeared. Her grandmother's too busy with her husband and her bookstore."

"What?"

"And the ex-prostitute who the granny hired to take care of the little cutie has had a most unfortunate accident."

"You ... you ..."

"Somebody has to look after the baby. Why not Flash? He likes little girls."

"This can't be happening, la." I'm dreaming this. It's the tea.

"I assure you it is happening. Even as we speak ... back in Cholon."

Tuki feels a sob rising in her throat. A huge lump of guilt. "Will you stop at nothing?"

"Of course I'll stop." Wen-Ling pours Tuki another cup of tea. That dreamy smile spreads over her face again.

"If I give you the ruby?"

"It's all up to you, Sweetie."

She feels the guilt swelling right behind her eyes, the urge to grab the dragon by the throat with her teeth, tear, drink blood.

But it's only for a moment ... and then her hand, drawn by some dark impulse of its own, stretches for her tea cup. She takes a long sip of the bittersweet tea. As quickly as the thirst to kill came, it leaves. Her mind just plain loses the thought, the will.

She's imagining Michael charging toward her on an immense horse when Wen-Ling bends toward her, takes her face between velvet hands. Kisses her on the mouth. Purrs.

34

"I CAN ALMOST SMELL her perfume, she's that close," says Michael. He doesn't know what's giving him this sense of optimism, but he's getting strong signals from his intuition.

It's almost sunset. The sky's a strange violet as the failed Cape Cod public defender, his father, and Meng wander along a line of about thirty stalls with young women selling black pearl jewelry in front of the cafes, bars, restaurants, and boutiques on the main street curving around the edge of harbor at Cat Ba Town. The steep overgrown hills of the island loom a deep purple beyond the lights of the town.

"But where?" asks Caesar. "Where's that girl?"

Michael looks at the shop houses to his right, the high-rise hotel, the throngs of Chinese tourists and European backpackers. Turns to his left and stares at the broad harbor. There must be a thousand fishing boats rafted together at anchor out there. And a floating restaurant.

"I was expecting a village like Woods Hole. This place is a cross between the Mardi Gras of Provincetown and the industry of New Bedford."

"How screwed are we?" Caesar seems to be talking to himself more than his son or girlfriend.

He has no interest in the jewelry for sale, and like his son he has taken to staring out at the fishing boats, probably wondering what the catch is here, how much these guys are getting for ground fish, what they are paying for diesel fuel. Just plain missing the screeching of the gulls and the roll of the deck as the Rosa Lee takes to the swells east of Nantucket.

Meng has been looking at earrings and necklaces, chatting up a vendor. But now she grabs Caesar's hand to wrench his attention from the sea.

"This girl maybe knows something about Tuki and Dragon Lady," she says.

"What's she know?" Michael feels a little stutter in his heart. All these trays of earrings make him think of Tuki's mutilated ear.

"I don't know yet." Meng nods to the vendor. "She say her memory not so good."

"But if I buy you a pair of earrings, maybe she remembers better?" Caesar's already reading the situation, the old street hustle he remembers from his days in Cholon forty years ago.

"This pair, American," says the jewelry seller in English. She has a big, gap-toothed smile on her face as she holds one of the earrings, a collection of three green pearl pendants next to Meng's ear. "Very beautiful. Just thirty dollars U.S."

*   *   *   *

"To hell with this." Michael's tired and hungry. Mostly he's frustrated.

For the last hour Meng and the Decastros have been rooting around in an open-air market building, following up on the information they got from the jewelry lady. The sellers here are packing up their wares after a long day. The fish and vegetable marketers have already gone home. The only merchants left are selling kitchen goods and Chinese-made clothing smuggled here on fishing boats, knock-off Levis and tank tops with logos for the Lakers, Magic, Heat. The lights in the market are faint, giving the place a clammy, chaotic feel. And the mosquitoes are getting fierce. People have been answering Meng's questions with one or two syllables, if at all.

"Well, at least we got you some great earrings, Darlin'," says Caesar.

"Didn't that earring girl say she saw Tuki and Wen-Ling right here just two hours ago?" Michael gives a soccer kick to a forgotten shrimp on the ground with his foot.

"She described them to a Tee, Kid."

"But she said they were walking arm-in-arm. How the hell does something like that happen. Arch enemies, like that? I should have known we were being served up a load of bullshit."

"Not bullshit." Meng put's a hand on Michael's forearm to calm him. "Maybe just old news. Trust me."

"How can you be sure, Darlin'?"

"We get very bad deal on earrings. So maybe better deal on Tuki news."

"Well, nobody here's talking." Michael looks around at the market. The last of the merchants are covering their wares with tarps and scurrying away.

Caesar's face twitches. "Hey, I got an idea."

"What?"

"I think there's someone we can trust around here."

"Well, Cristo, Dad. This is no time to keep us in suspense."

The older Decastro is already leading the way out of the market building.

"Where are we going?"

"We're fishing right?"

"Yes?" Meng sounds confused as they hit the main street and the tourist throngs again.

"And we're fishermen, right, Mo?"

"Dad ... ?"

"Well, then, there it is. We need to talk to some fishermen."

*   *   *   *

Thirty minutes later, Caesar has led his son and Meng, almost as if by instinct, to a marine railway and boatyard on the western fringe of Cat Ba Town. Now, with Caesar's own Vietnamese, and quite a bit of assistance from Meng in translating, he's gotten a conversation going with an old man who has been working by the light of kerosene smudge pots, pounding twisted coconut husks into the seams between the bottom planks of a seventy-foot, teak-wood shrimper.

The men have been complaining to each about how badly they get ripped off by seafood buyers and debating the merits of using tallow made from lamb fat as a calking compound. In other words, they have been testing the depth and breadth of each other's authority, experience, integrity. But now the men are talking about government fishing quotas and the Vietnamese guy has made a joke. He says that politicians know about as much about fishing as a deaf, dumb, and blind sea slug.

All three men burst into laughter.

Meng gives Caesar a curious look. Like is this conversation heading somewhere useful or it this just boys being boys?

"Darlin', ask him if he has seen a shiny, blue helicopter land on Cat Ba."

She tenders the question.

"Khong," says the caulker. No. Why do they want to know?

Caesar says something in Vietnamese.

The only words Michael catches are nguoi dep. He's heard that before, thinks it means beautiful girl ... or something like that.

The caulker nods solemnly, stops his work and stares at the wooden mallet in his hand for a long time. When he finally speaks, his voice is slow and measured, but clearly Caesar doesn't understand.

"Please," say father and son Decastro together, turning to Meng for translation.

"It true he not see helicopter. But ... maybe three day ago his brother fishing off northeast end of island near village called Viet Hai. Brother see helicopter land. Shiny and blue."

"Jesus." Michael feels a thick wad of guilt rising in his throat and doesn't know why.

"How can we get there?"

Meng asks the caulker. There's a long conversation in Vietnamese.

"Best by boat."

"How long does it take?" Michael's voice is shaky.

"Two hours, maybe three, depending on current," says Meng. The caulker has clearly already briefed her on this information.

"Does he have a boat we can hire?"

Meng asks the caulker.

"Da," she says. "Yes. Boat possible."

Caesar switches into halting Vietnamese.

"Vang." The Vietnamese nods … then continues in his native language.

"What did you guys just say, Dad?"

"I asked him if he could take us tonight, take us now."

"And?"

"He says it's too dangerous to run at night. But I think he wants us to come home with him for dinner."

"No kidding?"

"You got to love these people, huh?"

35

SHE DOUBTS SHE can sink any lower than this. She told herself that she was buying time to get out from under this fog of opium, time to plan an escape and murder. She let Wen Ling cradle her, nuzzle her neck. During each and every moment, she might have killed the dragon. But she didn't.

Who the hell knows why, la? I'm alone in the last bed. In the last suite. In the last beach hotel. On the last island. Of the last country. On the last day. She thinks.

She looks at a vase with a cut red orchid, thinks this is what she has become. A plant, severed from her roots. Trapped in a beautiful, fluted glass. With a false and temporary bloom. Living briefly on fluid alone.

She's already feeling the numbness, the wilting, the failure within, when a hand strokes her hair with spreading fingers.

"It's time to go," says Wen-Ling. She has just re-entered the suite from the hall door. Pale moonlight is shining in through the thin curtains over sliding door to the balcony.

"Now?" Things are so confused in her head.

Wen-Ling brushes back Tuki's hair from her ears, taking care with her missing lobe, kisses her on the forehead, and dangles a black pearl pendant necklace next to Tuki's left cheek. "I hope you like this, Sweetie. I just paid a lot of money for it." "Why?"

"That fucking American you used to love is here."

"Please don't hurt him, la."

"Why not?"

*   *   *   *

"Can we make a bargain?" asks Tuki. "If I take you to the ruby."

"Of course."

Midnight ... and Tuki's still not quite ready to leave the hotel suite, still in opium-induced slow motion. She's seated at a vanity in front of a mirror. She has on a pair of jeans and a gold lame top. She could swear to Buddha that it's exactly like the ones the whores at the Tiger's Tail wear, swear that Wen-Ling has made her wear this little number just to remind her who she belongs to now—what a slut she has become.

But maybe that can still change, thinks Tuki vaguely, if I start getting my fluids from the toilet bowl and the shower, not the tea cup.

"I want Hong Tam with me," she says.

"Naturally." Wen-Ling's standing at her back. combing Tuki's black hair. It's still damp from her shower.

"I want to see Michael and his father."

"Really? Even after we ...?"

"Yes."

"Then ...?"

"I don't want to ever see you again."

"Are you sure of that, Sweetie?"

"Do you want the ruby or not?"

"Just lead the way."

"I want a million dollars for Hong Tam's education and because she lost her father and her mother."

"You drive a hard bargain." Wen-Ling stops brushing Tuki's hair.

"Ni sua pa chorake," she says in Thai. It's one of her favorite proverbs, and it just pops into her head unbidden. "Escape from the tiger, meet the crocodile, la."

"I want the Heart of Warriors."

"We can go get it. Today."

"Where are we going?"

Tuki feels a small victory. It's her turn to smile a little inside. Sometimes she actually senses that there's a person behind the Dragon Lady mask. Maybe even a vulnerable little girl that tries to creep out into the sunshine after enough of the magic tea. And sometimes a person can actually find someone who stirs a little sympathy there.

"Tell me about my father."

"The black cat at the Black Cat."

"You said you used to smoke with him."

"Where are we going for the ruby, *bui doi*?" The Dragon Lady's back. She gives a hard stroke to Tuki's hair. For several seconds her roots feel on fire. But after days and days of dulling opium the pain is refreshing.

"How did you know my father?"

Wen-Ling turns her back walks out onto the balcony, stares out at the moon-streaked sea. Says something.

"What?"

The Dragon Lady suddenly wheels around, her white terry cloth bathrobe swirling through the air. "We were lovers."

"Lovers?"

"And partners."

"At the club? At the Black Cat?"

"We were in business together ... for a while."

"You knew my mother?"

"Knew her?"

"You hired her?"

"Who do you think introduced that little bitch to Marcus?"

Suddenly Tuki understands something she never quite got before. The real source of her father's apprehension and warnings about Wen-Ling from their first contact with her in Singapore two years ago. She wonders how much her mother has known, or at least suspected, all along about Wen-Ling's hand in the misery that has been visiting her loved ones. How much has her mother known about a nearly forty-year-old grudge?

"Then this is not just about the ruby." Tuki thinks that her cloying suspicions about Wen-Ling's deep and various motives are about to gain some shape and clarity.

"It is now." Wen-Ling picks up the receiver from the room phone on a night stand. "Do you take me to the ruby … or do I tell Flash he can have his party with that little girl?"

"Was my father dealing opium with you?"

"I'm calling Flash."

"Wait." Tuki knows she's out of tricks.

"Why?"

"The ruby's in Saigon."

"Where?"

"Not so fast, la."

"You think you are a very tricky girl …"

Tuki shrugs, remembers something she learned a long time ago in Bangkok about cabaret theater and the strip tease from the two drag queens, Brandy and Delta, who raised her. "A princess never undresses all at once."

"Then this princess is going someplace those Portuguese fisher friends of hers, or anyone else, will never find her lovely bones … for a very long time."

She feels her heart sink. She just wants to get back to Saigon. Home turf, where possibly she can find her old strength, an old ruse, to slay the dragon. Wen-Ling must sense this, and wants to keep her up north where she has the advantage of the Hmongs and her smuggling network to protect her, maybe put the bite on Michael and his father, too.

"Cave or floating village? Your choice, Sweetie." Wen-Ling wraps her in a hug from behind. The hairbrush smells damp and dirty pressed beneath her chin.

"Cave," says Tuki.

She's hoping that whatever she chooses, Wen-Ling will do the opposite. Hoping that she can find enough real water to drink in a floating village that she can stay clear of opium tea. Hoping, too, that a floating village might be some place her fishermen lover with his sea sense might think to look, might not get himself killed.

36

THE SUN HAS BEEN up for two hours when the crew of the shrimp boat heaves an anchor ashore and drops Michael, his father, Meng on the rocky coast of a fjord on the northeast side of Cat Ba. The caulker and fisherman who wined and dined them last night at his home points to a narrow, paved road. He motions with his hand for them to follow it north into a lush valley of cultivated fields and rice paddies between steep limestone pitons.

Michael's posse is not walking for even five minutes before a collection of wooden houses appear alongside the road. Children come pedaling toward them on bicycles offering bottles of cold water and little baggies of candied ginger, coconut, lotus seeds for sale.

Caesar immediately starts negotiating with the kids for their goods.

"Ask them if they have seen the helicopter." Michael's voice is a bit shrill.

The nearness he felt to Tuki back in Cat Ba Town has been replaced with a jittery feeling, something like jet lag. Maybe the bun thang—fried noodles with egg, chicken, prawns—that he ate last night at the fisherman's home was laced with MSG or something else that has left him feeling like every vein in his body is pulsing with tiny acetylene flames. He has this terrible feeling that Wen-Ling has her spies everywhere, knows he's at Cat Ba, has already started the process of vanishing with Tuki again.

His greatest hope is that maybe if the blue helicopter came here before, it will come back to this village again for Tuki and her captor. And when it does, he and his father will be waiting. But what they do then, if such a thing actually happens, is anybody's guess. It's not like they have a weapon besides the pair of net hooks that he and his father snagged from the shrimper and have hidden beneath the waistbands of their shorts.

"Did you ask them, Dad?"

His father and Meng shoot him hard looks. Like haven't you learned anything about a civil way to pursue your questions in this country?

His father's got tears of sweat running down his cheeks as he hands Michael a bottle of water and several bags of candied ginger. It must be over ninety degrees already this morning. There's no wind. The blades of grass along the road are dripping with dew.

"Sorry," says Michael. "This just sucks."

"You hear me complaining, Buddy Boy?"

"No, but Cristo ..."

"Like people we know seem to be dropping all around us, huh?"

"Yeah."

"You think this is bad? You should have been here in the last war."

Last war? So this is how his father is keeping himself together? He's gone totally into combat mode. Sergeant Caesar Decastro, 716th Marine Police Battalion, reporting for duty. Again.

"Dad? What are the odds that we aren't going to find ...?"

His father shakes his head, as if Michael's bringing up something so toxic that to even speak this fear aloud will bring bitter curses or death swarming down on their heads.

"I think Meng's asking about the chopper now," he says.

She has stepped away from the two Americans and is down on one knee at eye level with the kids, talking quietly while sharing the contents of a bag of candied lotus seeds with them. She seems to know that parents make these kids account for all the candy and that they can't just help themselves to the tempting treats.

More muffled conversation. Then, between bites, the children's voices suddenly rise an octave. Their words come fast, with a rushing of breath and the windmilling of their arms over their heads.

" May bay truc thang." They echo each other.

"Yes," says Meng smiling. "Helicopter."

"Hell ick coat tore," say the children, arms spinning again. "Hai nguoi dep. *Bui doi*, vang. Thu hai."

They see it," Meng says softly to the Decastros. "Last Monday helo drop two pretty women near ocean, one is *bui doi*."

"Monday?" Michael tries to remember what today is. "That was four days ago."

"Yes," says Meng. "Children say speedboat pick up pretty women."

"Which way did it go?" Caesar seems to be searching a chart in his mind.

"South. Cat Ba Town."

"Cristo." Michael kicks up a cloud of roadside dust with his Nike.

"You mean they were back there in that town all along?" Caesar looks ready to bite his front teeth through his lip.

"Maybe they still on island somewhere," says Meng.

"What makes you think so?" Michael's trying to ram his mind back in gear.

"Children say village fishermen see same speedboat that meet helicopter race by here last night. Late."

"We just missed Tuki," says Caesar.

Missed. That word. Michael wishes he could never hear it again. Wishes it did not always poison his soul with longing … or guilt about Colón and that evening in Chatham when she rubbed his hand against her cheek, closed her eyes, offered him her world.

*   *   *   *

"Do you still miss Tuki?" she asks.

The white walls and oak floors of the tavern room at the Chatham Bars Inn seem to be spinning.

"Could you just hold me?" He's sorry he asks for what he really needs even before the sound of his voice withers and breaks.

Yemanjá Colón's eyes burst open. They're huge, dark, wet, dripping with hurt. She draws back her hand from his.

"I'm already somebody's mami."

He knows that she's talking about Ricky, her son in second grade. Knows that she needs to be held, too. But held the way adults hold each other, the way it is in movies they both sometimes watch on lonely nights. Movies about saudade, risk, romance. Backbreaking craving.

"I've got to go."

She pushes back her chair from the cocktail table, stands up. She's already three steps toward lounge exit when he goes after her and grabs her hand from behind. Spins her toward him.

"Stay," he says. "Please."

She pulls him into a kiss. It happens so fast that their lips lock before he can exhale. In front of about twenty patrons and God.

*   *   *   *

"If they know we are on the island, they must be trying to hide," says Caesar.

"They wouldn't stay in Cat Ba Town. Someone would see them." Michael's starting to rise out of his memory and regret, getting his brain working a little.

"So where they go?" Meng seems at a loss. She opens a bag of candied coconut for the kids, bends on one knee in front of them again, starts talking rapidly in Vietnamese.

The children are breathless, rushing their words as before. Alternately covering their eyes with their hands then breaststroking the air with their arms.

"What the hell's going on?" asks Caesar.

"Children say best places hide on Cat Ba are in caves or floating village."

Michael and his father look at each other confused. "Floating village?"

"House boats. All tie together."

"They are fishermen? In the floating houses?" Caesar's eyes widen as if he's starting to get the picture, maybe wishing he lived in a floating village on Cape Cod right now.

"Yes. Many fishers."

Michael thinks about Wen-Ling. Ever since he has known her, flight—travel—has been her M.O., from the first time he met her two years ago on the night train from Bangkok to Penang in Malaysia. She's a mover. Movers look for multiple escape routes. Caves don't usually have lots of exits.

"I'm going to bet against the caves," he says.

"Where's the floating village?" Caesar asks.

Meng gives a little smile, seems to be glad she's helping now. "Children say half-hour by boat."

37

MAYBE ONLY THE BUDDHA can save us now. Tuki's standing on the deck of a houseboat this morning, staring at the dark shapes, larger than humans, circling beneath the calm sea. Fins cutting the surface of the water.

She breathes in the overwhelming scent of stinking, scaly plaa. Thinks about the growing unlikelihood that anything besides divine intervention—not even the Heart of Warriors—can save her, Hong Tam, Michael, his father, her mother from the dragon. Her gaze darts away from the predators schooling around for the fish that Wen-Ling's tossing in the water, skips away from the thrashing, the tearing of flesh. The little brownish clouds of blood.

She surveys the maze of mist-shrouded, limestone islands surrounding the raft of more than forty houseboats. This bay off the north side of Cat Ba called Ha Long—Descending Dragon—looks like something out of a fantasy. She wonders if she's still feeling the effects of opium this morning as she fakes drinking from her cup of the terrible tea.

Wen-Ling nudges her back from behind. "Just get on with it. In the water, *bui doi* … or tell me exactly where the ruby is in Saigon."

The morning mist is cool. The slate-gray water looks darker, still to the diva. She's stripped to her bra and panties, feeling naked to the world here on the teak deck of the little, green, floating house.

She feels the whole affair rocking beneath her bare feet. Five ragged fishers look on. Three men from a small boat tied to the house, two older women from inside one of the windows. They're waiting for the show to begin.

"Last chance, Sweetie. Where's the ruby?"

Tuki closes her eyes, shakes her head no. She's not giving up the ruby. Not before she gets back to Saigon. Not before she sees Hong Tam and Michael again. Not before she's back on home turf where the monks at Xao Loi can help her. Not unless she can hand it over in person. No deal, la. Sharks in the water or not.

"Then swim for your life, Sweetie."

The barrel of Wen-Ling's pistol jabs the small of her back, knocks her off balance. The next thing she knows she's plunging deep into the dark, cloudy currents of the bay. Eyes wide open, tea mug dropping from her hand. The water warming her even as she sinks. The Heart Sutra unraveling in her soul.

There is no suffering, no cause of suffering,
no end to suffering, no path to follow.

She's deep into the part about no attainment of wisdom, and no wisdom to attain when the first predator brushes against her legs. A second bangs against her hip. Then one comes straight at her face out of the milky haze ahead.

Body is nothing more than emptiness,
emptiness is nothing more than body.

She's about to close her eyes, waiting to be torn open by rows of razor teeth when the torpedo racing toward her veers, stops. Looks at her eye to eye … with a gaze that almost feels sentient, curious. And something harder to read, but not totally threatening.

For the first time she realizes what she's truly seeing, not what she imagined she was seeing. No doubt what Wen-Ling wanted her to imagine, to fear. The slim, finned, muscular gray creature before her is not a shark at all. Nor are the other creatures that have been feeding on the thrown fish. They are dolphins. And now this one's nudging her with its head against her belly, pushing her toward the surface. Toward light, air.

> *No eyes, no ears,*
> *No nose, no tongue,*
> *No razor teeth, no shark …*

She breaks out into the shimmering mist. Breathes deep. Strokes the dolphin's back with her right hand as it wallows at her side, the touching a purely instinctive reflex. Something in her mind's starting to see the world in crisp outlines for the first time in nearly a week.

Wen-Ling's standing, tea mug in hand, on the deck of the floating house. She tosses out three dead fish to the dolphins, smirks. Obviously proud of having terrorized Tuki with this practical joke.

"Do you feel like the Little Mermaid?" she asks.

"Just watch me, la." Tuki dives. Aims to vanish. One way or another.

*   *   *   *

But the three fishers in their boat surround her with a net, pull her in, haul her back to Wen-Ling who's drinking her tea inside a floating, gray, teak shanty with a rusty roof. "How was your swim, Sweetie?"

"I hate you."

Wen-Ling smiles. "Want to see some new pictures?"

*   *   *   *

It's not yet noon. Tuki's wrapped in a rough, orange blanket. Seated on a sleeping pallet on the floor of the ramshackle floating house. Her back's against the wall as Wen-Ling sets the laptop in front of her. A slide show's scrolling. And the first image makes her gag.

It's a picture of the bar in the Tiger's Tail. Hong Tam's standing on it. Bare. Except for her black hair drawn up in folds. Except for the ruby lips, the eye shadow, eyeliner, fake lashes. She's blowing a kiss to the camera. Intruding an inch into the top, right corner of the picture is something gray. A cylinder. Only after squinting for several seconds does Tuki see that the cylinder is the barrel of a pistol nearly pressed to the child's head. It's hard to tell if the little girl knows the gun's there.

"How can you live with yourself?"

"It's your stubbornness that's hurting the child, not me."

"Please let her go back to her grandmother."

"But she's having such a good time. Look."

The computer has scrolled to a new picture. It's a street scene in Cholon. Tuki can tell by the golden Chinese characters on a red sign over a butcher shop in the background. In the center of the picture is an ice cream vendor's silver cart. Standing in front of it is Hong Tam, wearing a t-shirt with a picture of Mickey Mouse on it. She's holding a cone piled high with what looks like mango sherbet. It's starting to melt. The girl's smiling as she offers it to the man kneeling at her side with his left arm around her shoulder. He's smiling too, his pink tongue starting to dart out as he goes in for a lick. There's no mistaking who he is.

"Freaking Flash, la."

"She's really taking what the Americans call a 'shine' to him."

Tuki says something in Thai.

"What?"

"It's a proverb."

"Oh really?"

"You always reap what you sow."

"That's a proverb?"

"The Buddha sees all."

Wen-Ling shakes her head dismissively, takes a sip of tea. "I have a proverb for you."

Tuki stares into the dragon's face, waits.

"Like father, like daughter." She points an imaginary gun at Tuki's nose with her thumb and index finger, pulls the trigger.

"You're really going to suffer for this in the next life, la."

"What planet do you live on, Sweetie?"

"You'll see."

38

"THESE PEOPLE not happy we here." Meng's voice is almost a whisper.

She's huddling on the foredeck of the shrimp boat with Michael and his father as the crew heave their lines to a pair of frowning fisher folk waiting on the deck of what seems to be a floating school house. The students, if there were any, have gone home even though it is only noontime. No kids are visible anywhere among this nest of several dozen houseboats. They are rafted together beneath the cliffs of a limestone island shaped like an immense gumdrop.

"What's wrong?" Caesar rubs his hand, gentle, across the backs of her shoulders.

"Ten buon lau," she says.

Michael looks confused.

"Smugglers," says his father, obviously proud that he remembers this phrase from his MP days in Cholon.

Something clicks with Michael. These people in the floating village are coastal outliers, subsisting here on the fringes of the Tonkin Gulf, all but hidden and forgotten by the world and their government. They have easy access to deep-sea boat and ship traffic ... and nearby China. There are small communities on some of the islands off the Massachusetts coast back home that still have a reputation for their clannishness, for illegal drug trafficking. According to myth, most of Cape Cod was once home to wreckers and pirates.

Out fishing at the Canyons and on Georges Bank aboard the Rosa Lee he has watched on the radar scope while offshore lobster boats and trawlers heaved-to suspiciously for hours. He's observed them steaming in what looks like box patterns as if searching for something that's lost. One foggy night as a teenager on a summer haddock trip with his father, Michael had the midwatch in the wheelhouse and saw on the radar a pair of trawlers meeting up with a target that could have only been a ship. When he hailed another fishing vessel on the radio and asked if they were watching this rendezvous on radar, someone came on the frequency cautioning "Silencio, cabrón." Message received. Don't ask, don't tell.

Well. Cristo, it's happening again.

*   *   *   *

"Nobody want to talk to me," says Meng, returning to the shrimp boat from trying to engage the fishers who tied up the lines.

Michael has noticed. The fishers are jabbering intensely with the crew of the shrimper and pointing out to sea, but they have repeatedly turned their backs on Meng when she tried to ask them questions.

"They say not good time." Meng looks uncharacteristically pale, almost withered. Her jeans and yellow cotton blouse suddenly too big for her.

Is it fear or some dark intuition preying on her?

"They say maybe we find Tuki at floating village other side of island."

"This island?" Michael's finding it hard to believe that an island no bigger than Boston's Fenway Park would have another village on its far side.

Meng nods. "They call it Monkeys Castle."

Michael's wondering where all of the kids in this place have gone. Wondering, too, if a storm is coming. The sky is overcast, misty. Everything looks shadowy or on fire. "I'm getting bad feelings."

His father eyes the crew of the shrimper, sees that they are already taking in their docking lines. "Looks like our chaperons are too."

The shrimp boat's diesel barks, the exhaust stack spews a burst of dark smoke as the vessel slips away from the floating school. The old caulker/fisherman who has been so friendly in the past is now stony-eyed as he draws Meng into conversation.

"What's the matter, Darlin'?" Caesar is at her side.

"He say captain forget. Have important business back in Cat Ba Town. We go home now."

"Just ask him to take us around to the other side of this island, first," says Michael, "in case there's even a remote chance we can get lucky."

"Something tells me this is a bad idea, Mo." His father laces his fingers through Meng's. He draws her to him, kisses her on the forehead as if he's saying goodbye.

*   *   *   *

Michael's fully prepared to find nothing except sea and more of these weird piton-like islands when the shrimper rounds the Monkeys Castle to the north. But, to his surprise, he sees another floating village. It's nearly a clone of the one they just left astern. But it looks less prosperous and seems to be moored to the edge of a small beach. There's no school. The houseboats are smaller, with peeling paint. The sky seems darker here. The beach and the water, gray. He's wondering where to start when up ahead he spots a sailing junk tied alongside the deck of a house with a rusty roof. Through the mist he sees someone's waving a red sheet or towel on the beach.

It seems to be a signal. From a woman. A young woman. A pretty woman. Jesus Cristo, a nude woman. And now that she sees that she has his attention, she's wrapping her body in that red sheet. The wind's blowing her hair off her head in dark flames. It's wild, sunstreaked. Almost like Tuki's, back in the day when she was in her Janet Jackson phase, singing in the drag clubs of Provincetown. And like an image from another place and time. A shadowy image from Cape Cod. One he can't let himself bring into focus.

"Is that your girlfriend, Kid?" Caesar's pointing.

Cristo Salvador. Michael wants to shout.

"That her?" Meng has never seen Tuki before.

"Yes," says Michael. "Holy shit, that's her."

The shrimp boat is still a hundred yards away from her, when Michael sees Wen-Ling step onto a gangway leading from the dock of a small houseboat onto the beach with some kind of small submachine gun in her hands. She's pointing it at Tuki as a dozen men with automatic rifles rise out of boats tied alongside the house. And now a speedboat is rounding the Monkeys Castle from the East. Bright bursts of muzzle fire erupt from gunners aboard.

Caesar grabs Meng, pulls her to the deck and covers her as rounds buzz over their boat. The captain of the shrimper guns his engine, wheels into a lumbering left turn away from the island, the village, Tuki.

She drops the red sheet from her shoulders and is stretching her arms out toward the man she loves.

"Come on." He's shouting at her. Beckoning her. "Swim."

And she does.

One second she looks like a frantic child, naked on the beach, red sheet trailing in her hand. The next, she's a dark shape beneath the gray water. He can see her arms stroking together in sure arcs as if she was born to this water. She can't be more than fifty yards away when bullets begin hitting in little geysers all around her. The beautiful swimmer.

He wonders how long it will be before she begins to jerk and flail, sputter to the surface with blood darkening the water around her.

His brain's shouting the Hail Mary inside his head as he throws off his sneakers and dives over the rail for her.

The last thing he sees before he hits the water is Wen-Ling pointing her weapon at him and smiling. Then he's in the water and something's stinging his neck where it joins his right shoulder. He's swatting at it with his left hand when everything goes dark, silent.

39

WEN-LING STROKES the hair alongside Tuki's temple. They are both back aboard the junk.

"It's okay, sweetie. Only a flesh wound. You know I wouldn't let him die ... yet."

"I want to see him ... please." She's curled up on a plush, blue settee in the main saloon of the boat, wrapped in the red sheet again.

An hour ago the junk was tied alongside the floating house next to the little beach where Tuki was Wen-Ling's prisoner, where all the shooting happened. After Tuki surfaced, waving her hands, surrendering to save Michael, Wen-Ling's thugs dragged Michael from the water. He was bleeding from the neck. They staunched the flow of his blood with a rag and took him into the wheelhouse, even as the boat that he jumped beat a retreat from the gunfire. As it left, Tuki could see Michael's father struggling against two fishers in the back of the boat. He seemed to be trying to dive into the water after his son. But Tuki was not allowed to see Michael. She was pulled, soaking, aboard the junk. It cast off its lines immediately, started motoring west. Chasing the sun, weaving among the maze of islands in Ha Long Bay. The junk looks like one of the hundreds of boats that tourists charter for cruises through the bay, but the three staterooms of this boat don't carry people. One is filled with two-liter bags of heroin, the second has a cache of automatic weapons. The third is locked.

"I want to show you something," says Wen-Ling. "Come."

The Dragon Lady leads Tuki—still wrapped in her red sheet—by the arm to the locked cabin, keys the door. Her grasp is gentle on Tuki's wrist. She's really had enough of Wen-Ling's sending her these mixed messages—the violence and threats perpetually followed by tenderness, cheap sympathy.

Is this the shape of true evil, la ... and can I still kill it?

When the door opens, Tuki sees that the cabin has been furnished as an office. A teak desk, wooden filing cabinets, small couch, chairs. A ceiling fan spins slowly overhead. Music echoes from hidden speakers. The Supremes singing, "Baby Love." In one corner is a stack of black travel roller bags. The top one is open and filled with packets of American twenty-dollar bills. In the middle of the room in front of the couch is a coffee table. And on the coffee table is a green satin warm-up jacket. It's spread out, the back facing up. Stitched onto the back is a cartoonish image of a black cat with white lips twisted into a devilish smile. The right eye's winking.

"How did you get this?"

"I told you I knew your father."

"But this was the jacket ..."

"That he was wearing two years ago in Bangkok when Thaksin Kittikachorn's throat got in the way of my throwing star."

"Oh, la."

It was the night everything started to go wrong. Her Buddhist act of contrition. Her attempt to shed her bad karma. She had gone back to Thailand to return the ruby her Prem had stolen from his father.

*   *   *   *

She's face-to-face with his prick of a father, the billionaire producer of sleeping pills, the crusher of an only son. Here on the deck of the River House, bathed in the tangy scent of fresh-cut teak. It's bigger, more ornate, than the old house that she burned in anger, in revenge, a few years ago. The house where she loved her sad, sweet Prem. The heroin junkie who gave her up under pressure from the bastard standing in front of her now.

"Do not waste my time." Prem's father sounds impatient.

She glares at Thaksin Kittikachorn. Late fifties. Self-assured. But his eyes darting between her and the river.

He demands to know if she has the Heart of Warriors.

She feels in her handbag with her fingers, touches the cool stone. Remembers one night in a river taxi when Bangkok looked like a fairy world. Prem slipped the immense ruby into her coat pocket.

She asks this bastard if he will promise to return the Heart to the monks in Ayutthaya.

The father twitches, then promises before Buddha and his dead son Prem. Kittikachorn tells her they cannot be here long. Does she not see how dangerous it is for both of them to be at the River House like this? Alone in the dark without the protection of his bodyguards.

She takes the gem from her bag, cups it in her right hand. Is stretching out her arm to offer it to this tiger of a man. The lights of Bangkok and Thonburi are twinkling in the facets of the ruby when she feels something buzz past her ear. Kittikachorn's face blooms blood. He folds, tumbles over backwards.

She wheels, looking for a killer. Sees two silhouettes slipping back into the shadows where the house meets the porch rail at the far end of the deck. Sees the flash of a green satin jacket as one figure vanishes. Much later, after her father's murdered in Truro on Cape Cod, she learns that he was the man in the green jacket.

40

HE KNOWS he's dreaming but he can't wake up from the nightmare, from the memory. Maybe because he's afraid he'll wake to something worse. So ... he sinks into the familiar horror. The dream that comes so often these days with his night sweats, his fear of death.

He grabs Colón's hand from behind, spins her toward him.

"Stay," he says. "Please."

Then they're kissing ... in front of about twenty patrons at the Chatham Bars Inn. He's sinking into the wetness of her mouth, feeling the warmth of her arms around his shoulders as if he's rescuing her.

He doesn't remember how it is that they got a room on the beach, or who paid. He just knows that they are entwined on an antique four-poster bed, a bright platinum moon staring through the glass door at them.

"Promise you won't judge me," she says, sitting up in the bed and pulling her sweater over her head, unclasping her bra. Sliding out of her panties.

"Cristo, you're lovely, menina."

She smiles, seems to like the way he laces his English with Portuguese. "Promise me."

He slithers out of his pants, his shorts. Unbuttons his wool shirt, but doesn't take it off. Instead, he reaches out his arms, slides his hands behind her neck, looks her in the eyes. Promises her. He's thinking she's the good Lord's gift to him, undeserved as a gift may be. No, seguro, he will never judge her. Who is he to judge? Just a poor, unspeakably grateful and lonely man. Completely unworthy of her esteem and this most amazing moment of intimacy.

"I've been dreaming this will happen," she says. "For a long time."

"You mean us, like this?"

She bows forward, puts her head on his shoulder, nods. She says he doesn't know much about her, except that she's Lou Votolatto's protégée, a detective in the state's CPAC unit on the Cape. That she has a young son, that she and Ricky live in New Bedford with her abuela, her grandmother.

"I know enough to know you're a quality person."

But he doesn't know her complicated history, she says. Not all of it. And she wants to start clean with him.

"I'm listening. No judgments." He folds her in his arms as they lie together in the moonshine.

She tells him as she has before, that her mother, half-Cuban, half-Jamaican, died at the hands of her drunken Puerto Rican father. Killed accidentally while making love to her drunken, philanderer of a father. Beaten, asphyxiated. Maybe for pleasure.

But there's more to the story that she hasn't told him until now.

She had been there at the killing. She watched. Just a child standing in the doorway. The witness at her mother's room. Wanting to shout, Fuck you. Fuck you. Leave her. Leave her alone, Papi. She wanted to kill him. Kill her mother, too. Kill the whore. Stop them both. But she said nothing.

"I wanted to taste the shame. Taste the lipstick and the cheap perfume of my father's putas. Wanted him to hit me, not Mami."

"I'm so sorry. Jesus."

Since Tuki vanished eighteen months ago from the Cape, he and Colón have met many times at the Indian mound in Chatham to walk along the windy beach, meditate on the marsh grass, the sea birds, the deep blue of the harbor. He thought of these interludes as a way to find peace. Colón said she came to talk to the dead, to listen to the dead. But even after all those meetings, he really had no idea these were the ghosts she was carrying.

"I wanted the slap. The punishment. The love. The killing. I want to

eat my father's black soul and my own."

"That's all over," he hears himself say. Hugs her tighter, kisses her hard.

But as he kisses her, he knows that he's trying to revive the desire that he was feeling five minutes ago … but is failing him now. His core trembles with jolting panic.

"Make love to me." Her voice sounds small.

Cristo. This woman is as vulnerable, as damaged, as he is. And now he sees that no matter how lonely he feels, how much some dark part of him craves this fine, strong body pressing against him, his soul is telling him that now is not the time or the place for romance. This woman deserves, needs, more than he's capable of giving.

"I can't … I don't dare."

Her hand slides down his belly to his thighs. Feels the sad truth of his maleness suddenly shrunken with fear and recrimination.

"You promised me you wouldn't judge."

"I'm so sorry." He's whispering.

"Please." She pulls a beach towel around her naked body and runs out onto the moonlit beach. The wind's screaming, blowing her tangled hair off her head in skeins. "Just leave me the hell alone."

41

TUKI'S STILL CAPTIVE on the junk. Still hugging the red sheet to her body as she curls herself into the corner of the couch in Wen-Ling's office cabin. Still feeling just plain stupid for letting her naked self on the beach be used to bait Michael and his father into a trap. Wen-Ling must have known that the Decastros would come looking for Tuki among the floating villages. Must have made sure that islanders saw their speedboat and could point the way that led the Americans into the ambush.

"You think it was an accident your father was at the River House when Kittikachorn died, *bui doi?*"

Tuki has thought this question through a thousand times. Once she and her father had reunited after three decades apart, she told herself that both of them were starting their lives over. He helped her to escape from the sadness of her impossible love for Michael and the horror of Prem's death in the aftermath of the Provincetown Follies murder case. Once they were clear of all that stinky plaa, they flew to Southeast Asia. She got the operation that made her fully a woman, they found her mother and Tran. Life was beginning in a fresh way... except that she still had the stolen ruby.

"My father knew I was going to the River House to give back the ruby, la. He followed me to protect me."

Wen-Ling sips her tea, paces the main saloon. "He told you that?"

"No, I ..." She feels stupid. All her assumptions seem so shaky now.

"Your father found me in Saigon when the two of you were in Vietnam looking for your mother. He said he had a way to pay me all the money he owed me."

Wen-Ling was more than a little surprised to hear from the man who had suddenly vanished from Saigon and the Black Cat more than three decades ago owing her over a million dollars. In the early days of the Black Cat, when Marcus and Wen-Ling were lovers, they went into partnership together to start the bar. Marcus used profits from Wen-Ling's opium and heroin business to underwrite the expense of rebuilding the little juke joint into Saigon's glorious rendition of the House of the Rising Sun. And he also used her drug money to support his gambling habit.

But when Wen-Ling saw him again two years ago, she gathered that he erroneously thought she was still after him, that a group of Thai thugs who had been shaking him down in New York were just a fresh incarnation of the guys she had sent to threaten his life back in the early seventies after he dissolved his partnership in the bar with her ... and dumped her for Huong Mei.

"The story of the stolen ruby just sort of fell into my lap, Sweetie, that day he came to see me at the Tiger's Tail two years ago."

Tuki feels herself starting to shiver as she hears how Wen-Ling was quite willing to let Marcus proceed under the delusion that she had been stalking him for decades. Especially when she learned that what he had in trade for his debt was a magnificent ruby, a national treasure of both Thailand and Vietnam. A stone that she might hold in ransom against the Thai, Lao, and Vietnamese government's efforts to drive the Hmong people and the opium trade out of the Golden Triangle. Hold in ransom for more private dream things, too.

"You really think your father was trying to protect you at the River House?"

Tuki's face is pale, icy. She doesn't know anymore, isn't sure any of this is happening, any of her crazy-crazy life has happened. Maybe its all just part of someone's opium dream. She'll never know for sure unless she dies, or Wen-Ling does. The old anger, the urge to kill flickers deep in her belly.

"Why are you telling me this, la? What does any of this matter now?" Tuki bolts off the couch. At this moment she wishes she could spit on her father's ghost.

Wen-Ling puts her hands on Tuki's shoulders, gently pushes her down until she's sitting on the couch again, looking out the window at the crimson ball of the sun sinking between two steep islands to the west. The music coming from the junk's speakers is a moody rock and roll song Tuki first heard in Brandy and Delta's drag bar in Bangkok, Lou Reed's "Coney Island Baby."

"Can't you see, I'm all you have? Not your father, not your mother, not that wreck of a fisherman-lawyer. None of them can keep you safe …"

Tuki closes her eyes, tries to think.

"Only I can keep you from harm now."

The diva says something in Thai. It's a proverb that boils out of her soul. Something about beware the dragon … speaking with forked tongue.

"Two days before Kittikachorn died in Bangkok, your father called me. Asked me to come to Bangkok. I was in Vietnam."

Tuki stares into Wen-Ling's black eyes, feels the flames rising in her belly.

"That old black cat said that if I wanted the ruby, I had to come to Bangkok right away because you were going to give it away."

"I don't believe you."

"He met me at the airport, we went to the River House together. After I had to kill Kittikachorn, he ran … and left the jacket with me. What more proof do you need?"

Tuki says that her father could have just asked her for the Heart. She probably would have given it to him.

"Except that he knew you had a collection of fake rubies and he had no idea which one of the stones you carried was the real one. He couldn't be sure you would trust him with the real one."

Oh, la. It was true. The night she had met Kittikachorn at the

River House, the ruby she had tried to hand him was a fake. The real one was hidden beneath a bush at a Buddhist temple in the Banglamphu district of Bangkok.

"You're trying to poison my mind … and my heart. And I don't know why. I already told you I will take you to the ruby in Saigon."

"How do I know it's not another fake?"

"I gave you my word, la," she says.

She feels the fire in her stomach burning the way it used to sometimes before she went on stage. Thinks there still must be a way to get out of this box she's in, a way to harness the bonfire that's searing her liver, her lungs. A way to take back the power, kill the dragon. And save Michael, Hong Tam, her mother.

Wen-Ling laughs. Like what's Tuki's word? Nothing but wind. "Do I have to let Michael Decastro die right in front of your eyes, to show you how deep in hell you are right now? To show you that I am your one and only way out?"

"Please, let me see him."

From the sound system, Lou Reed's moaning about the glory of love.

42

TUKI'S NUZZLING his chest when he wakes on the junk. It's dark now, and he has a vague memory of being dragged by some men into this cabin piled with plastic bags of heroin. He's lying on the cabin sole, but he barely notices the hardness of teak wood beneath him. He's sinking into the smell of her tangled hair—oranges, dampness, something sweet. The sharp scent of her fear.

"Don't die, Michael."

He feels the bandage on the wound at the base of his neck, then reaches up and strokes the back of her head. "It's you."

"It's me." She laughs with delight at finally hearing his voice. "Who else, la?"

"I love you," he says, wrapping his arms around her. The effort makes his vision blur, and he closes his eyes.

"I thought I'd never see you again."

He brushes back her hair, feels the tight African kinkiness at the roots. Looks at her right ear. The wound has almost entirely healed, just a thin red line where the skin has grown back together.

"We're going to get out of here," he says.

She nuzzles against him. "Only if we kill Wen-Ling."

He doesn't know why, but his mind slides away to the night almost two years ago when Tuki lost their baby trying to protect that damn ruby.

*   *   *   *

Eastham on Cape Cod. From outside the barn, he hears a thud like a blow to the body. The Thai mobster has her on the floor, is kicking her. Tuki grunts.

Another blow, another groan. Like his mother's moaning in her last days of cancer. Cristo.

When he rushes into the barn, she's lying on the ground, pulled into the fetal position. The thug's kicking at her knees, her belly. Pointing a Luger at her. Michael doesn't hesitate. He raises the shotgun in his hands, aims at the bastard's head, shoots.

Next thing he knows, he's on the ground holding her to his chest. She has not turned to engage him, just sits there in the blood, hugging her belly, whimpering as he embraces her from behind.

"It's all over," he says.

She just moans. Wipes her bloody hands on her face to quell the tears. Rocks her body. Finally turns and buries her face against his chest.

*   *   *   *

"I love you, la."

He holds her even tighter, shivers.

"You're hurt. You need a doctor."

"I feel fine."

He's lying. The pain at the base of his neck is a cold ache. Growing. He feels faint. And he knows she's right. Even if the bullet left a clean wound and is not buried in his muscle, a raging infection is just hours away in this heat and humidity.

She kisses his chest, his lips. "I don't mind dying if I'm here with you."

He tries to muster strength, optimism. Says he doesn't believe the two of them have gone through all of this misery, that God brought them together, just so they can die on a godforsaken boat for a ridiculous red stone.

"That's what I thought before I lost our baby."

The weirdness that she too is thinking about their lost child—and the darkness of what she's telling him—makes him catch his breath. The horror in what she's picturing about their entwining fates is so stunning that he suddenly moans. Then a memory fumes in his head. The day she rose from her coma in the Hyannis hospital after her beating and after losing the child.

*   *   *   *

"I had a little baby in me," she says.

He closes his eyes, turns his face away, wipes away tears from his cheeks, squeezes her hand tightly.

"I wanted it to be a surprise."

He drops to one knee next to the bed, presses his cheek against hers. Prays for another child to come into their lives.

*   *   *   *

"This is all my fault. I have a stolen treasure and I had no right to fall in love with you, la. Or bring you into this nightmare. I'm a poison who …"

He eases out of their hug on the cabin sole of the junk, notices for the first time that she's wrapped in a red sheet as if she were trying to be a Buddhist monk. His eyes look deep into hers. He wants to confess his own guilt, too. About his drinking and fighting back on the Cape. The shotgun episode in Woods Hole. And his mistake that night with Colón. Worst of all, his countless failures to protect Tuki, protect the people she loves. Her father and Tran have been lost because he was so blinded by love and guilt, saudade. And ego. Blinded by his ignorance about Southeast Asia and the evils of the Dragon Lady, too.

"I'm sorry for everything," he says. "Except loving you."

"Do you mean that?"

"I swear on my mother's memory."

"Do you think she would forgive me for loving you?"

He sees the tears in her eyes, draws her back into a hug. Grits his teeth for a second against the pain flaring in his neck.

"My mother would love you like a daughter."

She pulls him into the sweetest embrace, says that she will forgive him anything and everything if only he will love her unto death. His guilt starts to rise off him in winged waves.

"But now what?"

She tells him that if they are separated again, he must go to Saigon. To a place that sounds something like Za Loy to look for her. He can ask the monks for help.

"If I am gone …" she looks deep into his eyes, and he knows that when she says gone, she means dead, "ask the monks to help you find Wen-Ling. Do not tell them that you must kill her."

"What?"

He remembers just a month ago back on Cape Cod swearing to Colón and his father that he was done with violence forever, sickened even by the thought. It has been one thing to defend himself and Tuki's family against Wen-Ling, but what Tuki's asking is something different.

"Kill the Dragon Lady," she says, "or many, many more people will die."

He thinks he understands. He's been to the Golden Triangle, seen the poppy fields. Seen all those bags of heroin here on the junk, too. Guesses that he has only the vaguest sense of the drug empire Wen-Ling works for, possibly controls. And he knows that Tuki has been forever scarred by watching her first love Prem fall victim to a devastating heroin addiction.

But still, what Tuki is asking him to do is bewildering, horrifying. He did not come here to fight with drug lords. That's for the police, the government. He came here to get Tuki free of this violent world, not become a warrior in it.

"Please," Tuki's says. "Promise me."

He's not sure how to respond, searching his mind for something to say, when the cabin door bursts open.

"Look at the love birds." Wen-Ling's voice oozes disdain.

"You're just jealous, la."

Michael feels Tuki stiffen with hatred, defiance.

"Those days were over, *bui doi*." There's an odd wistfulness in the dragon's voice. "When you father left me in Saigon a long time ago."

Michael doesn't understand what he's hearing. The urge to stand up and defend Tuki from this devil is all that he knows right now. So he's staggering to his feet when the Dragon Lady charges him. She's dressed in what looks like a golden karate gi cinched with a black belt.

"Time to die, lover boy." she says, spinning and planting a brutal kick between his legs.

"No." Tuki's screaming as he doubles over.

From the corner of his left eye, he catches the blur of Wen-Ling's hands, pressed together, chopping toward his bloody neck.

43

"GET IN the helicopter, *hui doi*."

She's still feeling half-drowned by the memory of Wen-Ling pushing Michael's lifeless body off the junk an hour ago. Suffocating, too, from what Wen-Ling told her back in that office cabin. Dragged down by the knowledge that her father's connections with Wen-Ling were rotten from the start. And they had not ended at the Black Cat in Saigon in the early 1970s. Her dad had met with the dragon on at least two occasions in Saigon and Bangkok two years ago. He was the one who informed Wen-Ling that his daughter, this strange con lai diva back from America, had in her possession the Heart of Warriors.

"As I've said before, I'm all you've got, Sweetie."

Tuki's face trembles with grief as she climbs into the blue chopper. Her throat aches from the crying. For her father and his foolishness again. And, especially for her sweet Michael. Michael, who came all this way to slay the dragon for her. Michael, who's floating facedown in Ha Long Bay. She feels as if the blades of the helicopter are shredding her soul into tiny pieces as it lifts off from a patch of beach on a tiny island in the misty bay. She thinks that she's finally beginning to understand Wen-Ling. The Dragon thinks the only way to make sure she gets the ruby is to stop these Americans from chasing her once and for all. The only way to show Tuki that she is absolutely, one hundred percent on her own is to kill, maim, or abduct everyone she loves. The only means to get revenge over her loss of the man she loved is to make his daughter suffer a thousand emotional deaths … and there are probably other reasons she still cannot fathom.

The helicopter's rotor is spinning fast now, creating an awful muttering.

"Next stop, Hanoi airport," says Wen-Ling. "Then private jet to Saigon. Would you like to see your little niece and Flash … before you take me to the ruby?"

44

THE FIRST THING he sees is his father's face hovering above him next to a middle-age Vietnamese man. The Asian guy has a stethoscope plugged into his ears, seems to be listening to Michael's lungs.

"How do you feel, Mo?"

His mind's starting to focus. "The Dragon Lady shot me ..."

"She left you floating for dead."

He remembers Wen-Ling's junk and the shrimper his father and Meng rented. "You picked me up."

"In the nick of time."

"Cristo."

"Exactly. I begged those shrimpers to turn back and look for you." "I could have died."

His father turns away, clearly doesn't want to talk about the details of pulling his shot and lifeless son from the water.

"Where's Tuki?"

"This is Dr. Nguyen. He just saved your life."

"Dad, where's Tuki?"

"Wen-Ling must still have her."

"We have to go to Saigon. Right now."

"One step at a time."

"Where are we?"

"Haiphong."

"Really?"

"You've been unconscious for twenty-four hours."

"What?"

"The doctor removed a round buried in your neck."

"Dad, I …"

"We have to make sure we've killed the infection."

"We have to find Tuki."

"I've been consulting with a professional."

"What? Who?"

"I called your old pal Detective Votolatto."

"You called the Massachusetts State Police?"

"Unofficially."

"How's Lou going to help?"

"We're in a war. We need intel and allies."

"Tuki wants me to kill Wen-Ling."

"See what I mean?"

"What are we going to do?"

"You want to fold your tent and go home?"

"I can't leave Tuki."

"Then we're in for one hell of a fight."

"I don't know … Maybe we need to go to the police."

"Huong Mei already did that back in Saigon. You see any help on that front?"

"Could be she didn't tell them about us."

"So we waltz into a police station and announce that we are a couple of American fishermen come to help a half-breed, former drag queen protect a ruby that probably rightfully belongs to someone else?"

"You've got a point."

"No shit."

Michael feels his belly churning, a mean crankiness coming over him. Everything's whirling out of control. This freaking country. This freaking war.

"Where's Meng, Dad?"

"At a temple."

"Why?"

"Praying for you. What do you think?"

Michael feels a sharp anger in his throat beginning to tangle with the pain in his neck and shoulder. "She's not my mother, you know?"

Caesar looks sad, embarrassed. "Why don't you cut that shit?"

"Because it's like I hardly know you anymore ... since she ..."

"What?"

"Ever since you found her, you've become ..." He throws his hands in the air.

"What?"

"Some kind of love-struck fool."

Dr. Nguyen vanishes from the room, clearly wants to get out of the heat.

"Now you know what it feels like being me, watching you, Mo."

The words are jackhammer blows to Michael's brain.

"You're a Decastro. Your mother always said that we were fools for love."

Michael remembers the scent of Tuki's hair—the oranges, the lemons—and the scent of his mother's hair. Colón's hair too. Other women. Sometimes the scents get all mixed up in his mind. "Mom really said that? About herself, too?"

"Why do you think she stuck by me all those years?"

"Because she loved you."

"And because she knew that I was nothing but trash fish without a woman to die for ... and only a couple women could ever fit that bill."

"You're saying she would be happy that you found Meng again?"

"And happy you aren't giving up on Tuki."

"Dad ..."

"Meng will never replace your mother."

"But she makes you happy?" He almost says like Tuki makes me happy ... in a thousand ways that make no sense.

"We would probably be dead already without her help."

"But if we have her help, what can Lou Votolatto add?"

"You ever dealt with a kidnapping before?"

Michael shakes his head no.

"Votolatto has. Quite a few."

"But …"

"We don't have time for buts. Meng's really afraid for Tuki. She says she has heard the Black Hmongs call Wen-Ling a nickname that has nothing to do with Robin Hood. They call her the Creeping Death." Michael thinks of Peter Pan and Captain Hook. The crocodile approaching. Like a ticking time bomb. "How soon before we can leave for Saigon?"

"The doc says maybe you'll be out of here this afternoon … if you eat your Wheaties."

*   *   *   *

Huong Mei's just getting ready to pull down the metal shutters over the bookstore's plate glass display window and close her shop for the evening when Michael, Caesar, and Meng roll up in a taxi from Tan Son Nhat Airport. Tuki's mother actually tries to close the front door and hide inside when she sees Michael get out of the cab with a bandage on his neck. But Caesar sticks his foot in the door, and Meng fires off something shrill in Vietnamese.

"Please leave my family alone." Huong Mei pushes against Caesar's chest.

Part of Michael wants to grab this woman and shake her, tell her that he, Meng and his father are all that stand between her daughter and granddaughter … and certain catastrophe. He wants to say that he doesn't give a flying eff about a stolen ruby … He's here to protect the woman he loves. But another part of him makes him bite his tongue because he has no idea the emotional torture this woman has been through of late … and has been through because of America's terrible meddling here four decades ago.

Caesar takes her by the wrists, falls on his knees. Starts saying things softly in Vietnamese.

Michael turns to Meng, who's the last out of the cab. "What's he doing?"

"Begging … promising her things he probably never can give her

… asking if she hear anything from Tuki or granddaughter."

Huong Mei spits in his face, shouts a phrase at him. Repeats it several times, then spits at Michael, too. "Ke giet nguoi."

"Her heart it so broken," says Meng.

"What did she call us?"

"Killers."

"Someone else is dead?"

Meng shakes her head. She doesn't know.

Michael's father is on his feet, hands pressed together bowing in supplication. "Xin loi," he's saying over and over again. He's so sorry. Just like his son.

Huong Mei has a cell phone in her hand, is punching in some numbers.

"Get back in cab," says Meng. "We go now."

"Why?"

"She calling police."

"Just what we fucking need." Caesar wipes the spit from his face. "Cristo, now what?"

"I think we have to go see our old friend Flash."

"We can't just going walking into that bar."

"This job for me." Meng's voice echoes with somber resolution, as if she's sensing her destiny. Miserable though it might be.

45

"DON'T WORRY, la. Everything's going to be okay." Tuki's in the apartment over the Tiger's Tail.

It's seven o'clock in the evening, Saturday. Tuki and Wen Ling are just off the dragon's private jet after delaying a day in a Hanoi hotel penthouse while Wen-Ling took care of urgent drug business. The former Patpong diva's down on her knees, hugging her niece to her chest, squeezing, soaking up the child's warmth. She's talking softly—consoling—waiting for her own tears to clear. Several minutes pass before it occurs to her that Hong Tam speaks very little English. But, of course, the child understands. Her arms are around her auntie's neck and nothing can pull them away. Except the Dragon Lady.

"Okay, nguoi dep," says Wen-Ling to the child, unclasps Hong Tam's arms from Tuki. She tells the child in Vietnamese that its time to go back to Uncle Flash and her new aunties. The little girl clings to Tuki.

Flash and two hookers stand smiling, beckoning to the child, from the doorway leading out of the apartment and down to the bar. Once again, the women are wearing look-alike red vests and minis, gold lamé tops. And Hong Tam is dressed to match. With ruby lipstick, eye shadow, liner.

The sound of "Midnight Train to Georgia" is rising from the bar downstairs. It cuts Tuki, burns her skin. She wonders if Wen-Ling has had it played to taunt her. And she's struck by a sense of déjà vu, feels as dark and unsettled as the Saigon River. The air's thick as smoke. Full of the unforgettable scents of Cholon. The ginger and the charcoal fires … the roasting pork, pungent fish sauce, steaming noodles … motorbike exhaust … the stale beer … the river.

"I want the ruby now, *bui doi*."

Tuki thinks of the gem, hidden in the sand of the incense burner at Xa Loi pagoda. She told Michael to go there. The monks would help him find her. Would help them both get free of the Dragon Lady once and for all. Or, if she was already dead, point the way to Wen-Ling. She knows that it was outrageous—very not as the Buddha wishes—that she asked Michael to slay the dragon, extinguish the evil. And maybe she is suffering for her wish now. Michael was so close. She held him, felt that warm, rough cheek against hers. Only to lose him again.

The ho must die, la.

Sometimes revenge is just, she thinks. Her burning the River House ten years after Prem abandoned her, that was just. But revenge is a vain hope now. Her heart shudders as she remembers Wen-Ling's karate chop to Michael's neck, the awful crack … and his body pushed into Ha Long Bay. Back to the sea he loves like he loves her, back to the mother of waters.

Bodhi!
Svaha!

Which means...

Gone, gone,
Gone fully over.

His soul must be very lost. Like mine, la.

"Are you crying, Sweetie?" Wen-Ling cups Tuki's chin in her hand, looks intently into the *bui doi*'s face.

"I have to pray first." She's still kneeling, pulling Hong Tam tighter to her chest.

The dragon sighs. "Do you remember me saying that I was going to let Flash rip out your heart and eat it for dinner after he fucks your dead body?"

"I have to get down on my knees before Buddha."

"Do what you want, Sweetie. But you know all those things I said Flash was going to do to you? He wants to do them to your pretty little niece first. You care to watch?" Wen-Ling flashes her pistol like you will watch. "Or you want to take me to the ruby?"

"Please don't hurt my baby." The words come from somewhere in her core. The memory comes, too.

*   *   *   *

"Look around you," says Tran. "All these people watching us. They think we're a family."

It's a year ago. The Saigon zoo. Off Nguyen Binh Khiem Street., just a few blocks walk north from Tran's apartment. Six o'clock in the evening and the botanical gardens pulse with people strolling, sitting on benches, eating at picnic tables. Everyone trying to escape the heat and noise of Saigon here, among the tall shade trees and the breeze blowing in off the river. The air dripping with Vietnamese love songs sifting from hidden speakers.

"Of course we're family," says Tuki, thinking—brother, sister, niece.

"No," says Tran. "They think we are like those elephants."

Across the stone and concrete moat three elephants are parading around their grounds. They are in a line. Male, female, baby. The female holding the tail of the male with her trunk. The baby holding the mother's tail.

Tuki gets the picture. She's walking between Tran and Hong Tam. Squeezes Hong Tam's hand a little harder, Tran's hand, too. She's going to buy herself a bracelet carved with elephants.

"I love you both," she says.

Hong Tam is not yet three years old. Her hair's cut in a page boy, falling just above her shoulders. She's wearing the cutest little red spaghetti strap jersey and pedal pushers that her grandmother gave her for her second birthday. Snappy little orange DayGlo sandals that Tuki bought with Hong Tam from the night marketers in an alley off Le Loi.

"Love you," says the little girl and wraps Tuki's thighs in a hug. She bends. Kisses the child on the head, the hair and skin smell like baby roses.

"Love you, too." Tran drops to one knee, pulls his sister and daughter into the cradle of his arms.

Oh, la, she thinks. Is this what I have been missing all my life? Not romance, but a family? Maybe in his infinite wisdom the Buddha provides.

*   *   *   *

"Let Hong Tam stay with me."

"Are you taking us to the ruby?"

She pauses. Tries to meditate on a large candle burning atop a table in the corner of the living room. It's the size of a potted plant, purplish-brown, shaped like the praying Buddha. The top of the head's half-melted away, wax running down the cheeks. Tears.

Her thoughts turn again to Michael. He will not meet her at Xa Loi now. She heard the crack in his neck, saw him hit the deck of the junk like a sack of rice. She shivered at the heavy splash as Wen-Ling heaved him over the rail of the boat into the bay. Saw him floating facedown, his arms spread like wings, feet still wearing his black Nikes, dragging him down. Only his spirit will meet her at Xa Loi.

But maybe, somehow, it will be enough. If she prays hard enough and long enough, he will come to her, take her hand, show her a way to finally slay the dragon and save her brother's daughter. Then maybe the Buddha will wrap Michael and her in his six arms that are no arms. Guide them to the nowhere that is nirvana, to the no couple that is true union, to the no love that passeth love. Nothing in this world of flesh matters anymore, except getting this little girl safely back to Huong Mei.

But the temple is already closed for the night.

"Are we going, *bui doi* … or do I let Flash show this baby the meaning of suffering?"

Hong Tam doesn't see Flash because her back is still turned to him as she hugs her auntie. But Tuki can see, and what she sees makes her blood ache. The hookers are gone. But he's still standing in the doorway, barrel-chested and buzz cut, wearing wrap-around shades as usual. A menacing example of Saigon's Chinese population … with his sport shirt hanging open to expose a trio of gold necklaces and his hands massaging the bulge in his crotch, even as they begin to loosen his belt and unbutton his waistband.

"We can't go until tomorrow morning."

"Then your niece will be spending the night in Flash's bed."

The thug's starting across the room toward the child, one hand stretched out. The other unzipping his fly.

"I so horny," he says echoing a line he must have heard his hookers say ten thousand times to their johns.

"No." Tuki jumps to her feet, makes a shield of her body as she pushes Hong Tam behind her.

"What?" Both Flash and Wen-Ling look confused.

"Take me," says Tuki. "Please just let her sleep tonight."

The dragon and her henchman exchange glances.

"Tomorrow morning we go get the ruby, *bui doi*, or you watch your baby die. Piece by piece."

"Just leave her out of this, la."

Flash is now so close to her, she can smell the scotch on his breath, feel the hard bulge in his pants rubbing against her hip.

"Me so horny," he says again.

Tuki braces herself, tries not to feel his left hand rising up beneath her skirt.

"It's not safe to stay here," says Wen-Ling as if she knows something Tuki doesn't.

Flash says something—probably a curse—in Chinese.

"Call a cab, you pig. And get lost …" Wen-Ling runs the back of her hand against Tuki's cheek slowly. Very slowly. "This pretty lady and her niece are spending the night with me. We're going to the Luc Phuc …"

Tuki remembers her last time at the Fragrant Moment, another night when even the air she breathed seemed in short supply.

46

"SHE'S BEEN in there too long." Caesar Decastro's sitting next to Michael in a cyclo parked on the corner of Nguyen Trai and Ngo Quyen Streets. He's dragging on his third Winston since Meng went into the Tiger's Tail an hour ago.

It's slightly after ten o'clock. Saturday night. Cholon sizzles with the scent of roast duck, bia hoi, painted ladies, men on the hunt. And something else tonight. The burnt gunpowder from exploding firecrackers.

"What do you think we should do?" Michael's exhausted. His neck wound hurts.

"I think she's in trouble, Mo."

"You want to go in there?" Michael can see three bouncers at the door. He remembers that the last time they were here, Flash's thug pulled a piece on them.

"Got a better idea?"

"We could wait until the place closes, jump the dude after everybody's gone if Meng doesn't come out."

"Assuming he's the last one to leave."

"Yeah."

"Back in the day, lot of the club owners lived upstairs over their bars. That's where he'd have Meng."

A string of fire crackers goes off. There must be some sort of Chinese festival happening in Cholon. Michael feels himself jump.

"I'm starting to hate this place all over again." Caesar throws his butt into the street. He hands a dollar to the cyclo guy. "We stay here, Chum."

"You think we're in over our heads?"

"We have been for weeks."

"Maybe Meng's making some progress in there," says Michael.

He's trying to cheer himself up … and calm his father, whose left leg has begun to bounce up and down with the jitters. *Can't really blame the guy.* Meng's into high-stakes theater tonight. She went into the Tiger's Tail posing as a rich *mamasan,* out to recruit Flash and his girls for some top-end escort work with a group of French business-men at a downtown hotel.

Her rationale was that she had all the right connections. She's Hmong like Wen-Ling and probably most of her intimates, speaks Hmong as well as Vietnamese and the Cantonese of Cholon. And, of course, she knows her way around places like the Tiger's Tail, hav-ing been a bar girl before her affair with Caesar. Meng claimed she had ways of finding out if Tuki was around. Might even be able to buy her.

But still, Meng's only one woman going into a pit of reptiles. What if someone in Wen-Ling's crew recognized her from a close encounter up north in the Song Da Valley? And, surely, Wen-Ling must have her trolls on high alert after the showdown in Ha Long Bay.

"I don't like the smell of this, Mo."

The cyclo driver taps Caesar on the shoulder, asks in English if they want "good massage with happy ending" while they wait. Thirty dollars.

"How about a bottle of Johnnie Walker … and a set of nunchucks?"

*   *   *   *

It's now more than an hour and a half since Meng rolled up to the Tiger's Tail in a rented white Toyota Century limo, dressed like a reincarnation of South Vietnam's infamous first lady Madame Ngu.

Black *ao dai*, hair in a French roll, aviator shades, lots of bling. A half hour since Caesar and Michael got back from a quick trip to haggle with the night marketers off Phan Van Khoe for costumes of their own.

The Decastros have changed into cheap, gray business suits and knockoffs of old-school Ray Ban wayfarer sunglasses. Michael thinks they look like a cross between New Bedford mobsters and the Blues Brothers as they keep watch on the bar from their cyclo a hundred yards away. Michael can feel the sweat starting to bead on his forehead as he finishes a can of 333. The pains in his neck and shoulders are melting away to a vague throb.

Still no sign of Meng.

Caesar has already worked his way through a quarter of the bottle of whiskey and is snapping his newly purchased nunchucks to kill time.

"These things just slide up inside the sleeve of your jacket, Mo. Nobody knows you're armed until it's too late."

"You actually know how to use them?"

"I learned a couple of things the first time I was in country."

"Maybe this is a bad idea, going in there."

"You love Tuki?"

Michael rolls his eyes. Like *do you really have to ask?*

"Well, I love Meng … And I've seen the kind of shit that can happen to a girl in these places."

"So let's get on with it, huh?"

Caesar hands another two bucks to the cyclo driver, tells him to go away. Then he hails a cab. Tells the cabbie that he wants the guy to wait at the curb just one storefront east of the Tiger's Tail. And keep the engine running.

"Now or never, Buddy Boy."

*   *   *   *

The Tiger's Tail throbs with more than two hundred people. Rich Vietnamese, Chinese businessmen, Japanese on sex holidays, European ex-pats, American and Aussie johns of every stripe and age.

Dozens of girls working the crowd. A teenager in a G-string humping a pole at the far end of the bar. A rap by Ludacris pulsing.

In the center of it all is Meng. She's seated on a folding chair atop
the pool table. Across a card table from her, eyes fixed on hers, sits
Flash, wearing a white sports jacket, sleeves pushed up to the elbows.
His cheeks glow with booze. His left hand clutches an envelope.
There are nine empty shot glasses, face down in front of each person.
Meng holds a full shot of whiskey between her thumb and two fin-
gers inches from her mouth. She looks both regal and unworldly to
Michael, lost to him behind her aviator shades.

"What's going on?" he asks a young American wearing a Yankees
ball cap.

"Drinking contest. Between the *mamasan* and the guy who runs
the club. It's starting to get really interesting." The American waves
two twenties in the air, tells a bookie to bet it all against Meng.

Ten other guys are trying to get their bets down before Meng
drinks her tenth shot.

"What's at stake?" Caesar grabs the Yankees fan by the elbow.

"Her ass or his club, I think."

Michael's wound has begun to hurt again.

The crowd's starting to chant. "Drink. Drink."

"She's not really playing for the club." Caesar whispers in his
son's ear. "She's in this for Tuki. That envelope that Flash's holding
onto must be the key."

"Really?"

47

ELEVEN O'CLOCK. The darkened rooftop suite of the Luc Phuc shimmers with light from the street below. The pink walls look deep gray in the glow. Wen-Ling strokes the child's head as the Dragon Lady lies, propped up on one elbow. The queen bed squeaks a little with her movement, but Hong Tam's not disturbed. She's already asleep. Probably never even noticed Wen-Ling toss down three quick cups of opium tea.

"Tell me this isn't what we've both missed, Tuki," she says. Her voice sounds far away, dreamy.

Tuki can't believe she's hearing the Dragon Lady call her by her real name. It has almost never happened before. She's lying next to the little girl on the far side of Hong Tam from Wen-Ling. Eyes closed. She has been singing softly, an American lullaby that Michael taught her called "Sweet Baby James."

"I mean it. The glamour, the power, the money, the clothes, the men. Even the Heart of Warriors. They are all just substitutes for this, aren't they? The sound of a child sleeping easy next to you."

Tuki feels Wen-Ling's fingers grazing the back of her neck.

"We want to be mothers don't we?"

The fingers again. Tuki sighs. She feels dizzy with the knowledge that the Dragon Lady has tapped into her own desires, dizzy with fear about what's coming next. If only she could pounce on the wench right this instant, strangle her … But there's this child dreaming between them.

"I was so sorry when I heard that you lost your baby back on Cape Cod."

"Don't lie to me." Tuki's voice hisses.

"It's no lie." More of those fine fingers stroking her neck.

"You keep threatening to kill me, to kill Hong Tam."

"Just bitter words."

"I don't care what you do to me anymore." Tuki hears resignation and exhaustion in her own voice. "Just let Hong Tam go."

"Why don't the three of us go somewhere and start fresh? As a family."

What?

Tuki bites her lower lip as the dragon's fingers massage her neck. Can hardly believe the bizarre and shameless ways this woman tries to control her.

"No one will ever hurt us as long as we have the ruby. I have plenty of money. We could go to someplace like Bali or Tahiti."

Tuki reaches up, seizes Wen-Ling's hand. Stops the soothing fingers. "Why are you doing this? I'm going to give you the ruby, la. You can start your family with someone else."

"You think I haven't thought about that?" The words burst into the night air, little bullets.

Tuki feels Wen-Ling's hand grow suddenly oily with sweat.

"It wouldn't be the same … Couldn't."

Was that a sob, la?

"Please, just give Hong Tam back to her grandmother tomorrow morning."

"That's the problem."

Tuki really doesn't want to hear about Wen-Ling's problems. Real or imagined. "Immense desires bring immense suffering, la," she says. *Like what I feel because of Michael now.*

"You think I don't ask the Buddha for peace?"

Strange, but it feels like Wen-Ling's looking for real comfort here, not simply another opportunity for manipulation. The woman must be floating on her lavender cloud somewhere on the dark side of the moon. Lost in space out there ... or way down deep in herself behind the dragon mask. Tuki's off balance. She can't bear to feel another person's misery. Her own is so heavy.

"Listen to your heart. Give the girl back to Hong Mei."

"She doesn't belong with that cow."

Tuki thinks she's starting to understand. "Is this still about my father?"

"If she hadn't walked into his life ... I would be your mother."

I'd rather be dead.

"I gave the Black Cat everything. I gave your father my body and my heart. My money. My soul."

"The Buddha says what's passed is yesterday's rain."

"Give me a chance." The plea is strained, plaintive.

"You've killed people I ..."

"I have feelings ... for you and, now that she has come into my life, for Hong Tam." Wen-Ling has pulled her hand free, is stroking Tuki's cheek. "A mother's feelings."

Oh, la. This is madness and opium talking. "Then ... will you just let us sleep tonight?"

"Can I rub your head a little longer?"

Tuki can't speak. She's afraid that if she does, the dragon will hear in her voice that she's freaking out. Hear that this opium-crazed bitch has touched a nerve in her.

"Mama loves you."

Say What?

"My daughter."

This is too crazy, Wen-Ling is too crazy. Only praying can help, la. Tuki knows that she should pray to the Buddha. But what she does is put her hand over Wen-Ling's and guides it to her temple. Best to distract the lonely, hungry dragon right now. Tomorrow will be soon enough for killing.

48

"THIS IS ABOUT to get ugly, Kid."

The Decastro men, doing their Blues Brothers imitation, are pushing through the crowd toward the pool table and the face-off between Meng and Flash. Meng has just finished her eleventh shot of Jack Daniels. She's sweating so much her black *ao dai* is spotted with perspiration stains. But she's still sitting tall, impassive behind the mask of her shades. If she has seen Caesar and Michael, she has given them no sign.

It's Flash's turn to drink. The guy's eyes have narrowed to slits. He's swaying in his seat as the barmaid holds the tray in front of him, offering him the next shot of whiskey. His left hand still clutches the white envelope. The bookie is scooping up hundreds, maybe thousands of dollars in bets. Pole humpers, working girls, johns have all stopped their mating dances and turned to watch the show. From speakers in the corners of the pool room, Bruce Springsteen's raging about being born in the USA.

"Watch Meng's back, Kid."

"What are you going to do?"

Caesar Decastro pats the sleeve of his jacket where he has the nunchucks hidden. "Make sure Flash doesn't try something cute. He's got a little gun in his jacket pocket."

"Drink. Drink. Drink." The crowd is totally into this.

Michael moves behind Meng, sees that the thug who pulled the
.45 on his father here a few weeks ago has bellied up to the table right
behind Meng.

Up there under the bright, orange light over the pool table, Flash
has taken the shot from the barmaid. He's holding it in his right
hand six inches in front of his mouth, staring at it like he's not sure
what he's seeing. Or not sure how many glasses he's seeing.

"Drink, Drink. Drink."

Flash sways in his seat, almost spills the shot of Jack. His left
hand has started to squeeze the envelope.

The crowd moans. They think he's going down.

Michael sees the thug at Meng's back reaching under his loose
sport shirt. He's almost certainly fishing for a gun.

Meng says something to Flash. Just four syllables. Maybe in
Vietnamese or Cantonese. Maybe Hmong. Michael has no clue. But
he can tell by the tone that she's challenging her adversary.

Flash rubs the sweat from his eyes with his free hand.

"*Cho chet*," he says.

Michael gets it. Like *fuck you, bitch.*

"Then drink, *ban toi*." She smiles. "Drink."

Flash growls. Throws back the shot.

The crowd's screaming … as the son-of-a-bitch winds up and
heaves the empty glass at Meng.

She catches it. With both hands. Right in front of her nose.

Like a catcher snagging a foul tip, thinks Michael. *Amazing.*

The bar's roaring.

Flash slumps in his seat, blinking. Swaying.

Meng rises to her feet, still holding the shot glass in front of her
nose. Triumphant.

As she stands over Flash, he topples off the chair. Hits the pool
table with a thud, bounces to the ground, splays out on his back. Still
clutching the envelope in his left hand.

She climbs down from the table with the help of a half dozen
patrons. Bends, to put the empty shot glass upside down on his forehead, is reaching for the envelope in his hand … when the dude's
eyes open. His right hand goes for the gun in his jacket pocket.

Zap.

That's what it sounds like to Michael when his father breaks Flash's forearm with the nunchucks.

Zap.

When Michael smacks the .45 from the bouncer's hand with a bottle of 333.

Zap.

When Meng seizes the envelope and dives for the man she loves.

Zap. Zap. Zap … Zap. As Caesar, swinging the nunchucks with one hand, carrying Meng doubled over his shoulder with the other, beats a path to the door.

Zap.

As Michael slams the door of their waiting cab.

And the Blues Brothers, Madame Ngu—crumpled white envelope in hand—plunge into the traffic and smoke of snapping firecrackers on Nguyen Trai Street.

Meng jams her fingers down her throat, vomits whiskey through an open window. Caesar tears open the envelope and reads the words printed on a bar napkin inside.

"Luc Phuc Hotel," he says, directing the cabbie. "That's where Tuki is."

"That hole again?" Michael's looking out the back of the taxi.

Four police cars are rolling up to the Tiger's Tail. Lights flashing, sirens wailing.

49

TUKI WAKES to the sound of sirens, sees from the digital clock on the nightstand that it's 12:37 Sunday morning.

"I'm really sorry I have to do this, Little One," She hears Wen-Ling say.

And then she hears Hong Tam scream. It's a long scream, a loud scream. A scream Tuki will do anything to stop. A daughter's scream.

By the time Tuki's fully aware of the place where she has awakened, aware of the nighttime lights of Saigon seeping into the penthouse of the Luc Phuc, the dragon has already gathered the child from her bed and is carrying her out onto an open balcony, holding Hong Tam like a shield in front of her.

Wen-Ling's shouting down into the street from up here on the top of the four-story building. Her Vietnamese is too fast, too fluid for Tuki to fully comprehend. But she understands enough. She understands that the Dragon Lady is telling the police gathered below that if they try to enter the building the child will not come out alive. She's not sure how the police found them here. Maybe something happened at the Tiger's Tail tonight, the police got called, Then when the police started to squeeze Flash, he offered them Wen-Ling, the kidnapper and killer, to take the pressure off himself.

Maybe her mother and her stepfather have brought the police onboard since Hong Tam's abduction, Tran's death, and Nguyet's death … if not after Tuki's disappearance. With Michael gone, maybe his father turned to the police in his grief and desperation for justice. *But, really, la. What does it matter why and how the cops are here now?* The point is they are, and they are acting with the kind of caution—not rushing the building with a few men—that suggests they have been forewarned about how dangerous Wen-Ling can be. They are gathering for an organized assault that promises to be a slaughter unless she does something.

Tuki rises on all fours ready to pounce. The Dragon Lady stands less than a dozen feet away.

"Don't try anything stupid." Wen-Ling holds her pistol to the base of the little girl's head.

Hong Tom is still screaming … and the absolute shrillness of it seems to be driving Wen-Ling toward some emotional cliff. Tuki, too. But Tuki has not been drinking opium tea. Her mind, if not her heart and soul, is still somewhat grounded on planet Earth. And she can see Wen-Ling's gun hand shaking. Her chest heaving with fast, shallow gulps for air.

"Take a deep breath," she says to the dragon. "The Buddha says imagine the sound of one hand clapping. We can get out of this, la."

"I'm not afraid to die." Wen-Ling's voice sounds otherworldly. "With my family." She must be wrapped deep in her opium blanket.

"Why don't we just forget about the ruby. And do what you planned—go to Bali."

The dragon steps back into the room from the balcony, still clutching the shrieking child to her chest. Still holding a gun to her head.

"It's too late. The ruby was our ticket out."

"Don't give up. We can go to Bali." Tuki can't believe she means this, but she does. Anything to save the child.

Wen-Ling doesn't seem to hear Tuki's change of heart. She says that the police don't care much about what happens to the little girl. Their bosses only concern is the ruby. It's a national treasure that the Vietnamese have wanted to get back from the Thais for a very long time. And by now, thanks to Michael Decastro's father, or possibly

Flash, the police must know that at least one of the two women hiding on the top floor in this hotel has the ruby ... or can get it. The police are not here because people have been killed or a child has been kidnapped, not here because a *bui doi* is being held hostage. Not here to arrest a Hmong opium trafficker. It's all about the Heart of Warriors.

"There must be a way out of here. Let's just go."

"All my life has been leading up to this place, this moment ... with my family." Wen-Ling has a glazed look in her eyes. "This is the way our world ends."

Tuki picks up the Dragon Lady's cell phone, holds it out to her. "Call your jet. Get it ready. We can sneak away."

Hong Tam's still screaming. Ear-drilling shrieks.

"We can go tonight. The three of us on a quiet little beach in Bali before the sun sets tomorrow."

"We must pass over to the other side together. Seek the ancestors together. Beg forgiveness for our earthly sins together." Wen-Ling seems to be talking to herself as she slumps onto the bed with the child.

Tuki hears her brain shouting that she only has seconds to change the polarity of this conversation before the Dragon Lady shoots them all. In the blink of an eye. She would welcome death, its dark eternal reunion with Michael, but not at Hong Tam's expense. The child must be given her life back.

"Do you think you could break into Xa Loi pagoda tonight?"

"What ... ?" Wen-Ling looks like she's drowning in the Hong Tam's screams.

"Can you get us out of here and across town to Xa Loi?"

"You want to die there ... before the altar to Buddha and the *bodhisattva*?"

"I want to get you the ruby. I want to buy ... our family ... freedom. I want to go to Bali."

"The ruby's at Xa Loi?"

Tuki swallows to find her voice. "In an incense burner."

Wen-Ling rubs her eyes with her gun hand, holds Hong Tam

with the other. She seems to be rising out of a dream of death. "You're telling me the truth?"

"I don't have much choice if I want to get the three of us to Bali, do I, la?"

Hong Tam's screaming has changed from long wails to fits and bursts. Each new explosion sets Tuki's teeth on edge.

"Take the baby." The dragon thrusts Hong Tam at her auntie and grabs her cell phone.

The moment Tuki wraps the child in her arms, the screeching starts morphing into heavy sobs.

Wen-Ling's got her gun on the two of them.

"What are you going to do?"

A policeman's shouting up from the street in harsh Vietnamese, using a bullhorn.

"Shut up and let me think," the dragon says in Thai, of all things. She starts pacing in front of the bed, stops. Extends her arm to full length pointing the pistol at Tuki and the little girl.

"Please don't shoot us."

Wen-Ling winces, she takes a deep breath, grabs the pistol with both hands to steady her aim and closes her eyes.

A bullhorn barks outside in the street.

"Put some clothes on … I need to make a call."

"We're going to Xa Loi?"

"There's a secret stairwell," Wen-Ling pulls on a tile rack in the bathroom. The wall behind it swings slowly open, revealing dark stairs. "And a tunnel."

50

"YOU CAN'T go in there, Michael."

"Why the hell not?"

"You want to get killed for real this time, *hombre?*"

It takes him a second to realize that the person who's gripping his forearms with both hands, who's standing like a wall between him and the entrance to the Luc Phuc is absolutely the last person he would want to see right now. Or maybe ever. Yemanjá Colón. Cape Cod detective. Former confidante. Kindred haunted soul. The woman whose heart he tossed back in her face.

"Don't say anything," she says. "Just count to twenty in your mind."

"What in the name of *Jesus Cristo* are you doing here?"

"Your father called Lou and said you were in deep *mierda.*"

"Lou sent you?"

"Not exactly."

"What's that supposed to mean?"

"We talked about it."

"Talked about it?"

She still has him by the arm, but she turns her face away, stares up to the balcony of the penthouse on the Luc Phuc. "I just decided to come."

"I don't get it. You hate me."

"Yeah," she says softly. "I hate you … but a lot of people love you …"

"I don't need rescuing …"

Colón nods to the hotel. "Well, someone does."

"You came with these cops? You told them about me, my dad? The ruby. And Tuki?"

"It's a brotherhood … with sisters."

"Well, right now they're the last thing we need."

*   *   *   *

It's a half hour of shouts over the bullhorn with no response from Wen-Ling, no answer to the calls to the penthouse phone, before a SWAT team storms the hotel. Another twenty minutes before the cops in riot gear come out and proclaim the place secure, empty. No Wen-Ling, no Tuki, no Hong Tam.

The crowd of hundreds of onlookers from the streets of Cholon has begun to dissipate, no more action here. It's almost two in the morning.

"Damn it all to hell." Michael's leaning against a parked cab on the street. His father's cuddling with Meng in the back seat, feeding her bottled water. From time to time, a back door of the cab opens. Meng leans out, spews. Michael tries not to notice. He sucks coffee from a plastic cup. Mixed with condensed milk and gobs of sugar, the beverage tastes more like a warm milkshake than anything else.

"They got away." Colón has just come back from talking with the leader of the SWAT unit. He speaks some English.

In her black slacks and ruffled white blouse, long black hair cinched back in a ponytail, the glow of sweat on her cheeks, she looks to Michael like a cocktail waitress at some high-end Cape Cod watering hole.

"I told my father not to get cops involved. That meant Lou … and you, too. I thought he got the message."

"Don't you remember all the other times you went off on some kind of quest for vigilante justice?" There's a fierce defensiveness in

Colón's voice. "Quite a few people died. Some of them, I hear, you had feelings for."

Michael feels his heart seize as he remembers the lovely Awasha Patterson, who took a bullet for him at an ambush in Harwichport that was not so different from how this night might have gone without the police. Remembers, too, how the Thai mob executed Tuki's first love, Prem, and her father when he tried to avoid bringing in the cops to help.

"This isn't America."

"No shit, *cabrón*."

"Look. I'm sorry. Okay? I feel terrible for all the hurt I've caused you."

Kissing her, his core trembles. "Make love to me." Her voice sounds so small, fragile. "I can't ... I don't dare. I'm so sorry."

"Please. Just leave me the hell alone."

"What's happening here ... It isn't any of your business."

She puts her hands on her hips, juts out her chin as if she didn't hear his last sentence. "Your girlfriend sure hangs out with some sweethearts, Hot Shot."

Ouch.

"What's that supposed to mean?"

"The Luc Phuc is a brothel of the first order. Whips, chains, costumes ... and about a million dollars worth of heroin stashed in an elevator shaft."

"She's been kidnapped," he says. "These people are anything but her friends."

"You sure of that?"

"Absolutely."

"Then how do you explain what the cops found on the hotel security camera tapes?"

"What?"

"They've got pictures of your *novia* and that Chinese-looking glamour girl walking down the hallway to their room. Arm in arm, with a little girl in tow."

He thinks of the report he heard at Cat Ba. Tuki and the Dragon Lady walking down the street all chummy.

"Looks like Tuki may have changed sides."

"No." He's trying to resist the heart-shredding illusion.

"Then what's with the arm-in-arm stuff?"

"She's doing anything to stall for time … trying to stay alive."

For a nano-second, Colón's face drains of all its intensity and bravura as if she feels a wave of empathy for Tuki. But then she's all tough and sassy again.

"Well, she better come up with her A game fast."

"What are you talking about?"

"You know how most kidnappings end?"

Michael chokes on his ice coffee. "You got any good news?"

Colón bites her lower lip, says it hasn't been exactly a picnic ingratiating herself with local law enforcement, but a wink and a wiggle still go along way in the squad room when you want friends and information,.

"The cops think nobody's dead yet. They think there must be some kind of secret tunnel they used to escape."

"The city's full of them." Caesar Decastro has gotten out of the cab, has been listening to his son and Colón trade jabs.

"Dad, do you remember Detective Yemanjá from the Cape?"

"Detective." He shakes her hand. "If you really want to help, you can ditch your friends in uniform … and come with us."

"I don't know … I … The police are going to want to talk to you and …"

"There's more at stake to the cops here than a double kidnapping."

Colón looks baffled. "Lou said you were military police …"

"On these very streets. Forty years ago."

The detective's eyes widen. It seems Caesar has way more cred with her than his son does. "What have you got?"

"Those tunnels. The opium boys and the V.C. used them to move product and arms around Cholon. The one's I saw back in the day … they seemed to be connected with weed wackers."

"Weed wackers?" Michael's totally out of the loop with the cop talk.

"*Botánicas*," says Colón. "Herb shops."

"They're usually somewhere near the Ben Nghe Channel so they can smuggle things in and out on little boats."

"You think there's a *botánica* right down the block from here?" Colón's words race with adrenalin.

Caesar nods to the cab with Meng in it. "We've got to get there before the Gestapo."

51

TWO-THIRTY in the morning. It has started raining on the streets of Saigon.

"We can't stay here." Wen Ling nods to the darkened back room of the herb shop.

There are shelves on every wall stuffed with hundreds of small bundles of herbs, bottles, little cotton bags of notions. Corked jars with lizard entrails, bird claws. Baby cobras in wine bottles. A dried-out carcass of a dog on the floor, separated into pieces. Legs stacked together. Heads turned upside down. Lips grinning obscenely. The air smells like dust, fermenting rice wine, rotting chicken skin.

Tuki hugs Hong Tam to her chest. "She's shaking with fear."

"The police will find us. Trust me."

"She needs to rest."

"We have to get to the ship."

"Ship?"

"You want me to carry her?"

Tuki hugs the child tighter. "What ship?"

"The police will be watching the airport. We can't go there. Not now."

"You have a ship?"

"The *Bangkok Venus*."

"Where?"

"In Khanh Hoi."

Tuki pictures it. The ship's probably one of the tramp freighters she has seen tied up to the wharves south of the city in District Four, the area separated from the rest of Saigon by the murky waters of the Ben Nghe Channel.

"That's a mile from here," she says. "We have to cross a bridge over the channel."

Wen-Ling doesn't answer. She's jabbering into her cell phone.

Hong Tam has begun to fuss and whimper again.

The Dragon Lady claps her phone closed. "No time. We must run."

"Where?"

"Across the street. There's a broken place in the seawall my people use."

"What?"

"The boatman's waiting. He's nervous. There are already police on one of the bridges."

"Boatman?"

"He can take us to the *Venus* … if we go now."

Tuki has a vision from a Vietnam War movie, maybe *Apocalypse Now*, of a sampan being sprayed by a hail of automatic weapon fire. Everyone dying except a puppy. Hong Tam's starting to convulse against her chest.

"Maybe there's another way."

Wen-Ling pulls out her pistol and aims it at the little girl's head. "You want to make your peace with Buddha here and now?"

A siren screams from somewhere near. Tuki tries to inhale every liter of air left in this house of the dead. Wen-Ling's still on the edge. Playing at two games at once. Self-preservation and self-destruction.

Does she know that the Buddha says there is no difference, la?

*   *   *   *

The ship is not what she expected. From the outside it looks like a standard container ship waiting to be loaded in the morning by the cranes hovering over stacks of truck-size metal boxes on the wharf.

But beneath the usual assortment of industrial-looking cabins for the operation of the ship and quarters for its crew is a passage through the engine room into a large machine shop closet. Inside is a door with a keypad entrance. Beyond is a secret warren of rooms that seem to Tuki like something out of a James Bond movie.

Several of the cabins hold neatly stacked two-liter bags of heroin. But at the heart of this maze is an ultra-modern bachelor pad complete with a bar, white leather sofas, a trio of five-hundred-gallon aquariums, an oval-shaped king-size bed, indirect lighting on the down-low. A giant flat-panel TV screen's playing the Michael Jackson *Thriller* video in surround sound. The audio swirls softly through the room.

"You like it?" Wen-Ling pulls the fluffy, red comforter up around Hong Tam who is already nodding off in the big bed.

"Is this for real, la?"

"It's where we spring our trap."

"What do you mean? I thought we were leaving on this ..."

"My people tell me that your boyfriend's father has joined forces with the police."

Knowing Michael's past aversion to the institutions of law enforcement, Tuki kind of doubts what she's hearing. But maybe this is a time to be silent and let Wen-Ling believe what she wants. Maybe there's some advantage for Tuki and Hong Tam in Wen-Ling's thinking that she's up against a united front of enemies ... even if this may not be the case.

"When do we go to Bali?"

"Have you forgotten Xa Loi and the ruby?"

It's bizarre, but she almost had. Perhaps in revealing the place that she hid the Heart of Warriors, she had started letting go of an obsession, started letting herself imagine a life without being a guardian to a beautiful rock.

"When those fools come for us, they are going to be in for the surprise of their lives ... while we are collecting our ticket to paradise at Xa Loi, Sweetie."

"I don't understand."

"Have you ever heard of chlorine gas?"

Pictures on the TV a few years ago. Some terrorists in Iraq had deto-nated a truck-load of gas canisters in Baghdad. Fifty people or more were taken to hospital with problems breathing.

"You have it here?"

"Enough to kill a hundred."

"But … why? How?"

Wen-Ling looks at her with sad eyes. "Once someone comes into this room without entering the right code on the key pad, the door behind him closes in ten seconds. The gas goes off automatically."

"This only happens in movies, la."

"You still don't get it, do you?"

"Why would you want to …?"

"For the same reason you've held onto the ruby for so long. For protection. The war didn't end for me just because the Americans left or Saigon fell to the communists."

Tuki feels her whole body starting to lock up. "Why don't we just get the ruby and go?"

"Because those bastards smell our blood now. You think the police want anything less than our heads tonight?"

"But …"

"Do you know what the police are going to do to Hong Tam once they've cut souvenirs from our dead bodies?"

Tuki cringes.

Wen-Ling draws her gun from beneath her blouse again, kisses the end of the barrel then presses it to Hong Tam's head, above her right ear. "We can still end this right here with just …"

"Don't."

Tuki hears her voice erupt over the faint Michael Jackson melody drifting from the sound system. Hong Tam stirs.

"How do we get to Xa Loi?"

"A van's coming for us any minute … with a couple of guys who can break into anything."

"I won't leave the baby."

Wen-Ling touches Tuki's arm. Her fingers are dry and cold. "You think I would?"

"But if she wakes she'll …"

"I gave her something to help her sleep."

"How do you know the police will fall into your trap?"

"I've baited it."

Tuki's lips purse in confusion.

"I kept that little jewelry pouch that you had with you the night Flash cut your ear. And now some of your pretty things are missing …"

Tuki sees it. A trail of cheap bling. An earring, a necklace, maybe a bracelet or a costume ring dropped like crumbs in the tunnel—as if lost by a woman in flight. Everything leading to the wharf. And the boatman. Just fifteen minutes ago the Dragon Lady sent him back to get a handbag she said she left near the crack in the seawall on the Ben Nghe Channel. She promised him another hundred dollars for his trouble.

Wen Ling winks. "It's just like honey for the big bad wolves."

52

"I'M SORRY, Mo." Three AM and Caesar Decastro's shaking his head in self-recrimination, sucking on an unlit Winston. He has just sent Meng off in a cab to recuperate at her apartment. "If I had known my call to your buddy Votolatto would bring that spitfire over here. Or that she would call in the Saigon cavalry. I ..."

The spitfire, Colón, has just broken a front door window with the heel of her shoe to unlock the door. Is charging into the herb shop facing the Ben Nghe Channel. The Decastros stand on the sidewalk out front keeping watch for anyone, Wen-ling's thugs or the police, who might be looking for them.

"What made you think, for even a second, that calling the cops—even Cape Cod cops, was a good idea?"

"*Cristo*, how was I supposed to know that *she* would show up?"

"That's the point. When you get the cops involved, you never know what's going to happen next."

"Look, I'm sorry. I said I'm sorry. I thought I was helping."

Michael Decastro rubs his forehead with the thumb and fingers of his right hand and turns away from the sounds coming from inside the herb shop. Colón must be breaking open another door. "You hear that? She's gone crazy."

"Maybe that's just what we need. Reinforcements. New energy." Caesar inhales deeply as if sheer will can suck tobacco from the cold butt between his lips. "This freaking rescue mission of yours is really starting to wear me the hell down."

Michael thinks about the absurdity of the bizarre love triangle that has begun smoldering around him in the last hour or so. He adores Tuki more than his own life, but he feels more than just guilt about the Latina tiger who has suddenly shown up to wade into the *mierda* with him. And what the hell good comes from adding yet another person to this catastrophe?

"You think Colón's going to help anything?" His voice is high and way too loud.

"Hey, pipe down and get in here," Colón barks. "I need you."

By the time the Decastros find their way into the back room of the shop, Colón is holding a thin silver bracelet in her hand. "Recognize this?"

"No," says Michael.

"I found it on the floor by those stairs. They go down into a tunnel."

"You think the bracelet's Tuki's?" Caesar.

"Didn't you once tell me she's obsessed with elephants?"

"Among other things," says Michael.

"Well, look." Colón shines her light on the thin, silver band.

Squinting, Michael can see that the bracelet is engraved with a parade of tiny elephants, linked trunk to tail all the way around. "So …?"

"She was here. With the Dragon Lady," says Caesar, the old cop intuition kicking in. "Maybe she's marking her trail for us."

He sees it. They came through the tunnel from the Luc Phuc, left through the front door. That's why the metal security shutter was not drawn down to protect the glass. The women must have gone from here to a sampan in the channel.

"Hey, there's a guy in a boat down there." Colón is already out the front door and halfway across the street, jogging toward a broken place in the seawall lining the Ben Nghe channel.

"Now what?" Michael's feels like he's sinking deeper into a swamp every second.

"What do you think, Hot Stuff? We have to stop that son of a bitch." She freezes the boatman in the glare of her flashlight.

Right. Stop the boatman. Waste the Dragon Lady. That's what he's thinking as he dives for the bow of the boat. Without a thought to his wounded neck ... or even a memory that he came to this country swearing that he was done with violence once and for all.

* * * *

It only takes Caesar about two minutes of firing nonstop Vietnamese at the boatman, while waving sixty dollars, to convince him that he has been set up by the Dragon Lady. Convince him, too, that the cops will be here any second to haul his skinny butt off to a torture tank unless he takes these three crazy Americans to the ship where he dropped the *bui doi*, the little girl, and their captor.

Eight minutes later the boatman rows the Decastros and Colón alongside the *Bangkok Venus*, where a pilot's ladder stretches from the deck twenty-five feet down to the water.

"At the risk of repeating myself," says Michael, "what do we do now?"

He's sitting on the floor in the sampan, squeezing the right side of his neck with his hand, which has been oozing blood since he dove into the channel and grabbed the bow of the boat.

"Can you climb?" asks Colón.

* * * *

By the time he reaches the deck, Colón and his father have collared a sailor on watch in the bows. Colón has persuaded the sailor to lead them to the Dragon Lady and her hostages or feel his larynx crush beneath the cord that she has wrapped twice around his neck.

"Something's not right," says his father as the sailor leads them through the engine room and into the machine shop.

"What do you mean?" Colón still has the seaman's neck firmly in the grip of her cord.

"There's nobody down here but us. There should be at least one engineer."

Michael has just followed the others through a door in the back of a large metal closet stuffed with spare generator parts. He's staring off into a side cabin, seeing hundreds of bags of heroin packed in grey fish totes, when something clicks in his head. This is the Dragon Lady's inner sanctum, and she would guard it with a small army unless …

"*Jesus Cristo.*" He sees the sailor who Colón has by the neck, eyeing a gas mask hanging from a hook on the wall. "This is a trap."

"Fuck a duck." Caesar Decastro's already turning back toward the engine room, when the air begins reeking of chlorine. Colón launches herself like a wedge against the edge of the closing door.

53

THE SECURITY FENCE around Xa Loi pagoda looks daunting in the rain and darkness of three-thirty AM. There are twelve-feet-high iron bars, curved outward at the top to repel vandals, maybe stop tanks if necessary.

But less than a minute after rolling up to a back corner of the property in a panel truck, Wen Ling's two burglars have cut a man-size hole in the fence with a torch. Seconds later they are ushering Tuki toward the hole in a place where the truck and several huge shade trees hide the intrusion.

Lord Buddha, forgive me my trespasses, she thinks.

Then her mind shifts to more earthly obligations. The Dragon Lady's plan is for Tuki to sneak in, grab the ruby, and return to the truck where her niece and Wen-Ling are waiting to flee Vietnam for paradise. But here. Now. This temple. It may be her last, best chance to save Hong Tam and kill the dragon. A place to take back control. A place free of all of Wen-Ling's network of snares. A place where Tuki has one last card to play. The trouble is, she has no clear scenario in mind. Just intentions. To end things here. If only Michael were alive … she feels sure he would be coming here to help her. Maybe he still will be here. In spirit. Lord Buddha willing.

"I'm not going in there alone." She stops in front of the fence.

"Go. Get the stone." Wen-Ling's voice comes from the open

passenger's window of the truck. More hiss than words.

"I won't leave my niece."

"Are you crazy?"

"You can shoot me if you want."

These words are a huge risk given Wen-Ling's erratic moods tonight, her flirtations with killing them all. But Tuki's betting that the thrill of being this close to snatching the ruby will overrule every other emotion in her enemy ... and leave open some opportunity she can seize.

The dragon opens a door in the truck. "The child's asleep."

"I'll carry her."

"No, just ..." Wen-Ling's hissing again. "I'll do that ... god damn this all."

*   *   *   *

The joss sticks stuck in the sand urn at the entrance to the temple have burned down to mere stubs. The rain is coming harder now, beating on the roof. Tuki wipes her wet hair back from her forehead, slips out of her sandals, and drops to her knees.

"What are you doing?" Wen-Ling holds the child to her breast and leans against one of the square pillars of the temple doorway.

"Praying." *That Buddha will show me the way to end all your evil ... Form is emptiness, emptiness is form. Bloody murder is ... liberation.*

"Get up!"

"This is a sacred place, la."

"We don't have time for this."

"Don't you think you should pray, too?" Tuki's stalling, still feeling for her opportunity.

Wen-Ling doesn't answer. She seems to be considering.

Out of the corner of her eye, Tuki, still on her knees rocking in prayer, sees the Dragon Lady lower Hong Tam to the ground, cover the sleeping child with her shawl.

"I'll get down on my knees when you show me the ruby."

54

"DON'T JUST STAND there like a pair of *cabróns*." Colón's coughing, lying on her back on a metal catwalk in the ship's engine room with her blouse pulled up over her head. "Piss on me. Piss on my face."

Michael looks horrified at the woman writhing in pain at his feet. She wedged her body like an arch between the door jam and the closing automatic door to Wen-Ling's inner sanctum so that Michael and his father could escape by ducking under her belly. And she was exposed the longest to the chlorine spewing from a nozzle nearly right over her head.

"She's right." His old man's exposing himself, claiming that he learned about this pissing business in an army chemical warfare class. During World War I, soldiers in the trenches discovered that they could survive chlorine gas attacks by breathing through urine-soaked cloth. "Piss on her, Mo ... before the chlorine turns her throat to fish meal. Piss."

And so he does. Like his father. Until Colón stops squirming in pain, until her chest stops heaving and she lies still. Her soaking white blouse a death mask over her yawning mouth.

"*Cristo*," says Caesar Decastro.

"Is she dead?" Michael feels a tremor growing in his belly as if he's going to puke.

"No ... I'm not dead." Colón sits up and pull the wet blouse off her face. Her skin has an odd glow in the light of the engine room. Her hair slick, black, astonishingly radiant. "But I sure wish one of you *pendejos* would tell me how I can get my claws into that *puta* Wen-Ling."

"There's a place called Za Loy," says Michael. The words just spew from his mouth unbidden, triggered by the emotions he's feeling from Colón, seething in his own chest, too. Anger and the desire for vengeance.

"If I am gone … ask the monks to help you find Wen-Ling. Do not tell them that you must kill her."

"Where's this Za place?" Colón.

"I don't know."

"Xa Loi. District Three. It's the city's most famous pagoda," says Caesar.

"So that's why she told me to ask the monks for help."

"It's after four in the morning. What time do the holy people of this world wake up?"

*   *   *   *

"No more traps," says Colón as their cab drifts by the main gate to Xa Loi on Ba Huyen Thanh. She nods at a suspicious panel truck parked in the shadows of some large trees alongside the temple's security fence.

"These places always have a back entrance where the monks can come and go from their residence in private." Caesar.

"How do we find it?" Michael voice cracks.

"The driver will know," says Caesar. He has a hundred-thousand-dong note in his hand and leans forward toward the cabbie.

55

JUST A FEW weeks since she was here reciting the Diamond Sutra and burying the Heart of Warriors in the incense burner ... But it seems like another lifetime altogether when she last bowed before this altar and the immense statue of the golden Buddha.

And now she remembers again that rubies are the sixth treasure in the Buddhist sutras. Remembers that supposedly the Heart of Warriors has powers to ease transitions, provide clarity, inspire loyalty, cultivate courage, engender love.

Love, la. Not like she feels for Michael ... His soul waits for her, maybe even here. But love like she feels for that little girl sleeping by the pillar, waiting for her auntie to give her back her life. Love that can drive away all misery. Love that can focus her mind on only one thing. Saving the child. Saving her baby.

She prays again for the courage of Thich Quang Duc when he burned himself alive in the street. Even in these deep early morning shadows the Buddha glows. She finds a fresh joss stick among the burning stubs, lights it, props it in the sand of an urn, wishes that she had an apple and orange to leave in a tureen as gifts for the monks. Then she bows her head, closes her eyes. Falls to her knees, begins reciting the Diamond Sutra. Her eyes close. She knows she should be keeping one eye on Wen-Ling, but first things first. Prayer. The dragon can wait. After the immense suffering the Heart has brought her, she wondered if it can just once do its fabled magic for her.

Lord Gautama, la, help this stone ease tonight's transitions, provide clarity, inspire loyalty, cultivate courage, engender love ... like a drop of dew, a bubble in a stream, a flash of lightning.

Her mind's eye sees the brass incense burner before her with its ornate dragons on the sides and tops. Sees that magnificent ruby buried beneath the sand in its belly. Sees Wen-Ling standing anxiously at her back, right hand clutching the little pistol. *The one I must turn against her.*

"If you want the ruby, put your gun on the altar." Tuki opens her eyes, stands up, pivots to look into Wen-Ling's dark eyes. Can't read them.

"Do you think I'm a fool?"

"I think you want the ruby. I believe you want to start a family. Bali waits for us." *Will she buy this pep talk, la? Is she still planning to kill me, if not the child?*

"How can I trust you, Sweetie?"

"The monks will be waking soon."

"Show me the Heart of Warriors."

"If I show the ruby, will you put the gun on the altar?"

Wen-Ling licks her bottom lip hastily, then nods.

Tuki lifts the lid off the incense burner with one hand, reaches within, fishes, finds the ball of paper prayers for the dead that she left here. Uncoils the paper, takes out its contents, leaves the prayers in the sand. Now she feels the stone. Hard, cold, sharp.

"Here," she says, holding the ruby in front of her in the palm of her hand.

Its facets catch the glow of the joss sticks, until the center of the stone looks ablaze with dozens of tiny flames.

"Oh my god."

"Feast your eyes, la."

"You were actually telling the truth." Wen-Ling stretches out her free hand to touch the stone.

Tuki steps away. "The Heart is yours when the gun lies next to the bowl of fruit ... and you get down on your knees and pray with me."

"Okay," says Wen-Ling. Her voice is shaking, maybe with elation, maybe with fear. Or something more complex.

But Tuki has not even a second to consider. Not even a second to exhale the breath she has been holding.

The very instant Wen-Ling puts down the pistol and Tuki hands her the ruby, the former reigning diva of the Patpong seizes the gun, points it at Wen-Ling's nose. Fires.

The sound of the hammer striking the empty chamber makes a soft click.

"You didn't think I'd put down a loaded gun, did you, *bui doi?*"

"Fuck you, la."

Wen-Ling stands three yards from Tuki, squaring her feet for a fight. Her eyes sag a little with disappointment, but her lips and jaw seem cut from marble. She's clutching the ruby in one hand, a throwing star in the other.

"I really had high hopes for our little family," she says.

56

THE MONK who answers the alley door to the residence is a bleary-eyed boy who was probably sleeping at his post as night guard. Since the secret police and special forces of the South Vietnamese army raided Xa Loi in 1963, alleging anti-government activity, vandalizing the main altar, and stealing the charred heart of the martyred Thic Quang Duc, the residents of the pagoda have been more vigilant. But tonight a certain complacency seems to have infected the youngster. When Caesar asks him if he has seen a pretty *con lai* woman and a little girl, he says, "*Xin phep*," "excuse me," and vanishes into the monastery.

Michael's giving his father a look like he's ready to tear dragon flesh with his teeth when an old man in a saffron robe comes to the door.

"Can I help you?" he asks in English.

"We're looking for our friend, a *con lai* ..."

"We've been looking for Tuki, too."

"The Darhma Telegraph strikes again," says Caesar softly.

"But she is not here ... has not been here."

"We saw a truck out front." Colón's voice has a throaty urgency.

There's some kind of commotion deep inside the residency. Two young monks run up and start whispering in the old monk's ears.

"Excuse me," he says. "It seems someone has cut a hole in our fence during the night."

"You've got a dragon in there." Michael's starting through the doorway. He can smell the blood.

"Please take off your shoes."

57

TUKI STANDS before the golden Buddha, folds her hands in prayer, bows her head. She closes her eyes against the first glow of the morning light through the temple door and waits for the *tonki*, the throwing star, to cleave her body.

She starts to chant:

> *There's no decay, no death ...*
> *No suffering, no origination, no cognition.*

"Stop with the drama, *bui doi*. Don't think you get to die like a martyr."

Tuki opens her eyes, glares at the Dragon Lady. "The Buddha is with me, la."

"I really didn't want to kill you, you know that?"

"I think you don't know what you want besides that stone."

"I told you. I want a family. Children."

"Let Hong Tam go."

"That child is mine."

"She'll find out about what you did to her father and me someday, you know?"

"I don't think so."

"The monks will tell her."

"She'll never set foot in this country."

"The monks are everywhere."

Wen-Ling says nothing.

"And when she finds out what you did, then she'll kill you, la."

"She will learn to love me."

"The Buddha says that love and trust are like the flower and the root of the lotus. Without the one, there is no other."

"Buddha lived in a fantasy world."

"He's not the one who drinks the opium tea."

"It clears the mind."

"And clouds the heart."

"What would you know?"

"I know it's because of the opium that you lost my father."

Wen-Ling takes Tuki's words right on the chin, winces.

"He would never have turned to my mother if you had not been so lost in your dreams."

"He smoked too. Drank the tea."

"So how could you two ever connect?"

"Shut up."

"My mother was his anchor in reality."

"He didn't need an anchor."

"I'm proof that he did."

Wen-Ling winces again. A direct shot to her soul.

"Don't think you can die in peace."

"You can't hurt me anymore."

"Well, consider this. You won't be seeing you Michael in Nirvana."

"What?"

"He's still alive. He's been trailing us all night. And when he gets here, he can weep over your dead body."

"You whore. *Gai diem.*"

"Close your eyes, Sweetie."

"Just let me see my baby one more time." Tuki tries to stretch her gaze to the far end of the temple where the child lies sleeping by the pillar.

The rain's drumming on the roof. Thunder echoes over Saigon. Lightning flashes in the distance.

"Come," says Wen-Ling. She throws an arm lock around Tuki's neck, holding the throwing star to her jugular as she turns toward the child. "But let her sleep."

*   *   *   *

"Freeze!" Colón's command echoes through the temple.

She has produced a pistol. It looks like a nine-millimeter Sig Sauer. And now she's got the gun aimed right at Wen-Ling and Tuki as they kneel, almost as one figure, beside the little girl sleeping by the pillar.

The crack of thunder echoes through the temple. Three monks and the Decastros hit the floor, mistaking the thunder for a gunshot.

"Don't move another freaking inch," says Colón, standing her ground, "or I'll blow your ass into little pieces, *hija de puta*."

"Who's the cowgirl, Michael?" Wen-Ling remains on her knees. But she has snatched the little girl from her sleep, holds the dazed child in front of her next to Tuki. Shields. Both captured in the same armlock across their necks.

"You tried to gas the wrong girl, ho." Colón's aiming her pistol at the Dragon Lady with both arms extended.

"Looks like Michael has a new girlfriend, Sweetie."

"More like you've made a new enemy," says Colón. "And she's a cop."

"You think you scare me?"

"I'm holding the gun."

"And I'm holding a razor-sharp *tonki* to these necks …"

"I can blow your eye out at thirty yards."

"You're police. You won't shoot first."

"Don't bet on it."

Wen-Ling shrugs. "Unless you want to see these cuties both bleed to death … you're going to let us walk out of here."

Michael sees Tuki's eyes reaching out to him. He feels his own telling her that he loves her, beyond reason. That everything will be all right. That he's sorry about Colón. Really sorry. That he's sorry he has not kept her safe. That somehow he'll tear this dragon to pieces. That when the reptile's dead, he'll eat a graveyard full of dirt for one embrace. For one chance to fold in his arms the diva who stole his heart, with a Whitney Houston song about eternal love. Stole his soul away one hot night on a swinging bed in a hut at a beach in Malaysia.

Her eyes are deep and unblinking in the first light of morning. They hold him. Whisper something to him. Her lips are moving, singing maybe. A song he can't quite hear yet. As her left hand starts to rise from her side. Like a claw poised to attack.

He feels a terrible, cold ripping begin in his body. The pain starts with the wound at the base of his neck, but it goes deep into his chest, deeper still. Right down through his gut to the roots of his legs. Everything's wrong. He's the one who should lay into the dragon now, not her. He's the one who should kill. Maybe even *needs* to kill, and for a dozen reasons. He's ready. If he could only figure out how to do it.

So he shouts. To save her, and save himself. "No. Don't."

*   *   *   *

But she does. Because she sees him. Really sees him. Hears his voice. Feels his love. Feels, too, the regret, the yearning for forgiveness, the need for atonement seeping from those sweet Portuguese eyes. And she forgives him. Forgives him of anything, of everything. Even though it's nearly too late for such earthly cares now.

She knows that she's already moving away from Michael, the Dragon Lady, and Hong Tam faster than time. Already in her *bardo* dream. Between life and death. She sees the killing gash over Tran's heart. His washed flesh, combed hair, her earring and some pieces of rice in his mouth. And she knows that this too is her body's lot. She's on the very edge of a new life. Where she will find everyone she loves again. Even if they will not know her at first.

There's nothing left to do here except save the child. Her auntie Tuki is the only one who can do it.

So her left hand channels the strength of a hundred elephants. She seizes Wen-Ling's right wrist … and the hand that holds the *tonki* to her throat. The arm that binds Hong Tam by the throat, too. And with one fierce jerk she casts it off. It seems to vaporize.

And the *tonki* sails free.

It spins against the flickering sky. In a slow, wobbling arch.

She does not feel the cut where the sharp edge of the throwing star slices open her neck as she casts off the dragon's arm, nor the warm blood surging from the wound. She only feels Hong Tam jolting fully awake and breaking free of Wen-Ling. Only hears the soft thud of bullets, hitting the dragon. One after the other. Six shots. Not from the American woman with the pistol, but from the rifle that her mother shoulders.

Then a song rises in her.

Her eyes close. The stage lights come on. Red and golden and warm.

She's singing with Tran and his band. The lights of the city twinkling outside the glass windows on the top floor of the Caravelle Hotel. Tonight she's wearing a silver *ao dai*.

And here comes Tran on the piano. A midnight train from Georgia. The bass is in, too, and she's singing. *Ooooooooo. El Lay …*

The heat's swirling through her belly, her chest. The spotlights flash with bursts of silver amid the gold and red. Her voice low. Sultry. But not straining. Singing about leaving a life. About going back to a simpler place and time.

The spots throw a reflection on the big plate glass window looking downtown toward the river. And she sees her mother in the glass. Sees Misty strutting the runway bar at the Black Cat. She's wearing a silver kimono stitched with little red dragons. Her lips glisten bright crimson. Liner accents the shape of her eyes, her long black hair is pinned up in loose folds. A goddess. Pure body heat. Losing herself in the song, the dance. And cradling a little baby.

Tuki feels the soul of the music, hears her call and response with the woman in the glass. With Tran singing backup, too. And she sees Michael sitting out there in the audience, smiling that big foolish grin of his. Like the first time he came to one of her shows at Provincetown Follies more than five years ago.

He's rising from his seat, he's coming to her. Carrying a baby against his chest. Their baby. A little girl with a shock of wild *bui doi* hair. Like the baby Misty carries in the glass. Tuki feels Michael's arms, her mother's arms, Tran's arms. Her baby's arms drawing her to them. Their voices saying her name over and over as their hands press against the bleeding gash on her neck.

She's on that train. Going back. Going forward, too.

Sashaying across the stage in her *ao dai*. Kissing up to the mic, showing some leg. Feeling this man's loving arms. His hands. Their child. Her brother and mother, too. Bringing the night down, the fire up.

Sweet Buddha, be with me, la. Saigon's burning again.

58

MICHAEL'S TREMBLING. He stands on the foredeck of the sampan as the old Buddhist monk from Xa Loi finishes reciting the Heart Sutra and hands him the funeral urn. He's surrounded by a clutch of friends and family in suits and dark dresses. At nine o'clock in the morning it's so hot that everyone's dripping sweat.

He passes the urn to Tuki's mother, but she pushes it back to him.

The chocolate waters of the Saigon river ripple around the boat, make a noise like whispering. The sound of motorbikes and the morning rush hour seems a distant moan.

"She want you do this. She love you so much."

He feels the tears starting to well behind his sunglasses, clinches his jaw. "I failed her."

"Gautama say it not possible make mistake." Once again he hears Tuki coming through her mother's words. Huong Mei wraps her arms around Hong Tam, who wears a dark blue *ao dai*. The little girl looks up at Michael with wet, beautiful eyes.

Michael tries to conjure a vision of the woman whose ashes he holds. The woman he loves. The woman who he failed to save. The one whose forgiveness he still craves. He tries to hear her songs. But nothing's coming. Instead, he hears the sound of Houng Mei's rifle firing into Wen-Leng. The howling of the little girl, the monks, his own voice. The only thing he sees is that goddamned ruby clutched in the Dragon Lady's hand as she falls, leaking blood from her chest and mouth, blank eyes staring into space.

He feels his father squeeze his hand. "Let it go, Mo."

"I can't do this, Dad." He wants to say this is too much like the day he said goodbye to his mother. The day they scattered her ashes from the *Rosa Lee* onto Buzzards Bay.

"You want me to help you?"

"Say something for her." His voice catches in his throat.

Meng has both arms around Caesar's waist, hugging him, forcing back tears with closed eyes.

"Do this," she says.

"I wish I had a butt," says his father.

"I've got you covered." Colón pats her black clutch purse. She has been standing back a bit from the mourners holding a bouquet of roses to throw on the water. Michael asked her to be here, but it's clear she feels out of place.

"Please, Dad." Michael's voice cracks as he tugs a little on his father's left hand.

Caesar clears his throat.

"A lot of people think the American War in Vietnam was a mistake and a terrible tragedy," he says. "It was … But that war built a bridge between two peoples who love freedom and who live on other sides of the world from each other. Because of that war some of us found understanding, tenderness. We found love among strangers. And from that love there came children. Wonderful children like Tuki Aparecio. Some people call them *bui doi* … but I call them gifts. Tuki was a gift to a troubled world. A gift to all of us." Tuki's surrogate mothers, the two old drag queens from Bangkok, start to weep.

"Gift, la." Her mother nods. "*Mon qua.*"

"*Mon qua,*" Michael hears himself say. He closes his eyes.

And there she is. Not the diva of Provincetown Follies strutting the stage. Not the Queen of Bangkok's Patpong. Not some glorified image of a smoldering sex goddess, but his girl.

She's looking very mermaid in her silver string bikini, reclining on a large, smooth rock in a mountain creek that spills into the pale ocean near the lighthouse at Maku Head. Penang Island, Malaysia. This morning she's golden. Her hair black, wavy. Tucked behind her ears, slick like her skin from swimming.

He's breaststroking against the current rushing around the rock, playing peek-a-boo with a pair of curious sea otters ... before he scrambles up beside her. His green surfer jams drip with water.

She takes his hands, draws him toward her.

"Look at me, la. I'm a girl, Michael. Just a simple girl. No more ... you know? Don't you finally want to kiss me?"

He feels her warm cheek slide against his, smells the coconut on her skin. She presses her lips to his. He tastes hot, smooth plums. Then her tongue finds him. And his mind curls into a tiny ball. His hands lock in hers as she pulls him prone on the rock. His nose to her nose. His arms to her arms. Chest to her chest, hips to her hips, bare thighs to her bare thighs. Her toes. His arches.

The otters, the rushing stream, the ocean waves, the wind in the palms, the monkeys in the trees, the butterflies in flight, must be pausing. Stopping. To witness this kiss ... growing wings in paradise. It's a kiss that both begs forgiveness and forgives. Forever.

"*Mon qua*," he says again and opens his eyes. "She was a gift. An impossible gift."

Then he does something he never thought he could ever do. He holds onto the feeling of that first kiss and its forgiveness for a little longer. Finally, he uncaps the urn and lets the love of his life go.

The ashes settle on the waves, float for a second. Tiny diamonds. Vanish.

The monk chants.

> *Gaté,*
> *gaté,*
> *paragaté,*
> *parasamgaté.*
> *Bodhi!*
> *Svaha!*

Tuki's mother turns her gaze on the old monk. They seem to exchange a sad and knowing glance, as if they share a deep and secret understanding. She murmurs the final words of the Heart Sutra in English. Her voice is firm and measured. Maybe for the sake of Michael and the other Americans. Maybe because she's afraid to let her voice show that the pain of this letting go is tearing her to pieces.

Gone,
gone,
gone over,
gone fully over.
Awakened!
So be it!

Michael knows that's its time to cry. Cry like he did when they scattered his mother Maria's ashes. Everyone around him is weeping as they take roses from Colón and toss them on the water. Tuki's mother, her stepfather, Hong Tam, Michael's father, Meng, Colón, the monk. Even the boatmen. But the tears won't come for the man who loved her. Just a stabbing darkness in his chest.

59

"WE'VE BEEN TALKING with Huong Mei," says Caesar. "Meng and I want to be godparents for Hong Tam."

"What does that mean?" Michael's not really listening. His mind's drifting over the bizarre events that have been unfolding since he scattered Tuki's ashes. He stares at the iced coffee in front of him. He's barely seeing his father and Meng sitting across from him.

His eyes squint around at the other café tables beneath the sunbrellas of this upscale restaurant hidden in a courtyard of District One. The place, apparently, used to be an opium refinery, during the French occupation. Meng likes it here, for the quiet. Her apartment's just around the corner. She's back at her supervisory job at the post office, but now she's on her lunch break.

Part of Michael half expects plainclothes police to rise up and arrest him at any moment. The authorities in Ho Chi Minh City have seized the Decastros' passports for the last ten days while they claim that they are completing their investigation into the deaths of Wen-Ling and Tuki. The interviews have been hell. The cops want to believe that Tuki was a drug dealer like Wen-Ling. That maybe Michael and his father are dealers too. Only in the last few days have Colón's friendships with some police detectives and Huong Mei's husband's position in the communist party seemed to bring a less-aggressive posture in the cops

This morning the Americans learned that Huong Mei will not be charged with any crime in the killing of Wen-Ling. The police are keeping it out of the papers. Huong Mei was a mother protecting her child, her grandchild. End of story. No one will be asking her about her relationship with the Dragon Lady, the Flower Hmong's Robin Hood. She will never have to explain to anyone except her husband, maybe, that secret look between herself and the monk at Tuki's funeral … or how she knew to come to the temple with a loaded rifle at just the right time to shoot the Dragon Lady. She will not have to explain that somewhere in her heart she hid a fear for nearly four decades , a fear that a bitter, shadowy woman from her past would come back to exact revenge. Come back to steal not just a ruby, but her children. She only has to say that she knew the past had come to collect old debts the day she heard Tuki mention Wen-Ling's name to Tran. That was the day Tuki disappeared. "All mothers have their secret grief," Meng said when she heard the news about the police dropping their investigation of Huong Mei. "Better for future those secrets die with mothers." Maybe she, too, is thinking of the *con lai* child who she lost so long ago during that dirty war.

"I don't think they're keeping us here because of the killings," says Michael to nobody in particular.

He thinks the police are holding their passports because of the ruby. Colón told him an hour ago that she has heard through the grapevine that the stone the cops found clutched in Wen-Ling's hand was a fake. The government of Vietnam claims that the real Heart of Warriors belongs to them. They think the Decastros may know where it is. And they want it. Like right now.

"Mo, are you listening?"

"What?" Michael's gaze rises from the dark cloud of iced coffee he has been staring into.

"I said that Meng and I want to be the little girl's godparents. You know, like send her presents and letters and emails and videos. Bring her to the States to visit when she's older. Maybe come for college."

"No offense, but don't we have more important things to think about?"

"That little girl needs a family. All she has is a grandmother and grandfather. Tuki was like her mother, you know? That makes us ..."

Michael feels that black stabbing in his belly again, remembers the child that he and Tuki lost.

"We need to get these cops to let us out of this ... country. We need to go fishing."

His father gives him a sad look. "Yeah, Buddy Boy, we do. But we need to make peace here, too ... I've waited a long time for it."

"I'm sorry," says Michael, grasping the aching in his father's voice. "Godparents. Great."

"You're cool with it?"

Michael shrugs. "Yeah, sure. She's a great kid ... You just have to excuse me. I'm a little beaten up, you know, Dad? And pretty pissed off."

"Colón told me about the fake ruby and the government," says his father. "I think she's trying to cut some kind of deal for us right now."

"What do *we* have to deal with?"

"Not us, *her.*"

Michael shakes his head. "I really don't understand."

"Colón's pretty sure she knows where the real stone is."

"What? Where?"

"Why don't you ask her yourself?" Caesar Decastro nods toward the alleyway leading into this secluded courtyard.

Colón's walking toward him with determined strides. She's wearing a cheap, gray business suit, looking very *Law & Order.* And next to her is a monk in his saffron robe. The same old monk who greeted them at Xa Loi the morning Tuki died, the same monk who celebrated her funeral in the sampan.

The monk, who had prayed for so many years with Huong Mei to help her find peace and forgiveness for abandoning a child. The monk who had prayed for eighteen months with Tuki, too. The monk who knew through the Darhma Telegraph the violent details of Tuki's kidnapping. Who called her mother to rush to Xa Loi as soon as Michael came looking for Tuki ... As soon has he heard the temple had intruders.

EPILOGUE

SPRING. MAY, ACTUALLY. Cape Cod has never looked so good to Michael. Chatham has never looked so good. The trees, the leaves on the vines, the brush, the marsh grass surrounding the trail into the lonely clearing on the edge of Stage Harbor known as the Whispers. Everything radiates green and new life. Marsh flowers bloom. Violets maybe. A delicate purple. The wind blows in off the Atlantic, ruffling the harbor into a plain of shimmering light. The air's cloudless, azure blue.

In the sandy clearing, Yemanjá Colón sits facing Michael. He lies on his side, tracing images of fish in the soil with a twig. Her legs are drawn in beneath her, on the ancient Indian shell midden surrounded by a sandy mix of quohogs and stone chips. The air is thick with the scents of salt and clams and flowers. It's a warm afternoon. Bees are making their ways from blossom to blossom. Strands of Colón's long black hair stir in the wind.

Michael thinks that there's always something piercing and scary in the way she stares at him. This is the first time he has seen her since they got back from Saigon in January. He has been fishing with his father on the *Rosa Lee*, trying to heal. Trying to put Vietnam and Tuki at rest in his heart once and for all. Trying to forgive himself for his failings. But now Meng's visa has come through. She's here on the Cape, and his father will not be going offshore any time soon.

So Michael's left to his own devices. And this morning it was either go to the Captain Kidd's in Woods Hole for shots and beers … or see if Colón wanted to meet him here the way she used to after Tuki left him broken on the Cape before. When he called her this morning, he didn't really think she would come. But he hoped.

She laughed. Said sure. She'd see him at two. At the Whispers. She guessed she could use another meeting of what they used to call the Cape Islands Lonely Hearts Society.

As he looks at Colón, her big watery eyes, hears the pain seeping through her sassy bravado and sarcasm, he feels his soul aching for his mother, for the sister he never had. Most of all for Tuki … While this fine woman that anyone would cherish unloads on him about her on-again-off-again relationship with another lost soul named Corby, who lives on a tugboat in Quissett harbor. How she fears that the guy's a binge drinker like her father. How she thinks she's going to end up dead like her mother. How her *abuela*, the Cuban grandmother she lives with says that she and little Ricky deserve better. How she's addicted to the sex with this man …

"I bet you're really glad you ask me to meet you here to tell you this *mierda*, huh?"

"You want to know the truth?"

"Is Michael Decastro finally going to level with me?"

"In some weird way, I think listening to you helps."

"Grieving?"

"Yeah … and maybe starting to forgive myself for a thousand mistakes."

"We have a strange friendship, don't we?"

"Why did you come to Vietnam?"

"Like *la verdad*?"

"Yeah."

She takes a deep breath, looks away from him, out to sea. "I still had strong feelings for you. I thought if I helped you get your girl back, I could put you behind me."

"Oh."

"Yeah. Oh. Oh shit, look how that turned out."

They both laugh. The absurdity of their lives, their choices, their connection.

"You did something good over there in Saigon. You saved a little girl's life."

She shakes her head. "Tuki saved her life."

"But you had the gun. You stopped the Dragon Lady in her tracks."

"I was just lucky. She fell for the scam."

"What do you mean?"

"That gun. It was just a toy."

"A toy?"

"How in hell do you think I could have ever gotten my hands on a real weapon in Vietnam?"

"You were bluffing when you called Wen-Ling out?"

"*Claro que sí.*"

"She had a throwing star. She could have …"

"Maybe that's why Tuki did what she did, when she did."

"You think she knew your gun was a fake? Knew Wen-Ling wouldn't be fooled long."

"The girl knew the power of illusion … and its limits."

Michael feels a huge hole opening in his chest. He's never quite understood Tuki this way before. But Colón's right. From start to finish Tuki's life, her magic, rooted in illusions. Drag. Make-up. Wigs. Props. Stage smoke. Colored spotlights. Winks. Wiggles. Love songs. Her soul was a pure and nearly unquenchable fire. A joy to behold. A thing to cherish. Maybe even a holy presence. But the rest of her was a collage of make-believe. A wild blend of every diva from Whitney Houston to Charlie's Angels. With a bag full of fake rubies. It's so odd seeing her this way. Realizing that it was the illusion, as well as the holy fire, that charmed him. That he loved. He feels a little bit like a sucker. But a loyal sucker. "That's how you knew where to look for the real ruby," he says.

"What?"

"You knew that Tuki's ace in the hole was always her ability to conjure the imaginary. You knew that she was offering up a fake to

Wen-Ling in the temple."

"I took a guess. Illusion was in her nature, right?"

"And so was Buddha."

She nods, continues staring out to sea.

"You knew that Tuki must have given the real Heart of Warriors to the monks."

"They didn't know they had it. Remember, we had to do some looking."

"But you found it. In the incense burner."

"Buried in the sand beneath a little ball of paper that must have held the fake. The monks said the paper was inscribed with prayers for the dead."

Michael says nothing. He follows Colón's eyes out to sea. A flock of terns wheels in a gyre above a school of bait. There's nothing more to talk about with respect to Tuki's illusions or the Heart of Warriors. The monks of Xa Loi gave it up willingly. They said it had bad *karma*. And besides … form, substance, beauty? They're all illusions. Better that this glorious red illusion go to a national antiquities museum where such temporal things are prized, than to remain in the temple where it would forever bleed like an old wound that will not heal. Better that it buy the release of the Americans from the complex sorrows of Vietnam … and let them go home once and for all.

"I'm still torn up," says Michael.

"You have a right."

"And … I'm so sorry for all the ways that I hurt you."

"I know."

"Can I hug you?"

"Not yet, Slick."